Protect Me

Immortal Vices and Virtues: Her Monstrous Mates

Heather Hildenbrand

Protect Me
By Heather Hildenbrand
Copyright © 2023. All rights reserved.

Edited by Dawn
Cover Design by TwinArt Cover Design

Blurb

I ran from my cruel fiancé…and found myself in the arms of three powerful shifters.

When I throw myself at the mercy of the Ringmaster in No Man's Land, I'm only seeking temporary refuge. A place to hide from the corruption and death that waits for me back home.

Three months. That's all I have until the protection the circus provides me expires.

My bodyguards? Three shifters who look at me like they want to eat me for dinner.

They want my body.

My heart.

And even as the attraction I feel for them is stronger than anything I've ever felt, neither of those is mine to give.

Not anymore.

The past I'm running from still holds me captive. But in the arms of my protectors, I've never felt more free.

Chapter 1

Sway

Breath wheezes in and out of my lungs as I hobble down the empty street. This particular section of No Man's Land is a stark void compared to the crowded party I've left behind. Trees surround me, the soft dirt muting my footsteps, slow as they may be.

Every step sends pain shooting up my limbs and ricocheting through my skull, but then sitting still isn't much better.

I'm a wreck.

Robert was drunker than usual, and shit, maybe I should have known better than to refuse him when he was so far gone, but I couldn't do it.

Not anymore. Never again.

I'll die first. As evidenced by the sheer number of bruises on my body and the fact that I'm only barely clinging to consciousness. Every pump of blood from my pounding heart is an anvil dropped on my brain.

When I ran, I had no destination. Hell, I've spent the last four months telling myself running was only going to make things worse.

But then I realized it couldn't get much worse. Not while I still breathed. So, I ran. And somewhere along the way, the circus became my end goal.

I have no idea why I chose it.

No Man's Circus isn't exactly the haven I need right now. Hell, the Ringmaster is known for being cutthroat and merciless. But he's also reputed to be a fair businessman. If I can appeal to his logic or at least to his love of money, then maybe, just maybe, I have a shot at escaping this nightmare of a life.

It's the only chance I have left. I can't go back. I won't.

Up ahead, the trees part enough that I can see a large tarnished archway beckoning me. The Big Top is in the distance, the top of it barely visible behind the crumbling apartments and trees still standing between me and my salvation. I pick up my pace—which isn't saying much considering my left leg is probably broken, forcing me to drag that foot a bit. The closer I get, the harder my heart pounds. Fear is a lump in my throat and a brick in my stomach.

I'm so damn close to what I can only hope and pray is asylum.

And if not? Well, then at least, I won't be suffering anymore. One way or another I'm escaping Robert once and for all.

Somewhere behind me, a male voice roars my name, "Swayyyy!"

The fear snakes through my insides, sending my bones quaking. I stumble and fall. The ground scrapes into the palms of my hands, but it's nothing more than a whisper of an ache compared to the rest of the agony.

Tears spring to my eyes, burning on their way down my bloodied cheeks.

More pain. So much pain that I nearly give up right here. But the sound of voices murmuring urgently somewhere among the trees sends me surging to my feet.

I push on, pleading with whatever gods or goddesses are out there to let me live through this night. I may not deserve it, but I can find a way to make up for what I've done. There has to be a way.

The voices of my pursuers grow louder. Closer.

My pulse hammers.

Finally, I lurch forward, landing in the soft dirt beneath the large iron archway. It's covered in vines, but I can make out what used to say *Garden View Apartments*. Just ahead, the Big Top looms, a tall tent that stands in what was once the courtyard enjoyed by the humans who likely inhabited those buildings prior to Portland's fall fifty years ago.

Portland, Oregon is nothing like the city the humans

once built. Now, decades of supernaturals vying for power and warring for their own corrupt causes have left it a shell of what it once was.

New boundary lines were drawn, and thanks to the portal that opened up here, Portland became yet another No Man's Land. It's ruled by no House, which is why I ran straight here rather than back to my own people—or his. None of them would have allowed me my freedom. At least here, I have a fighting chance.

I may not have the protection of a House, but there will be no one to turn me over either.

For most, the circus signifies entertainment. A way to pass the evening. But for me? The crumbling walls of these apartments combined with the red and white stripes of the Big Top signify hope.

Magic prickles along my skin as I pass through thin wards that most others likely don't even notice. My magic gives me an advantage there because I can sense things others cannot. I hold my head up just a bit higher, knowing that the Ringmaster has likely been alerted to my presence. The last thing I need is for him to see just how weak I am.

I know it won't be long before he shows up to investigate the after-hours breach, but I don't stop to wait. As long as I am out in the open, I'm still in danger.

The corrupt men hunting me will catch me unless I get out of sight. Remaining where I am is signing my own death warrant. Then again, a swift death would not be unwelcome at this point. But neither Robert nor his men will deliver that to me.

No, they want me to suffer. They want me to commit evil along with them. When I refuse, they'll only go to greater lengths to convince me. They'll break me. And that's what scares me most. Because I know they can.

If I'm lucky, the Ringmaster will take pity. But I chase that thought away. The Ringmaster's reputation paints him as shrewd in his dealings. There will be no pity. Only opportunity. If I can convince him I'm valuable, he'll keep me. If not, he won't. It's as simple as that.

At least, with him, I have a chance to offer value beyond the magical gifts that will *never* be available. Not to him and not to anyone. Not even for the price of my life.

As Robert is so furiously figuring out right about now.

Asshole.

I sniffle, shoving down the guilt I shoulder for the part I played in Robert's downfall. If it weren't for me, he'd likely still be the charming man I'd met all those years ago. The one with a quick smile and bright eyes.

The image of his twisted expression as he slammed his fist into my jaw assaults me, and I clench my hands into fists.

My own fury fuels me, and I manage to make it

nearly to the entrance before my body finally gives out. My knees buckle, and I go down hard, crying out sharply at the sudden pain it brings. I bite it off quickly, terrified I've alerted the asshole to my location.

But before I can twist around to see if I've brought him running, a heavy iron door opens in the center of the crumbling apartment complex. A figure steps out. Male, from the silhouette of him. And bathed in the light emanating behind him, though shadows make it impossible for me to make out features, the first stranger is followed by another. And a third. Security. The Ringmaster wouldn't come out here himself. These must be his guards.

I don't say a word. If I open my mouth now, all that'll come out is a scream, and I refuse to give in to the pain just yet.

The figures approach as a single unit, and I'm able to make out their shapes. Definitely males. I manage to look up at them through blurred, puffy eyes before the adrenaline driving me finally wears off and I sprawl onto my side in the dirt.

"Whoa," one of them says. The front man. He steps forward, and the other two spread out on either side of him in a sort of "V" formation like they've done this a thousand times before. Like they're trying to assess what level of threat I am.

Desperation has me whispering, "Asylum."

"What's that?" The front man steps closer, crouching down.

I see stark blue eyes set against a hard jaw. Handsome. Too handsome. My stomach tenses because, in my experience, men who look like him behave like Robert. And I damn sure don't want to find out if that's a stereotype or fact. But it's this or let myself be discovered here by the demon himself.

"Ringmaster..." My ribs squeeze with every syllable, and I shut my eyes against the pain. Wheezing, I wait to see if they'll grant my request.

"What do you think, Duncan?" one of the others asks.

"She's asking for the Ringmaster," the front man says. Duncan, apparently.

"Is she drunk?" the third asks, mild humor coloring his tone. My fists clench at that, but I can't afford a reply.

"She's not fucking drunk, you dumbass," the second one shoots back. He steps closer, peering over Duncan's shoulder at me. Up close, I catch sight of multiple facial piercings glinting in the light against an angled jaw and green eyes that prickle my skin where they scan my body. I watch as he gets a closer look at my face, and his own expression registers shock.

"What is it, Kill?" the third one prompts, inching closer now too.

But Kill—whatever kind of name that is—doesn't

answer. He blinks, his green gaze resettling on mine, and a dark sort of fury flashes in their green depths.

"She's covered in fucking bruises, dude." Duncan's tone has turned deadly. "Someone did a real number on her."

"I can fucking see that," the third snaps. "Drunken fight?"

"Do you smell liquor on her?" Kill retorts.

"No," the third replies.

Out among the trees, voices sound—male voices—all of them working for the asshole who did this to me. I tense, my wheezing cut short as I hold my breath and wait to see what my fate will be.

"Someone's out there," the third one says. "They might have done this to her. We should get her inside until we know."

"I've got her." Duncan reaches down and scoops me into his arms like I weigh nothing at all.

But the jostling makes me whimper, and I hear a, "Take it fucking easy," from the one called Kill; like he's actually angry at his friend for furthering my pain.

"He's just trying to fucking help," the third puts in.

They banter in a grouchy yet easy sort of way, and I wonder if these men are more than co-workers. Family, maybe. Their familiarity, even in the way they fuss at one another, suggests they're bonded somehow. The thought sends a pang through my already aching body. This one's more of a hollow echo in my chest. A deep sort of longing mixed with the grief of loss—for a bond I'll never have. That I can never afford to let myself look for.

I don't complain again, mostly to keep them from changing their minds about harboring me. Instead, I focus on deep breathing that doesn't sound like one of my lungs is drowning in its own fluids. Every inch of my skin hurts, but I also can't help but notice how safe I feel as I'm carried by the front man of this security trio, no matter how grouchy he is about having to help me.

The three men continue grunting at one another while we walk, and I lose all sense of direction as we make a few turns down a series of halls.

Finally, we stop, and one of the men knocks sharply on a door.

From the other side, I hear, "Come in."

I'm carried into a warm space that practically glows orange from a fire crackling in the large hearth. From this angle, I can't see much else beyond the ceiling, but I can sense there are others present here.

"What the hell happened?" a female asks. She doesn't wait for an answer before rushing over and looking down at me.

Through my swollen lids, I meet her eyes and find a surprisingly friendly face peering at me. Her near-white hair is pulled up in a messy bun, and her cheeks are slightly flushed, but she doesn't flinch away from the sight of my battered body. Instead, her kind eyes flash with a fury that seems out of place on her otherwise soft face.

"What is this?" asks a gruff male voice from somewhere behind the woman.

"Found her outside," one of my three rescuers says.

"Who did this?" the female demands.

"Liv, calm down," the gruff male warns.

"D's right," says the man holding me. *Duncan*. "You can't let yourself get worked up."

"Do not start with me, Duncan," she warns. Before he can answer, she leans in close to me and smiles. "I'm Liv. Can you tell me your name?"

"Helen," I lie through a busted lip. It's my mother's name. I cannot let them know who I really am because the one hunting me has friends all over, even in No Man's Land.

"Helen, can you tell me who did this to you?" she presses.

I don't answer that. Instead, I say, "I'm looking for the Ringmaster."

Liv smiles wryly. "Well, you've found him." She nods toward the figure behind her. The gruff-voiced male straightens, and alarm spears through me.

Shit. The Ringmaster is here? Watching me get carried around like a rag doll?

I scramble, trying to free myself from the strong arms holding me, but they only tighten their grip.

"Put me down," I insist.

"Not happening," Duncan says.

"I am ordering you to put me down." The words—and the bitchy tone I use to say them—completely exhaust me. But Duncan gives in and sets me on my feet.

I'm vaguely aware of Liv nodding to give him the order to do it, but I ignore that. Instead, I pretend it was all me and that Duncan gave in because of how scary I sounded. That feels better than this helplessness.

The minute Duncan lets me go, I wobble, knees buckling.

"Dammit." Duncan is there immediately. But he doesn't swoop in and grab me again. He only yanks a chair underneath me so that I sink into it rather than the floor.

He remains directly behind me, close enough for me to reach back and touch him if I wanted to. Which I don't. The other two stand on my left, too far back for me to see their faces. Liv, the woman, takes the chair opposite mine. As she sits, I note the large, round belly she cradles with her hand.

My mind tries to put all the pieces together, including who all these people are to each other, but the pain is making it hard to think. Exhaustion doesn't help.

No one else speaks.

I exhale, shaky but determined. Then, I lift my gaze to the man standing beside the hearth. He glares at me, his piercing copper eyes narrowed on my face. His dark hair is cut short on the sides and left a bit longer on top, and scruff darkens the lower half of his face. Even so, I note the strong, stubborn set of his jaw and the raw power emanating from him.

Of fucking course this is the Ringmaster. Everything about the man demands respect even when he's silent.

My head starts to throb, but I force myself to hold his stare. There's a hardness about it that I've never encountered in anyone else before, but it's not cruelty. I hope that means he'll have mercy. Or at least just give me a chance to prove my use.

"I have come offering my services," I say when it's clear he's not going to speak first.

"Your services?" he asks, arching a brow in challenge. "And what exactly can you offer?"

He's fishing to find out what type of supernatural I am, which means he's not able to sense me. No one else can, but still, after everything I'd heard about this guy, I'd wondered. *My first stroke of luck. Perfect.* I lift my chin. "I'm a performer. This seems like a place where my talents could be useful."

"And what exactly are you?" the man asks. "You don't look like you have much to offer me. So, unless you are—"

"I am a performer," I interrupt. "A talented one at that." Years of learning to cope with my anxiety led me to the silks. While I've never performed for a large audience, I'm damned good. Good enough to make my way here until I can figure out my next move.

"Talented?"

He doesn't believe me—that much is clear from his voice. I can't blame him. I look like a hot mess, and it's not like I'm up for proving my skills right now. Fear licks at my mind. If this doesn't work—

"Arial. Mainly silks, but I am experienced on the lyra, too."

Liv's eyes light up. "D, the lyra. We need—"

"Quiet," he says, but it's not nearly as forceful as he is with me.

She scowls but continues to watch me.

I look back at the Ringmaster. "I'll do whatever you need. I just..."

"Need a place to hide?" he finishes.

I don't argue because, hello, hot mess. I can't exactly deny I'm in a bind here.

"I'm not going to pretend there isn't something in it for me," I say, refusing to cower.

He grunts.

I have no idea what that means. Hopefully, I get points for honesty.

"I don't give freebies," he says at last.

"I'm not asking for a handout," I snap.

"Well, you're also not in a position to prove your worth, are you?"

"D," Liv hisses, but he ignores her, clearly waiting

for me to say something.

Behind me, Duncan, the one who carried me here, is utterly silent. Not that he owes me any favors but damn. The man found me collapsed outside; the least he could do is try and buy me some time, right? Even as I think it, I dismiss it, though. Since when can I count on a man to have my best interests in mind?

Easy answer. Never.

My entire fucking body feels like I was just run over repeatedly, but I straighten as best I can. "If that's what you need, I'll show you. Take me to the Big Top."

"No. Absolutely not," Liv snaps as she turns to D. "She is in no state to perform."

The Ringmaster eyes her with amusement glistening in his gaze. "She says she can."

"D," Liv warns, and I get the sense he's playing with her somehow and she knows it. Either way, watching her refuse to back down to a creature like him is impressive as hell.

"Fine," he says, turning back to me. "Answer me this. What are you doing here?"

"I told you; I'm offering my services."

"And whoever did this to you? Will they come looking for your *services* as well?"

I flinch but otherwise don't dignify that with an answer.

Liv gives him another exasperated look.

He clears his throat. "You have three days to

recover. You'll have one audition, two minutes. If you prove unskilled, you'll be asked to leave, no arguments. Do you understand?"

I keep my breath even, mostly to hide my excitement but also to keep from hurting my bruised ribs more. "I understand."

"If you can perform as you say you can, I will give you three months. That's all I can offer you. Nightly performances, five days a week—once you're fully healed, of course."

"Thank you." Hope soars, inflating my chest and straightening my shoulders.

He nods. "At the end of the three months, you're no longer my concern. We have no room for two aerial acts at this time, and I don't do charity." He glances at Liv, and she gives him an approving smile.

"I'll take it." The weight on my chest that's been threatening to crush me eases slightly. I inhale, still wheezing but lighter.

Duncan speaks up from behind me. "She needs a healer, boss."

The Ringmaster frowns but nods. "Put her in a room. I'll send Adaya over to take a look at her." He turns back to the fire, making it clear this meeting is over.

But Duncan doesn't move. "Sir, there were people in the woods outside the grounds." The Ringmaster turns back. "I think they might have been looking for her."

My breath catches. Shit. Had I really believed they'd keep that to themselves?

"Check it out," the Ringmaster says. "Settle her first, though."

"What about the wards?" Duncan asks.

"Take her to Uma on your way," the Ringmaster says as he looks me up and down. "Shouldn't be too hard to get blood from her right now."

"You got it, boss," one of the other guards says.

"Blood?" I ask, fear burning a hole inside of me. But they don't answer me, and I don't press. Whatever they need the blood for seems small in comparison to what's waiting for me if they throw me out.

Duncan comes around and scoops me back into his arms. I don't bother protesting about being carried. Now that I've secured my safety, I can afford to admit how badly I'm broken.

Besides, the Ringmaster only gave me three months. And I have a feeling all my complaining will do is make me look weak in the eyes of such a powerful man. The last thing I need is for him to throw me out before I can prove myself. I didn't come this far only to let my asshole fiancé win. I have three months to heal and figure out my next move.

Three months to figure out how to escape my fate. I will not be used to burn down the world. He'll have to kill me first.

Chapter 2

Duncan

The woman in my arms bears the marks of a victim, yet the fire in her soul suggests someone who is anything but. Her face is battered; nearly every inch of her body is marred in some way, whether it be her black eyes, the scratches on her cheeks, or the split in her pouty lips.

Whoever did this to her deserves to die.

Based on the hardened expressions my brothers wear, I know they're thinking the same thing. Ahead of me, Bracken doesn't say a word as we make our way to the staff quarters. The fact that D even gave her a chance is a precedent I wasn't prepared for. He's never granted asylum without an audition— or at least proof that the newcomer can deliver.

Liv's influence has softened him. Not a bad thing. The fucker could do with some softening.

Still, I don't want to think about what will happen to her if she can't perform in three days. D might have shown mercy for now, but he won't break his word. If this girl can't wow him, he'll put her back on the street in a heartbeat.

What will happen to her then?

And why the fuck do I care?

Uma arrives just as we pass back through the Big Top. Her dark hair is braided back as usual, and the cloak she wears is a deep violet that nearly matches the shade of her eyes today. They change with her mood, which is incredibly helpful when you're dealing with a powerful witch who could level this entire place with one pissed-off afternoon.

"Fuck, she looks horrible," she comments as she reaches into the bag she carries and withdraws a vial to draw Helen's blood.

"What is that for?" Helen asks, her voice barely above a whisper.

"The wards," Uma replies as she wipes the newcomer's arm with a sterilizing pad and slides the needle into her skin. Helen doesn't even flinch, likely because, compared to what she must already be feeling, a blood draw is nothing. "This will allow you inside them where it's safe. No one else can touch you here," Uma adds, eyes flicking to the damage someone has done to her.

"Thank—" The woman's eyes roll back in her head, and she loses consciousness.

"You already call Adaya?" Uma questions.

"D did."

She nods and puts a cap on the vial. "Liv's old apartment," she tells me. "Give me a few, and I'll get the wards altered to include her."

"Thank you."

Uma turns on her heel and rushes upstairs toward the apartments at the back of the Big Top. They're the only ones that are inhabitable, and they serve as the homes of every performer under contract here.

"Do you think it was a random attack?" Killian questions.

"Doubtful," I tell them as I study her body barely covered by a man's dress shirt. "She knew her attacker."

"What makes you think that? No Man's Land is a cesspool of fuckers doing what they want at others' expense," Bracken replies.

"She's seeking asylum here," I remind them. "Which means whoever is hunting her won't stop. A random attacker would move on."

"Are we going to have another Ernesto situation?" Killian questions, referring to Liv's psychotic ex.

"Let's hope not," I reply. "It's been long enough. Let's get her settled before Adaya arrives."

"I'm heading back down," Killian says. "Going to try to get a beat on those fuckers."

"We'll be down as soon as she's settled," I tell him.

"Sounds good. I'll try not to have too much fun

without you assholes." He winks then turns and jogs back through the Big Top.

Holding Helen in my arms, I cross the boundary and into the apartments. Since it's warded for the performers' protection, only those whose blood has been included in the spell can pass through undetected.

We reach Liv's old apartment, and Bracken moves around to open the door for us. My lion surges to the surface, desperate to get free so he can hunt. I shove him back down momentarily even though I cannot wait to let him free the moment I get a chance.

We will hunt.

And when we find these assholes, they will be shown no mercy.

Bracken flips on the light, illuminating the small apartment consisting of a twin bed, a vanity, a chest of drawers, and a tiny nook kitchen that serves no culinary purpose. It may not be much, but thanks to the wards, she'll be safe from whatever hunts her.

And although the Big Top is not protected by the same wards, we'll be there for her performances, watching and ensuring all those under the protection of this circus stay safe.

I set her down on the bed, gently, though she groans in pain all the same. Then, I step back and study the rest of her. She's dressed in barely anything—a man's dress shirt that looks haphazardly buttoned as though she did it in the dark. Or in a hurry. The beast inside me snarls at the sight of her in a man's clothing. The reaction takes me by surprise, but I dismiss it as she whimpers. Her eyes flutter open, and she stares up at me.

My attention returns to her body. Her legs are bare and torn to fucking shit, her feet, too.

"Were you assaulted?" I ask, my voice barely controlled as my anger stirs.

Her dark chocolate eyes shift to mine. "I'm beat to shit," she deadpans. "I think that's a yes."

"Were you raped?" I clarify. "I can see you were attacked, but your attire leads to other conclusions."

She swallows hard. "No." Her gaze shifts from mine. "I escaped first," she whispers.

My hands clench into fists at my sides as I offer her a nod, fucking relieved that she got away even if I am still going to take great pleasure in punishing the fucker responsible for her pain. "Adaya—the healer—will be here shortly, and we will ensure you are brought clothing and food. Is there anything else?"

"Am I a prisoner in this room?" She looks from me to Bracken, who has yet to speak since we stepped inside. I can feel the anger radiating from him through our pride bond, though, and I know he's impatient to join Killian on the hunt.

"You're not a prisoner although your current physical condition would only suffer if you tried to leave." Behind me, Bracken clears his throat. I roll my eyes. "Circus policy dictates that you are not permitted to leave your quarters until we're sure you can make good on your skills. Once you have signed your contract, you will have the rights of everyone else here. Including access to the gym, Big Top, and dining hall."

"Contract?"

"Everyone here is under a contractual obligation," I tell her. "You sign it, or you leave."

Helen swallows hard, and I struggle to keep my gaze from her delicate throat—and the red handprints wrapped around it. She wasn't just attacked. Someone tried to kill her. "Thank you," she says. "For this." She gestures to the bed, but my eyes flit over her half-naked body, and my lust stirs. "Your name is Duncan?"

The way she says my name has something churning inside me, but I shove it the hell down. I don't have time for attraction with this woman. I have a strict 'no fucking performers' policy for a damned reason. Not to mention this woman is in no condition for it, anyway. "Yes."

"Who are you?" she asks Bracken.

Despite her injuries and obvious pain, her gaze is direct. She meets his eyes with no sign of fear. Though my beast can sense her nerves at being alone with us, she's hidden it well.

He clears his throat. "Bracken."

"Bracken," she repeats, "and Duncan. Thank you both. And please thank the other one—"

"Killian," I interject.

"Killian. Please thank him for me, too. You three saved my life."

"We're just doing our job."

A soft knock sounds on the door, so we all turn as Bracken reaches over and opens it to reveal the visitor. Adaya, the water fae who also serves as our healer when necessary, strolls in wearing skintight jeans, a white crop top, and a black leather jacket. "Boys," she greets with a kind smile that fades the moment she sees Helen on the bed. "You poor thing." She crosses the apartment and sets her medical bag down then looks to me. "You both can go now. I'll take care of her."

Neither Bracken nor I respond as we turn and leave the two women. I set a fast pace, strangely off balance and glad to be out of that room. If Bracken notices my hurrying, he doesn't mention it.

"She's a looker," he comments instead as we step down into the Big Top and head for the exit.

"She's trouble," I say.

Bracken chuckles. "The best women usually are."

"She lied about her name."

"Caught that, too," Bracken comments. "Though, given her current state, I can't exactly blame her for being untrusting."

"Agreed. Still, we need to figure out who the hell she is and what fuckers need to die."

Bracken chuckles but doesn't respond.

Killian is leaning against the building when we step

outside to join him, his gaze fixed on the tree line just beyond the apartment buildings.

"Anything?" I ask.

"Movement," he replies. "We might want to shift to check it out. See if we can catch their trail."

Shifting means trading our weapons of man for weapons nature gifted our kind. It also means we're a hundred times more deadly. So, I nod. Not wanting to ruin our clothes, the three of us strip down and place everything inside the Big Top. Then, I glance at the two men who are brothers to me in everything but name and blood, and as one, we let our inner beasts take us over.

My bones crack, snapping and bending to fit my new form as golden fur shoots out through my flesh to cover my body. My head grows, my body morphing until I stand on all fours. Massive paws with sharp claws appear, each one capable of shredding flesh with a single swipe. Instinctively, I shake my head, letting my mane flare. One look at Bracken and Killian and I see that they, too, are in their lion forms.

Our pride was one formed out of survival and circumstance. And, due to that, these two men are the only people in this entire fucked-up world that I trust with my life. Well, and D. But the friendship I share with that asshole is different. These guys are my family now. Even if we weren't born brothers, we are now.

I extend my enhanced senses, sniffing and listening to the world around me, every sound and smell now magnified, thanks to my beast. Right away, I note the coppery tang of Helen's blood still hanging in the air and staining the ground near my feet. The mere scent of it drives the animal in me fucking wild with a need I can't name.

It's not a reaction I've ever felt before, but there's no time to decipher it. I tell myself it's just rage—a thirst for justice. So, on four massive paws, I race toward the trees, all while seeking out a scent that is not hers.

It doesn't take me long to find them.

At least a dozen different scents: all of them male, all of them hunting her.

Here, I can trace her steps, so I follow, Bracken and Killian on either side of me. The scents begin to fade the further we get into the woods, which means they either continued going past the circus or took a different route.

Most of them, anyway.

I catch an unfamiliar stench. *Enemy.* Just ahead. *"Smell that?"* I ask the others through our pride bond.

"Smells like rot," Killian replies.

"Let's find him," I order.

We all race through the trees, sprinting as fast as we can until, just ahead, I hear the crunching of branches and leaves beneath heavy bootsteps.

The man is sprinting, and when he realizes we're onto him, he turns and waves a hand. Magic scents the air. A branch falls in our paths, but we jump over it.

Fucking Warlocks. I leap, my paws slamming into his back and knocking the fucker onto his gut.

He grunts, and I shift while Bracken and Killian remain lions. Before the asshole can move, I wrap my hand around his throat and squeeze.

"Any more magic and my brothers will rip your throat out," I snarl at him.

His eyes widen, and the scent of urine fills the air.

"Why are you in these woods?" I demand.

"Out for a hike."

"I can see the lie on your fucking face, asshole."

The man doesn't respond.

"Don't want to talk?" I growl, "Not a problem. I have ways of making wormy little warlocks become real fucking chatty."

THE WORM—WHOSE NAME IS APPARENTLY MITCHUM— wheezes in a breath. The air is cool in the small, empty warehouse. Dusty, too. We haven't used this place for anything other than storage in a long time. Tonight, we're storing something other than circus supplies. The chair he's strapped to creaks as he tries to move, not that he'd get anywhere without it. With three of us and one of him, his odds of escape are pretty much zero. Arms tied behind his back, pants and shoes stripped away, he's helpless as fuck—and he knows it.

Blood slicks his shredded skin, compliments of Killian and his affinity for causing pain. Before that, Bracken's knuckles bruised the man's cheeks and cracked at least a few ribs. Me? I'm more into the psychological warfare of it all.

Can I cause pain? Fuck yes. In fact, my dark history probably makes me an expert in it. But I prefer the satisfaction I get in mentally breaking someone when they deserve it.

And this asshole *absolutely* deserves it.

"Why were you hunting the woman?" I ask.

"I told you," he wheezes, "I was just out for a hike."

I lean in closer, bracing myself on the arms of the wooden chair the asshole is strapped into. Chains bind his wrists behind his back, making it impossible for him to use his magic against us. "See, now, how can I trust you when every word out of your mouth is a motherfucking lie?" I keep my tone cool, my voice low.

"It's not."

"Then what is this?" I question as I use the tip of my dagger to push the sleeve of his shirt up. The brand there—a dagger with a single drop of blood at the tip of the blade—signifies exactly who he is, not that most folks recognize the logo or the name of the gang it signifies.

"I like tattoos," the bastard replies with a smirk.

Leaning in even further, I inhale deeply then let my inner lion show in my eyes when I pull back. Mitchum stares at me, his eyes widening just enough that, combined with his quickening pulse, equals fear.

Good.

"I can smell her blood on you," I tell him. "And that makes me desperate to rip you apart. See, I'll start with that pathetic cock that dangles between your legs. Then, I'll move to your legs. Your arms. Until finally—" I take the dagger at my waist and drag it ever so slightly over his gut. "Do I need to continue painting this picture for you?"

"You do not scare me, asshole," he replies. "Not nearly as much as *he* does. So go ahead, tear me apart, scatter me throughout No Man's Land. But I'm not saying a fucking thing. Ever."

There's just enough desperation in his tone to make his meaning clear. Whoever he's working for has him more scared than even I do. And that means this whole thing is useless. I try not to let my anger get the better of me as I accept that fact.

"Shame." In a blur of movement, I slash my dagger over his throat. He gags and wheezes, head falling forward as blood soaks his shirt. Frustrated, I turn to face my brothers. "Fucker wasn't going to talk."

"Nope," Killian agrees, looking just as pissed as I feel about the dead end. "What do we do now?"

"We inform the Ringmaster that our newest arrival has some nasty people after her. People who are, apparently, far more intimidating than we are."

"That's troublesome."

All three of us turn as D strolls in. He's every bit the intimidating dragon though most have no idea the truth behind his supernatural heritage. As the only full-blooded dragon in Portland—that we know of—he commands our respect though my brothers and I give it freely.

D might be an asshole.

But the man is honorable to the core. Even if everyone else in the world merely sees a man who contractually obligates his performers, I see someone who gave me a second chance, who gives people like his mate and Helen a chance to escape whatever horrors they're running from.

"What happened?" D asks.

"The fucker was more scared of his boss than of us," Killian replies.

"What boss?" D asks, eyes narrowing on the guy's body. "He doesn't wear a House ring."

"No. But he was clearly referring to whoever hired him. He wasn't going to break. Even with the fact that he pissed himself when Duncan tackled him in the woods."

"Who the hell is this girl?" D questions, eyeing the dead prisoner.

"I don't know," I reply honestly. "But she seems to be important enough that Crimson Hunters are searching for her. And a warlock to boot."

D arches a brow. "You believe this man to be a Crimson Hunter?"

I nod and pull his sleeve up to reveal the gang's brand again. It's one I recognize from my past life as a contract killer. "He's a hired goon all right. Though, if I had to guess, he's fairly green. Maybe a pledge."

D ponders what I said, his copper gaze not leaving the dead man in our presence.

"What will you have us do, boss?" Killian asks.

"Liv is intent on giving this woman a chance," he replies. "But I'm not looking for a front-row seat to someone else's war."

"Do you have any idea what kind of supernatural she might be?" Bracken asks.

D shakes his head. "I do not recognize her scent, and if she'd had any active abilities, I imagine she wouldn't be as banged up as she is."

"We'll figure it out. With enough time, we'll get to the bottom of it," I offer. The fear that D will throw her out grows with each passing moment. And for some reason, I don't want Helen to leave. Not yet, anyway.

"See that you do," D replies as he runs a hand over the back of his neck. "Find out her real fucking name, too. We'll give her a chance and hope she's worth the trouble she will inevitably deliver to our doorstep."

Adaya's grip is strong as she pulls me out of the tub. The water sloshes as I step out, its color a muddy pink where the dirt and blood have been washed from my skin, thanks to Adaya's efforts.

I'm grateful for her help—and her friendly silence. The woman has a soothing sort of presence that puts me at ease. I can't remember the last time I felt this comfortable completely naked in front of someone. Maybe because I can't remember the last time I was with someone who didn't want something from me. Something I'd been unwilling to give. I shudder at that, and Adaya frowns as she finishes toweling me off and slips a gown over my head.

"Are you cold?" she asks.

"Yes," I admit because it's true. Even if it's not the reason for my physical reaction.

"Come," she says.

Shaking away thoughts of my past, I let her lead me back to bed. There, I climb carefully beneath covers that feel deliciously comfortable now that I'm clean and mostly out of pain. The tonic Adaya gave me earlier, combined with her healing efforts, has already made a huge difference. The twinges and dull aches are only a mild inconvenience. More importantly, I can breathe without wanting to cry, and that's a miracle compared to how I felt when she arrived.

Settling back against the pillow, I let Adaya pull the blankets up and tuck me in. She leans over, re-checking the stitches and securing bandages over the worst of my injuries now that I'm clean and dry.

"Thank you," I say quietly.

Her gaze flicks to mine, and she softens. "You were lucky to get yourself away from … whoever the hell did this to you," she says. Unlike the others, she doesn't push for more. "I've done what I can, but you'll need to take it easy for the next couple of days."

"And then?" I ask, biting my lip. "Will I be back to full strength and movement soon?"

"What kind of movement?" she asks.

"I need to be able to perform. To secure my place here with the Ringmaster."

"The Ringmaster is an ass if he doesn't let you stay," she says. My eyes widen, but she pats my hand. "You let me worry about him. For now, concentrate on healing." When I try to respond, she holds up a hand, "But yes, in answer to your question, you will return to full strength and movement soon enough."

I let out a breath.

She gets up and pulls a sachet of herbs from her bag, setting them on my nightstand. "You'll want to take these in tea. Goes down easier," she explains.

"Thank you."

A knock at the door has her looking back and scowling.

"Come in," she calls.

The door opens, and one of the three security guards from earlier steps in. The one called Kill.

"Killian," Adaya greets then goes back to packing her things.

His face piercings glint in the light as he shuts the door and strides closer to my bed. Where Duncan is more refined, Killian is all animal. I can see it in his eyes and the predatory way he moves.

"How's the patient?" he asks, mostly addressing Adaya, which makes me bristle in irritation.

"The patient is right here," I say icily. "And I'm fine."

His brow quirks—the one with a small silver ring through it. And, despite his rudeness, my stomach flutters at the way his sharp green eyes assess me. "Sure you are, love." He tosses the words at me casually—meaningless even—then turns to Adaya. "What's the damage?"

Adaya eyes him with disapproval, likely at his crudeness, but she says, "Two cracked ribs, a sprained ankle, a concussion, and a fractured arm. Not to mention all the bumps, bruises, and cuts."

"What kind of cuts?"

Something about his tone keeps me from interrupting. And even though he's not looking at me, I can see the murderous set in his expression. He's angry. Not at me; at whoever hurt me. It's such a startling realization that I forget to be pissed they're talking about me like I'm not even here.

"Shallow, mostly," Adaya says, "though the one on her shoulder required a few stitches. Must've been a blade of some kind from the looks of it."

The man—Killian—says nothing, but I can feel the rage rolling off him. The air practically crackles with it.

"I'm done for the night," Adaya continues. "I'll be back tomorrow," she adds, glancing at me. "In the meantime, make sure she takes the herbs I left for her."

"Dosage?" he asks as if he's done this all before.

"Every four hours. Make sure she doesn't sleep longer than that in one stretch."

"Concussion protocol," he says, waving her off. "I got it. I got it."

She nods, satisfied. "Be nice," she tells him and then lets herself out.

When we're alone, the man turns back to me, and I tense.

"You look a lot less than fine," he says in response to my earlier comment, and I scowl.

"You're no prize yourself."

He grins, and I know we both recognize the lie. Even in my pained state, I can admit that he's hot. But he also knows it. Which more than likely makes him an asshole.

"What do you want?" I ask, suddenly exhausted.

"Just checking on you."

"Checking on me," I repeat. "You mean securing the prisoner?"

"You're a guest. An employee of the circus until further notice. I'm here to make your transition comfortable."

"That's your official role? Hospitality?"

Smirking, he drifts closer, and I brace myself for some sarcastic comeback. Instead, he says, "I ordered you some soup from the kitchen. It should be up shortly."

"You ordered me soup?" My surprise derails me. Just like with his anger, I don't know what to do with the kindness.

"Do you want something different?"

"No, I... you didn't have to do that."

That same brow quirks, sending the same butterflies battering my ribs again. My breath catches, and I immediately berate myself for reacting to a pretty face. After all, that's what got me into this damned mess in the first place.

"It's my job to get you well enough to perform," he says.

I sigh, my head falling back against the pillow. "Fair enough."

It should have been a cue for him to leave. Instead, he lingers, studying me with solemn eyes.

"You ready to tell me who did this to you?" he asks quietly.

"I tripped," I say with zero believability.

"Then I'll fuck up whatever floor had the audacity," he says as he cracks his knuckles. "Just point me in the right direction."

I snort then immediately cover my mouth with my uninjured hand.

Killian grins at me.

I cannot tear my gaze from him.

"What?" he asks.

I shake my head, my thoughts fuzzy all of a sudden. "You're so pretty to look at, but then you start talking, and the whole thing is ruined." I clamp down on my mouth the moment the words are out, a little shocked at myself. But he surprises me by throwing his head back and laughing. The sound of it warms me in places I've felt nothing but icy fear for way too long.

"Ruined how, exactly?"

"You're so ready to commit violence," I say, which only earns me more laughter.

"You're a trip, new girl." His green eyes are warmer now, gleaming with something dangerously close to interest.

"Helen," I say, sinking deeper into the warmth that's spreading through me now. "Call me Helen."

"We both know that's not your real name. So why don't you tell me what it is?"

"No, I don't think I want to be that girl right now." I wave a heavy hand. "You wouldn't like her," I slur. "She's weak."

His eyes darken with intensity. "I very much doubt that, *Helen*. You do seem to have a lot of secrets, though, don't you?"

His question is carefully light, but I can feel the darkness in me coming up to meet it. And right now, I don't want darkness. "Killian," I say, testing out the syllables on my tingly tongue.

"That's my name, love."

"I know one of your secrets. You're nice even when you're grouchy."

He grins. "I'll take that as a compliment."

I lick my lips, trying to understand how in the world these things keep coming out of my mouth. The drugs, I remember lazily. The herbs Adaya gave me. They must have kicked in. And their effects are making everything feel loose—even my tongue, apparently.

I groan at that.

"You feeling better?" he asks knowingly, a small smile quirking his mouth. A very delicious-looking mouth if I'm being honest. I want to touch it. To feel if those plush lips are just as soft as they appear.

"Much," I admit, sighing happily.

The pain is gone. Now, all I feel is numb.

"You have a lot of piercings," I say.

"You haven't seen the half of them, love. Maybe one day I'll show you. When you're not under the influence." He winks.

My eyes widen at that, but even drugged, I can't bring myself to ask the questions his words elicit. Something about my face draws another laugh out of him, though.

He shakes his head then runs a hand through blond hair that hangs messily to his chin. Tracking the movement, I catch sight of several rings on his fingers and find myself wondering how it would feel to touch him with all that metal decorating his body.

Before I can formulate a response, there's a knock at the door.

He strides toward it and grunts at whoever's on the other side. Someone hands him a tray, though I can't see who. Then he's shutting the door and carrying the tray toward my bed.

"You can put it over there," I say, stifling another yawn as I point at the small counter.

"Absolutely not. You need to eat." He sets the tray on my bed, forcing me to tuck my legs underneath me or risk spilling everything. I sit up, ready to argue until the smell of the food hits me. My stomach growls, effectively nullifying my protests.

He flashes a smug smile and crosses his arms.

I reach for the spoon then glance up at him with narrowed eyes. "Are you just going to stand over me and watch me eat like some kind of prison guard?"

"I could feed you if you'd like," he offers with a grin.

"Let me keep at least some of my dignity."

He flashes me a smile before grunting and snagging a chair from the small breakfast table. He turns it backward before straddling it. Propping his arms on the wooden back, he says, "Is this better?"

I don't answer, momentarily distracted. His sleeves have ridden up to reveal thick tattoos that color his wrists and disappear beneath his shirtsleeves. I wonder briefly what they are and how far up his body they go. But then I catch myself and quickly look back at the tray instead.

No good can come of wondering.

Or, worse, looking.

"Whatever," I mumble and force myself to take a bite.

The soup is good. I taste vegetables and a hint of chicken, but mostly it's a heavy broth; warm and comforting. Killian doesn't say another word as I shove spoonfuls of the stuff into my mouth. I've eaten nearly all of it before I even remember I'm being watched. Suddenly, the feel of his gaze prickles my skin, and I look up again, my face heating.

"What?" I snap.

"What are you?" he asks, and the directness of his question catches me off guard.

"What are *you*?" I shoot back.

"Lion shifter. You want to see?"

I roll my eyes even as my heart thuds. Lion? Wow. I've never seen a predator that huge up close, and here he is offering. But I know better. He's fucking with me. I don't give him the satisfaction of a response.

"What are you?" he repeats.

"Sleepy," I say pointedly, setting the spoon aside and shoving the tray back.

"You don't trust me, fine," he says with a shrug. "But my pride and I are the reason you're not dead or worse. That's not nothing."

He's right, of course. "Doesn't mean I'm going to spill my secrets."

"Can't blame you there. But you should know the Ringmaster doesn't do well with secrets. Not under his roof. And you currently have even more than he does."

"You do everything the Ringmaster says?"

I mean it as an insult, but he doesn't seem bothered in the least. "I owe D my life," he says quietly. "And because of that debt and the respect I have for him, I will protect him. Even from you."

I don't know what to say to that. Mostly because my heart twinges with jealousy. What would it be like to have someone protect me that way?

I'll never know, so I shove it aside.

"I'm not a threat," I say, "Not to you or to the Ringmaster."

"Maybe not directly. But whoever's after you isn't going to stop, are they?"

I look down. "I don't know what you're talking about."

"Right. A damned floor did this to you. I forgot."

He stands, grabs the tray, and deposits it on the counter. When he starts for the door, I wrench my gaze up, startled and panicked.

"You're leaving?" I blurt.

With one glance at me, his expression softens. "I won't be far, love. You're safe here."

I can't bring myself to acknowledge my fear—the fear he's so easily spotted anyway—so I just nod and fold my hands tightly together.

His gaze lingers on me for a moment longer.

Finally, he clears his throat.

"I'll let you rest." He turns for the door, and even in my drugged state, I sense a hesitance. Like he doesn't really want to leave yet. But he does. And when I'm alone, I find I'm too tired to be scared after all.

Maybe it's his promise. Maybe it's the drugs. Soon, I'm sucked into a dreamless sleep that, for the first time in a long time, feels like peace.

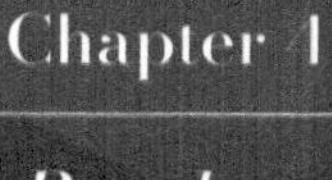

Exactly four hours after Killian last checked on her, I'm walking into Helen's room, a mug of steaming water in my hand. The sound of her even breathing tells me she's sleeping, so I move quietly, creeping inside and shutting the door behind me. Her form is slight in the bed with only pale light from the bedside lamp to illuminate her slumbering features.

I stop beside her bed, setting the mug down beside the herbs Adaya left before taking a few minutes to study her in the soft glow of the lamplight. The harsh lines of mistrust are gone now, her expression peaceful. Thick dark lashes, long dark hair, pouty fucking lips I long to trace.

Fuck me.

There's something about her, something that calls to

me. And my lion? Well, he's already decided she belongs.

The scent of her blood still clings to the air, and I bite back a growl, wishing like hell I could revive that fucking hunter just so I could break a few more bones and kill him again. I reach out and take a strand of her dark hair between the tips of my fingers and tuck it behind her ear.

A soft moan leaves her lips, and she arches into my touch. My cock hardens despite her injuries. And when her lids flutter open, those beautiful amber eyes peering straight up at me, I force myself to take a step back.

"Bracken?" she chokes out.

"It's time for your tea," I say. My name leaving her lips is so damned delicious it makes me want to groan.

She sits up, and the blankets slip from her neck and my mouth dries. The gown she wears is thin, and the swell of her breasts is on full fucking display. *Mine.* The lion in me snarls the word, and I shove it back.

No fucking way he picks this woman. What coincidence would it be that my mate would show up just as broken as I'd been when I came here?

"Sorry," she whispers as she pulls the covers back up over herself.

"Not a problem," I assure her. I put some of the herbs into the steel ball I brought up with the hot water and place it into the mug to steep. "How do you feel?"

"Like I was dropped from a building."

"Were you?" I question.

Her gaze narrows on my face. "I tripped and fell on the floor."

I grin. "That's what Killian said. Though, we've been looking for said floor and can't find it."

"It wasn't local," she replies as she leans back against the wooden headboard, blankets clutched to her chest.

"I know it doesn't feel like it, but you can trust us."

She peers at me through dark eyes with enough scars behind them that I know she's seen far more than she should have in this life. The darkness that surrounds her is soul deep. I wish I could steal it from her and carry that burden. After all, I have my own that I already shoulder. What's a little more?

"No offense, Bracken, but the last *floor* that told me that ended up nearly killing me."

A low growl escapes from me, and I close my eyes to gain control over a predatory drive that is demanding I hunt. Demanding I track and kill whatever put such fear in her heart. "We have nothing to gain from lying to you," I tell her.

"Not yet you don't," she whispers, then brings her knees up and lowers her forehead to them. She's so closed off, so burdened.

"If you don't tell us what happened, we can't protect you."

"I'm here," she replies when she finally lifts her head again. "That's protection enough."

"Three days is hardly enough time to recover from what happened," I argue.

"I'll be ready. I wasn't lying about what I can do."

Her confidence pisses me off for some reason.

"And three months from now?" My tone is harsher than I meant, but if we don't push her to open up to us, then there's no eliminating the threat. Which means, when she has to leave—I swallow hard, fear for what comes next smothering my ability to finish the thought.

"I'll worry about it then. Who knows, maybe the floor will have forgotten me by then."

"Men do not forget about women like you," I say.

Her gaze whips to mine. "Men?"

"We both know what kind of floor you're referring to, so at least, cut the shit on that front."

Helen swallows hard, and I worry I've pushed her too far. But she closes her eyes and breathes deeply then opens them and stares at me. "My name is not Helen."

"You don't say?" I feign surprise, and to my complete delight, she smiles.

"I'm not a great liar."

"That might be the first true thing you've said since I walked in here."

Another smile.

I reach for the tea, pulling the ball of herbs out before dunking it back in a few more times. Then, I offer her the mug and take a seat on the edge of the bed versus the backward chair I imagine is there because of Killian. Fucker's a rebel even in the way he sits in a damned chair.

"Thank you."

"You're welcome."

She puckers her lips and blows softly, and my cock hardens at the mental image of her on her knees. Lips puckered as she—

"My real name is Sway," she says, interrupting my thoughts.

"Sway," I repeat, her name like a whispered plea for deliverance from my own darkness.

"Yes."

"It's nice to officially meet you."

Sway takes a sip then groans. "That's perfect on my sore throat."

Fuck me, this woman is perfection.

"I imagine you'll be telling your brothers?" Her question jolts me back to the present. "Though, I have to say, you don't at all look like each other. Aside from the hair color at least."

"We don't have secrets," I tell her. "So, yes, I'll tell them, mostly because it helps us protect you. And we're not brothers by blood though we are a pride."

"You're all lion shifters, then? Killian told me that's what he was," she adds quickly as if she's worried I'll care.

"We are."

She takes another drink then clings to the mug. The blanket dips a bit further down, and I avert my gaze before I lose it and beg for her to let me show her how a real man treasures a woman. I could be gentle—at first.

Though, it wouldn't be just me she's having, and I can't speak for the others.

Duncan? Sure. He'd be tender in the beginning. But Killian? He's always a wildcard.

"Lion shifters." She sighs, her tone becoming more relaxed with each passing moment, thanks to the herbs in her cup. "I bet you guys are growly."

I grin. "You don't know the half of it."

She peers at me through a half-opened eyelid. "Who's the growliest? It's not Killian—he's too open and playful for that. And I can't say it would be Duncan either because he seems rather—refined."

"And me?" I ask, leaning in. "What do I strike you as?"

"An animal," she says. "Broody, moody, dark. So, I'd say you're the growly one."

The mug starts to tip, so I reach out and press a finger to the warm ceramic, straightening it so she doesn't accidentally dump hot water all over herself. "You have me pegged, Sway."

Her lips part, pupils dilating. "I like when you say my name." She takes another drink. "These herbs work fast."

"I like saying your name," I reply. "And that's the plan. We don't want you in pain."

"Is it that, or do you want me to spill all of my secrets?"

"I don't want to learn your secrets because you weren't able to keep them. I want you to tell me because you trust me."

"Trust," she whispers. A tear slips from her eye, so I reach forward and wipe it, my thumb brushing against her flesh. "I'm sorry. I—"

"Don't apologize," I say. "But you need to finish that tea."

She takes another drink. "I hope tomorrow is better. It has to be better, right?"

"It will be because you're here."

Her gaze narrows on me. "You surprise me. All three of you do." Her expression softens, and she adds, "You're so pretty to look at."

I stiffen because never in my life have I ever been referred to as pretty. I'm the monster that lurks in the shadows. A scarred, dark presence that will deal out death in the blink of an eye and without hesitation. She had it right earlier.

Duncan is the refined one.

Killian, the wildcard.

But me? I'm more than growly. I'm damaged goods.

She finishes off her tea before offering me the mug. I take it and set it on the table at her side then risk her slapping my hand away as I reach forward and brush a strand of dark hair from her face. Her cloudy amber eyes hold mine. "So pretty." She reaches forward with one hand and runs the tip of her finger down the scar that splits my left brow and runs the length of my face.

I freeze.

I've never been caressed.

I fuck hard. Carnal. Most women don't even look at me when I'm inside of them because I'm too much of an animal. But Sway watches me, unafraid. Which makes me wonder how much horror she's seen that she'd refer to me as 'pretty.'

"What happened to your face?" she asks.

And, for reasons I can't name, I actually tell her the truth. "I used to belong to a House that ran an underground supernatural fight ring. I fought to survive and took a broken bottle to the face for my trouble."

I tense, waiting for her to pull away. The story I just told her, however condensed, is one I've only told three others in this world. My brothers and D.

Her gaze furrows, but she doesn't drop her hand. "Your own people forced you to fight?"

"Yes."

"That's horrible."

I lean in closer so I can make out the flecks of gold in her eyes. "Then I suppose we have something in common. We both come from places we'd rather not go back to."

She drops her hand. "I like your eyes. Like the forest."

"I like yours," I reply then reach up to run the tip of my finger over the side of her face. It may be the herbs granting us this moment of trust, and while I won't take it too far, I'm enough of a bastard to try to use it to my advantage by sneaking past the walls she's erected around herself.

"I'm so tired." Her eyes begin to droop, and I realize breaking down those walls will have to wait.

"Then sleep." I pull my hand back as she scoots down further into the covers. "One of us will be back in four hours with more tea."

"Thank you." She looks up at me; then her gaze briefly drops to my mouth.

And because I'm an asshole, I lean in and press my lips to hers. A tender, quick peck that sets my blood on fire.

She moans softly beneath me, but before I can fully lose myself, I pull back. "Sleep well, Sway."

"Goodnight," she breathes.

After retrieving the mug, I slip back out into the hall. Killian and Duncan are already walking toward me.

"I know her real name," I tell them, flashing a smirk because I know it'll rile them up.

"You fucker. How'd you get that out of her?" Killian demands.

I grin at him then start walking toward the stairs. "She told me. I got a kiss, too."

"The fuck you did," Killian snaps.

I don't answer, just walk toward the apartment we share at the end of the hall. It's the only three-bedroom suite on the floor, the only larger apartment being D and Liv's upstairs. I push the door open and set the mug in the sink before turning to face my brothers.

The apartments are magically warded for privacy, so others are unable to hear anything inside once the door is shut.

So, as soon as it is, I cross my arms and give them one detail I know they're dying for right now. "Her name is Sway."

"Sway," Killian says, already smiling deviously. "Fitting. She sways me in throwing my morals to the side."

"What fucking morals?" I ask with a grin.

"Fair point. But I want her."

"So do I," I admit. "I think..." I trail off because it's too soon. "She's important."

"Dunc?" Killian questions, turning toward Duncan.

But he's closed off now. "I don't know enough about her."

"Bullshit," Killian says. "You know she calls to you, too. I can feel our pride's connection to her." He turns back to me, eyes narrowed in envy. "You seriously got a kiss?"

"I did," I reply with a grin. I can feel his jealousy, and it makes me happy as fuck. "She also called me pretty."

Killian rolls his eyes. "She called me pretty first, so fuck off."

I punch him in the arm, and he punches me back. When we're done wrestling, my gaze drifts to Duncan. "Whoever is after her is nasty as fuck."

"We already knew that," he replies.

"It's a man," I tell them. "Not that we didn't already know that, but she gave me confirmation. Based on what she told me, they were close at one point. Trust was a factor."

Duncan runs a hand through his hair. "Any idea what she is?"

"Nope. She is keeping that one locked down tight."

"At least, we have a name now," Duncan says. "Though we can't do much about it. Asking around will only draw their attention here."

"We'll have to do the investigation ourselves," I say. My beast stirs at the idea of hunting more of the assholes like the one we caught earlier.

"We tell D and Liv. No one else," Killian adds.

"Until we can put this fucker in the ground," I say, grinding my fist into my palm at the thought of it.

Duncan nods at me. "As long as she can perform like she claims, we have three months to figure it out."

"And the rest?" I can't help but ask.

"What else is there?" Duncan demands.

I shake my head at the way he's pretending not to want her. Before I can answer, Duncan grumbles something and stalks off to his bedroom. When Duncan's door shuts behind him, Killian rolls his eyes.

"He's being weird," I say.

"He's always like this when he has to get his hands dirty," Killian reminds me. "You know that. Give him a day or so to process, and he'll be fine."

He's right. Duncan's the methodical, clean-cut type, but that only makes him more ruthless. And more bottled up. He's wound tight as hell these days. "Fucker needs to get laid," I say finally.

Killian laughs. "Don't we all?"

Chapter 5

Sway

I come awake with a jolt at the sound of a door clicking shut. Heart racing, I sit up and blink, bleary-eyed at the sight of Killian striding across my room. The mere sight of him makes my pulse race faster, though, and I can't tell if it's due to the fact that he *is very much* a predator or because of something else entirely. Something I don't dare examine more closely.

"Whoa," he says when he sees my expression, "Chill, gorgeous. It's just me."

"Gods, you scared me." I force my breathing to slow as Killian sets a mug of hot water on the nightstand and goes to work adding the herbs Adaya left for me.

"Still a bit on edge, eh?" he asks, darting a glance at me.

I lean against the headboard, shoulders sagging as I

watch him work. "Those herbs make me sleep like the damned dead," I grumble.

He sets the metal ball of herbs into the water and then pulls up the chair he left earlier. "Better sleeping like the dead than being dead. Or wishing like hell you were because your body feels like it went head-to-head with a battering ram."

"You sound like you speak from experience."

He grimaces. "We all have our pasts."

I don't respond because that's one hell of a loaded statement. A few minutes later, he's shaking me awake again, and I straighten, realizing I've dozed off leaning against the headboard.

"Here," he says, holding out the mug for me. "Sway."

Doing my best not to react to his use of my name, I take the mug with wobbly hands, wrapping both palms around the ceramic cup to steady myself. The warmth helps wake me up, and I take a sip, enjoying the way the liquid soothes my throat.

Then, I look up into his expectant face and realize he's still waiting on me to respond.

"Bracken told you my name, then?"

"That's not all he told us."

I eye him warily, trying to recall what else I spilled while under the influence of Adaya's tea. "What?"

"He says you kissed him."

For a split second, I don't know what he means.

Then, the details of that moment come flooding back, and heat floods my face. "Fuck," I groan.

"Does that mean you regret it?"

My gaze snaps back to his. "None of your business," I say haughtily. "That's between me and him."

He leans forward until the chair stands only on its front two legs and he's close enough to reach out and touch. I should feel terrified at being alone with a man after everything Robert has done, but Killian is different. Despite the way he exudes power, I know instinctively that he won't hurt me. Instead, all I feel is attraction.

"We'll see about that, love." He lifts a hand and brushes his finger over my mouth then leans back again so the chair falls onto all fours.

I let out a breath, trying to decide whether to tell him to leave or not. That kiss with Bracken should never have happened. And it damn sure can't happen again— not with him and not with any of the other gorgeous, delicious lion shifters who've made it their mission to take care of me.

In fact—

Setting the half-empty mug aside, I push back the covers and swing my legs over the edge of the bed.

"Whoa, what the fuck are you doing?" Killian is out of his chair in a blink, hovering close enough that I very nearly edge back onto the mattress.

But I don't.

Instead, I shove him aside and stand, inhaling against the dizziness that washes over me.

"I'm taking a shower," I announce and then start for the bathroom.

Unsteady, I weave slightly left but manage to correct and somehow make it to the bathroom doorway. Bracing the wall for support, I hear Killian growl behind me. My lips quirk because, apparently, I was wrong; Killian can be growly too. And why does that excite me?

"Like hell you are," he says and marches up behind me. "You just took a shower when you got here."

"That was a bath," I correct. "And it was almost ten hours ago," I say, hoping my fuzzy brain is doing the math right. Besides, this shower is more to clear my head than clean my body, but I refuse to tell him that.

"You're too weak and unsteady to—"

I whirl, holding up an angry finger. "Let me stop you right there. It's my body. And while I did come here for safety, I didn't agree to being ordered around. I get to say what my body needs, and right now, it needs a shower."

His angry gaze flicks to my thin nightshirt.

"And another thing," I go on, pretending my skin doesn't tingle everywhere his eyes touch. "I'm done being drugged and put to bed."

His gaze snaps back to mine, a warning in his eyes now. "Are you sure about that, love? You've never been put to bed by the likes of me."

His tone is low and gravelly enough that I can feel his words scrape along my nerve endings. My mouth goes dry as I imagine him carrying me back to bed and climbing in with me. Of how close he'd have to press against me for both of us to fit in such a small space. Of capable hands erasing the memory of the very rough ones that were on me last.

I blink, shoving aside those mental images. Maybe a shower isn't enough. Better make it a cold one.

"I'm sure," I snap and then step back and shut the door in his face before I can change my mind.

I stand there, listening to see what he'll do and mildly terrified his next move will be to come crashing through said door and drag me back to bed. Terrified and incredibly turned on.

Ugh!

But instead, he's silent so long I wonder if he's left. Finally, he says, "I'm getting you some clothes. Stay awake and alive until I get back."

A moment later, I hear my bedroom door slam shut.

I grin like an idiot.

Point one, Sway.

THE SHOWER HELPS TO WAKE ME UP. BY THE TIME I'M done, I am more alert than before even as the herbs have numbed my aching body against the worst of the pain.

Killian hasn't returned. Or he hasn't made himself known, at least. Still, I am wary as I push the shower curtain aside, listening for some sound from the bedroom.

Reaching for the towel hanging on the hook, I grab it and wrap it around my body before attempting to step out. When that's done, I lift my right hand to the shower wall for support—and that's my mistake.

Steam slicks the tile's surface. My hand slips off it, and I careen forward. At the last second, I turn my body so I land on my hip rather than my face. The pain of hitting the tile floor is sharp and vicious, and a scream tears from my throat.

Seconds later, the door is ripped open, the lock breaking and the wood splintering as Killian shoves his way into the bathroom.

"Shit, what the hell did you do?"

I decide to let the question be rhetorical since I can't speak around the pain pulsing through me from hip to feet.

"Dammit, Sway." Killian reaches down and scoops me into his arms.

It isn't until I feel his palms against my exposed flesh that I realize my towel slipped off when I fell. Of course it did. Dammit. This is exactly what I'd tried to avoid. Now, thanks to the pain in my hip, I can't do anything to stop it.

"Easy now." Killian carries me back into the bedroom and lowers me to the bed.

The moment I'm in it, I reach for the covers, but he stops me.

"Hold on, let me see that bruise."

I ignore him, attempting again to pull the covers up, but he grabs my wrist, stilling me as he peers more closely at the new bruise blooming against an old one right along my hipbone.

"What are you, my doctor now?" I snap.

"If I were, I would have stopped you from taking that damned shower in the first place."

"I don't take orders from you."

He ignores that and brushes a fingertip over my skin along the edges of my aching hip. His touch draws a shudder from me, and even with the pain in my body, warmth pools in my belly.

"Did a number on yourself, didn't you?" he murmurs.

"The damned tile was slippery," I say, fully aware I'm taking my anger at myself out on him.

He looks up at me, a brow arched. "That's what happens when you get wet."

My skin burns at his words. And I don't miss the way Killian's eyes rake over me, taking all of me in with a single, sweeping glance. My nipples pebble at the awareness just as he finally lets go of my wrist. The moment he does, I pull the covers over me, wincing with the movement.

Frustrated, aching, hurting, I sink against the pillow and shut my eyes. Maybe it's all a bad dream. A hallucination from that stupid tea. Maybe I can just wait until the effects wear off and then wake up and find it's all just—

The mattress shifts as he sits on the edge of the bed beside me, so close his hip is pressed against my thigh. "Don't be embarrassed."

His tone is unexpectedly gentle and absent of his usual teasing or mockery.

I crack my eyes open. "Easy for you to say. You weren't found spread-eagle and helpless."

"If it makes you feel better, I'll take my clothes off and go lie on the tile so you can look at me. Will that make us even?"

My lips twitch even as a small voice in my mind screams 'Yes.' I shake my head. "Don't make jokes."

"Why not? Laughing is good for the soul. And you're brilliantly gorgeous when you smile."

I scowl. "Stop flirting. It won't work."

"That's yet to be determined."

I don't know what that means, but before I can ask, he nods at a stack of clothing folded on the dresser. "That's for you. Whenever you're ready for them, I'll bring them over. For now," he adds pointedly, "I advise staying in bed." He picks up the tea and shoves the now-cool mug into my hands. "And finishing this."

I sigh. "I guess I don't have much room for argument."

"Not a bit. Drink up, love."

When I don't move, his expression hardens. "If you don't, my brothers and I can take turns monitoring you from *inside* your room. That way, we can walk you to the bathroom ourselves next time. We'll probably fight over which one of us gets to wrap the towel around you, and you should know I'm clumsy enough to drop it from time to time."

Scowling, I tip up the mug and drink the cold tea. "You're an asshole," I say when I've drained the contents.

"Is that why you kissed Bracken? Because he's nice to you?"

"*Bracken* kissed *me*," I argue.

But the moment the words are out, I realize I shouldn't have said them.

A gleam lights his eyes like this is the detail he's been digging for all along. "Ah, I see. He stole it, then."

I say nothing.

"Well," he says, snagging the empty mug from my hands and setting it aside. "In that case, I'll have to take a page from his book."

He leans over, takes my face in his hands, and presses his lips to mine.

I have every intention of shoving him away, but the moment his mouth closes over mine, I lose that battle. My breath releases in a sigh, and apparently, my reaction is all the encouragement he needs to deepen the kiss.

He tastes like whiskey, like I somehow knew he would, and I find myself arching up for more even as my brain screams at me to stop. His hand slides around to the back of my neck, pulling me closer as his lips tease mine open just enough for me to feel the tip of his tongue lick my bottom lip.

My pulse is a steady drumming in my ears as lust slams into me.

I make a small sound that mirrors the desperation I feel.

But instead of trying for more, he pulls away. I blink, trying to focus my gaze even as my vision swims. This has nothing to do with the tea; that I know instinctively. No, this is all Killian. One short kiss and I'm drunk on him.

He looks down at me, his smirk full of satisfaction. "Take that, Bracken," he says smugly. Then, he stands and smiles down at me. "And sleep well, Sway. I'll see you soon."

Chapter 6

Duncan

I'm torn between wishing like hell Sway never showed up and fucking terrified that she's going to leave. Already, her mere presence has both Killian and Bracken acting like fucking love-struck idiots. It's been a while since any of us got laid, but damn.

She's turning things upside down, and it's only been a day.

While I try to figure out how to stop whoever's hunting her from finding her here, they're both locked in a ridiculous pissing contest over who's going to capti-vate the newcomer first.

I reach the top of the stairs, a steaming mug of water in my hand, though I stop before I open the door to her floor. Sway's battered face has been stuck in my mind since the moment we found her. And somehow, I know it won't get any closer to fading into the throes of my other bad memories so long as she's still here.

With a deep breath, I push open the door and start down the hall.

I make it nearly halfway to her room when my heart begins to pound. Something twists in my gut. Something is off. Wrong.

An unexplainable tightness in my chest has me rushing toward her door at full speed even as some of the near-boiling water spills over and burns the skin of my hand. I withdraw my key and unlock her door then shove it open.

Her scream splits the air the moment the soundproof barrier of the wards is broken.

I slam the door shut and sprint toward her as she thrashes in the bed.

"Please, no!" she throws up her arms, grasping at an invisible attacker.

"Sway!" I reach the bedside. Her expression is pained, tortured, her eyes shut tightly. *Nightmare.* "Sway!" I touch her shoulder, and she swings. Pain explodes in the side of my face. "Motherfucker!" Gripping my jaw, I turn my attention back to her and see her staring at me through wide, panicked eyes.

"I hit you." She scrambles back against the headboard then winces.

"Yeah, you fucking did." She packs a decent punch too.

"I'm so sorry." Sway pulls her knees up to her chest and sucks in a breath, her shoulders shaking with violent tremors.

I stare at her, trying to understand just what the hell—and then it clicks. She was brutalized by whoever is after her. Likely more than once. "You have a hell of a right hook," I tell her with a forced smile even as the side of my face feels like it's on fire. "Seriously. You hit harder than Killian."

Pressing the heel of my palm to my chest, I rub and try to loosen the knot that's formed there. Why the hell it's there at all, I don't know, but fuck me if it doesn't ache. "How do you feel?"

"Sore," she says.

"Likely because of all the thrashing." Reaching forward, I stick some herbs into the steaming mug of water. "This will help." I mix it then sit back to let them steep for a few minutes. She's wearing an oversized shirt that bares one of her tanned shoulders, and I get the urge to lean forward and brush my lips over the exposed skin.

Sitting here with her, I'm captivated by her beauty and the fire in her soul.

"Have Killian and Bracken been gentlemen?" I ask, clearing my throat and forcing my gaze from hers.

She snorts. "Killian saw me naked and didn't get handsy, so we'll say yes."

My hand tightens into a fist at my side as jealousy

churns in my gut. The fucker failed to mention that part of the story. "He said you fell in the shower." I shift my weight, leaning toward her. "Can I check the bruise?"

Sway eyes me warily then nods. "Why the hell not." With a pained expression, she scoots down and lies so that her hip is angled toward me. I draw the comforter down, baring tanned, toned legs. I reach the hem of her shirt and slowly draw it up over her hip, my fingers grazing her flesh as I go.

My cock hardens just enough to be uncomfortable, but I do what I can to keep myself turned so she can't see what she does to me. This woman is not mine to have.

Not ours to keep.

Therefore, I have no intention of acting on a damned thing.

A dark purple bruise, roughly the size of my fist, sits on her hip bone. "Damn. You did a number on yourself."

"That's what Killian said." She sighs. "What's one more, right?" It's meant to be a joke, but mention of the pain she suffered has a low growl rumbling deep in my chest. Quickly, I lower her shirt and pull the covers back up.

"Do you need to use the bathroom or anything?"

"Actually, yes." She throws the covers off again then moves her legs over the edge of the bed and tries to stand. She hisses through clenched teeth, so I reach forward and steady her. "Can you ... help me in there?"

I can tell how much it costs her to even ask, so I make it no big deal and offer a simple, "Yes."

Sway wraps an arm around my waist, so I do the same, holding her to my body as I take most of her weight and help her toward the bathroom door. Having her pressed against me is fucking cruel, but I don't complain. Because it's the closest I'll get to a connection with her.

As soon as we reach the door, she releases me and hobbles inside. The door shuts softly but then immediately reopens with a soft click. In the opening, Sway frowns. She reaches for the knob and tries shutting it again, but it only hits the doorjamb and swings out like before. A closer look reveals a busted latch mechanism, not to mention all the splintered wood around it.

She sighs. "Killian."

My brows lift, but I don't say anything before her cheeks flush and she says, "Will you, uh, turn around?"

"Of course."

I do as she asks and listen as the water comes on. I stand where I am, waiting for her to return. A minute ticks by until she clears her throat and says, "Okay."

I turn and offer my support again.

After helping her back toward the bed, I check the tea; then, as soon as she's settled, I offer it to her and take my seat again. I'm fully aware of the chair sitting beside the bed, but I ignore it and perch on the mattress instead. It's stupid, wanting to be this close to her, but I decide to allow myself this one thing.

Sway takes a sip and groans.

Once again, my cock responds, so I put both hands into my lap in an attempt to hide the growing bulge.

"I've been trying to figure you three out since I got here, you know."

Intrigued by that, I raise my brows. "I see. And what have you determined?"

"Killian is the troublemaker, Bracken is the silent muscle, and I think... Does that make you the leader?"

I catch myself smiling before I can stop it. "You could say that."

"It makes sense." Sway leans back against the headboard.

"How so?"

"You have a leader vibe to you."

"I have a vibe?"

Her gaze lands on mine, and I don't miss the way it momentarily flicks down to my mouth. Not surprising given both of my brothers have already taken their chances and kissed the woman. "You do. Calm and collected leader."

"Calm." I laugh. "That's a new one."

"I've yet to see you as anything but."

If only you saw me interrogating one of your hunters, beauty. "I have my moments."

"How long have you been here at the circus?"

"A long time," I reply.

She eyes me curiously, but no matter how beautiful she might be, I'm not going to share more than that. Not when she won't do the same.

"Not overly chatty, then?" she asks.

"You tell me what you are, and I'll tell you anything you want to know about me." It's a bit of a low blow, but I refuse to care. This is the job, dammit.

"I've already given you my name. You haven't figured it out yet?"

"No."

The relief on her face is evident, and I don't think she realizes just what she gave me. We were planning on asking around, but now that I know her name carries power—well—I'll be sure to use that power carefully.

She sighs, impatience in her amber eyes. "I'm looking forward to leaving this room."

"Is it not to your standards?"

Something dark flashes over her gaze. "Better than where I came from," she says. "But it's still a cage."

Still a cage.

My particular brand of torture has more to do with words and less to do with blades or fists. Which means that I have made it my mission to read people. Their expressions, body language—I live between the lines of what people say.

And she's not that hard to read.

Still a cage. She'd been held captive, yet she's spoken of being afraid to trust. Was it the one who broke her trust that held her prisoner? Did he have something to do with her entrapment? Or is it possible she has someone waiting for her, worried about her disappearance?

"Aside from the ones who chased you here, is there anyone else looking for you? Someone who can keep you safe?"

Her gaze lifts to mine. "No one." She shifts uncomfortably, and I know instinctively she doesn't want to answer these questions. "Do I still have three months, or are you already trying to find a way to get rid of me?"

"As long as you can perform, yes, you have three months. But I'm thinking about the future. Eventually, your time here will run out." And why the fuck does it feel like a sucker punch to my gut to think of it?

She takes another slow drink of her tea. "I'll figure something out."

I offer her a nod then sit in silence for a few minutes. "Do you want to talk about it?" I ask.

"What?"

"Your nightmare."

Her gaze darkens, and I get the sense that, for this brief moment, she's a million miles away. "There's nothing to talk about. You know I've been through shit, and that's what it was about. Vocalizing it won't make it go away."

"No. But sometimes it helps ease the pain to know you're not alone."

I almost snort at my words. I've never once lived by them. Hell, I'm the kind of stony silences and tight-lipped control. But something about her makes me want to carry her burdens. Or avenge them.

Her gaze holds mine. "I *am* alone," she says. "Maybe not physically right now, but you'll throw me out of here the moment I'm no longer of use. When that happens, it'll be up to me to figure out how to survive. Therefore, I am one hundred percent on my own."

I grind my teeth together. "As long as you are here, you are not alone," I tell her. "We will kill to protect you."

"You shouldn't."

"Why?"

"Because he can't be killed. Not easily, anyway." She sets the now-empty mug aside and draws her knees up.

"What is he?"

She shakes her head. "I want to sleep. Can I sleep?" Tears glisten in her eyes as she closes them, so I don't press. At least, not yet. Once she's stronger, we will push her for what we need to know. Until then, she needs to rest so that we get the full three months and not mere days to find out just who is tracking her.

And eliminate them.

"Yes." I get up, but her slender fingers wrap around

my wrist. At her touch, my heart thrums in my ears, and my lion surges to the surface. When my gaze meets hers, though, she does not shy away from the predator I know is reflected in it.

"Don't leave yet? Not until I'm asleep."

Her voice is small. Another favor she doesn't want to ask for, and yet she does it anyway. She asks it of me.

My gaze drops to her lips.

To those perfect, pouty, pink lips that I so desperately want to taste even if it lands me in the depths of the underworld to do so.

I lean in, and her gaze widens just slightly as it drops to my mouth.

Instead of closing the distance, though, I pull the covers up further and nod. "I'll be right over there," I say, gesturing to the chair.

"Thank you." She releases me and lies back, so I retreat into the shadows and sit down on a chair as Sway drifts into a hopefully dreamless sleep.

IT TAKES HER ALL OF TEN MINUTES TO NOD OFF. As soon as I know she's asleep, I stand and cross to her. She's peaceful now, her expression relaxed. So, I make sure the covers are pulled up then grab her empty mug and head out into the hall, locking the door behind me.

I'm walking past an apartment when the door opens, and a crystal-eyed berserker steps out. "Fiona," I greet.

Her expression flickers with something then smooths out again. "All good? I thought I heard a scream."

"New girl had a nightmare," I tell her.

She nods in understanding then falls into step beside me. Farther down, another apartment door opens and closes. It's late enough that most of the others have already gone down to the Big Top. Another day, and I'm starting it out already exhausted.

"You headed down to rehearse?" I ask.

"I am. Harriss is already down there, and he pissed me off this morning, so I'm looking forward to throwing some knives at him."

I grin. Harriss is a djinn who has a love/hate relationship with the berserker. As in, he's head over heels in love with her, and she hates that she feels the same. Of all the performers here, Fiona is the only one I'm honestly not sure I could beat should it come down to a fight.

The berserker is fucking brutal.

Luckily, the two of us are on the same side. In fact, she's the closest thing to a friend I've ever had beyond my brothers and D. The performers here, especially the ones who've been here a while, are more a family than a troupe. Sometimes, it's still a strange feeling to be part of something like this. But today, it only makes me think of what Sway said earlier about being alone.

While we walk, Fiona leaves me to my thoughts; another reason she and I get along.

We descend the stairs together until I reach the floor of my destination. Then, I wave her off as she continues down to the Big Top, and I make my way down the hall toward the gym. Killian and Bracken are both inside and shirtless, their torsos slick with sweat as they box in a makeshift ring.

I step inside, and both men stop and turn to me. "Damn, Dunc, what the fuck happened to your face?" Killian questions.

Reaching up, I gently touch my jaw. "Sway punched me."

My fingers brush over a tender spot at the top of my cheekbone, and I wince. There's undoubtedly a bruise forming. No wonder Fiona looked at me strangely.

Killian and Bracken exchange a look. Then Killian throws his head back and barks out a laugh. "So, Bracken and I get kisses, and you get clocked. That sounds about right."

"Asshole," I murmur as I set the empty mug down on a table. "She was having a nightmare when I got there. I walked over, and she punched me in the fucking face."

All humor vanishes from their faces. "Shit. Is she okay?" Bracken demands.

"I get punched in the face, and you're worried about her having bad dreams?"

"Fuck yeah." Killian stalks forward. "Is she?"

"She's fine," I tell them. "And I got a little more out of her." When both of them cross their arms, I continue, "She was held captive—and before you ask, I don't know for how long."

"Son of a bitch," Bracken says, expression dark.

Killian cracks his knuckles. "Makes me want to go hunting."

"According to her, this fucker after her is hard to kill."

Killian doesn't miss a beat. "Then I guess it's a good thing that we're all tough motherfuckers who like a challenge."

Chapter 7

Sway

When I wake again, I find a fresh mug on my bedside table, still steaming. Adaya stands at the counter, bent over her bag of herbs and amber tincture jars. I shift, pulling myself up to sitting, and find the movement much easier than I anticipated. Adaya turns and smiles when she sees me.

"You're awake."

"And feeling much less run over," I say, pleasantly surprised by how easily my limbs respond to movement. Even with the bathroom tumble setting me back, the pain is noticeably less than before.

"No thanks to your stubbornness, I hear." She glowers at me, but it lacks any real heat.

I smile wryly. "I tend to learn my lessons the hard way."

Her mouth quirks. "Something tells me I shouldn't be surprised."

"More tea?" I ask, nodding at the mug.

"Different blend," she says, and I take the mug, sniffing.

"Is it going to knock me out again?" I ask. The idea of sleeping anymore makes my stomach churn. I'm running out of time to prove myself to the Ringmaster and ensure my survival...for now.

"Exactly the opposite, in fact."

Relief hums through me.

"The herbs did their job," she says. "They offered your body a rest and recovery period that accelerated your healing process. This blend is to help wake you up again."

"I like the sound of that."

"I figured you might. Drink up."

I down the tea, chugging it before the bitterness can register. The idea of being up and around again is too tempting to pass up. When it's empty, I set the mug aside.

Adaya eyes it with approval.

"Now, eat." She carries a plate over, and my stomach immediately cramps and growls with hunger.

The eggs and toast are gone nearly as fast as the tea. When I'm done, I feel clearer and more energized than I have in a long time. Honestly, I can't remember a time in recent history when I felt as light as I do now. As unburdened and… well…alive.

"Whatever was in that tea, I need more," I say.

She laughs. "Come on then. On your feet." She bends down and pulls the covers off me. I squeak in panic when I remember, too late, I'm still naked, thanks to that spill on the bathroom floor.

"Oh, please," she says, "I've seen it all before."

I exhale. She's right.

You're safe, I remind myself.

Adaya helps me stand and dress. The clothes fit surprisingly well. A pair of spandex shorts, a sports bra, and a large t-shirt. Being fully clothed and on my feet gives me a sense of strength I didn't know I needed.

By the time I'm done, Adaya is standing back and watching me with a sort of approval.

"The herbs worked out well," she says. "How do you feel?"

I take a moment to move. Flexing my arms around and twisting at the waist. Nothing hurts badly enough to stop me, and that makes me smile. "Strong," I reply.

"You'll want to take it slow. Ease back into activity until you're sure you're properly ready."

"Can I perform?"

She puts her hands on her hips. "What part of *take it slow* did you not hear?"

I grin. "Hard lessons," I remind her.

She casts a glance toward the ceiling. "You're just as

hard-headed as all of them. Which means you'll do just fine in this place. All right," she says, marching over to grab her bag. "But don't be surprised when your body tires more quickly for the next few days."

"I'll be careful," I promise her, already excited to get out there.

She pauses at the door, her expression softening. "Whoever did that to you... I'm here when you need me, okay? But hopefully, for your sake, you don't."

"Thank you," I tell her.

She nods and slips out.

I blink back sudden tears of gratitude for the woman who healed me without knowing a thing about me—and without asking questions either. It's far rarer than it should be to find good, honest people in this fucked up world.

Before long, though, my eyes are clear, and the feeling of my sudden freedom makes it impossible to remain inside this apartment. I can move again, without feeling like I'm going to keel over from the pain of it. That's something I took for granted before that awful night. And it's not something I can waste in this moment.

I make it as far as opening the door and stepping into the hall before uncertainty halts me. Doubling back, I grab the key Duncan left for me that first night. Then I step back into the hall and lock my door behind me.

My door.

It's temporary, I know, but that apartment became a safe space over the last couple of days. I won't take that for granted, either.

Tucking the key into my sports bra, I turn right and head for the stairwell marked by a sign. All I can see on this floor are more doors that look like mine, which means the performing areas must be somewhere else.

I head downstairs on instinct and hazy memories, emerging from the stairwell on the first floor, which means my apartment is located on the second floor. I make a mental note of that so I can get back there later and then follow the sound of voices up ahead.

Halfway down the hall, a door stands open.

As I get closer, I realize one of the voices coming from inside is a familiar one. I stop in the open doorway and realize it's a break room of some kind. A counter lines the opposite wall with a fridge standing beside it. In the center is a table with a few chairs. I recognize Liv, the woman I met when I first arrived the other night. She's sitting at the table across from a male I've never seen before.

"Helen," Liv says, smiling brightly when she sees me. "I didn't realize you were up and around. How are you feeling?" She uses the fake name I gave her, which means that the three pushy lions either kept it to themselves, or she's choosing to keep it a secret from the other performers.

"I'm feeling much better," I say. "Adaya just cleared me."

"That's great. Oh, this is Brad; he's one of our performers."

The male turns to me and offers a friendly wave. "Nice to meet you." His light hair is styled perfectly atop his head, and his golden gaze shines brightly when he smiles.

"You too," I tell him then glance at their card game. "Sorry to interrupt. I was actually looking for the practice area."

"Oh, perfect timing. Brad can walk you over," Liv says.

"Are you sure? You're in the middle of a game."

"Actually, we're done." Liv lays her cards down and beams at Brad. "Gin."

"Dammit," he mutters, shaking his head. "You always win. Every damned time."

Liv grins. "See? Perfect timing."

Brad scrapes his chair back and stands. "I swear you cheat."

"I'm just lucky," Liv tells him.

"Lucky enough to clean up while I go swing around on the silks, huh?" Brad says with a smug smirk.

Liv's smile disappears. "That's evil, Brad. Don't rub it in that I can't go airborne right now. Besides, I'm growing a living thing. Have you done that? Didn't think so."

"Everything's a competition," he tells me, sliding past me into the hall. "Come on. The tent is this way."

"Thanks," I tell Liv.

"I'll come find you later," she says. "Glad you're feeling better."

I fall into step beside Brad, intrigued by his comments to Liv. "So, you do silks?" I ask.

"Not typically. And honestly, we're not very good at them, but with Liv out of commission, we've had to take over. Until now, thanks to you."

I smile. "Who do you perform with?"

"My sister, Kleo."

"What do you do when you're not filling in?"

He mimes throwing something. "We throw sharp things at each other."

"That sounds dangerous."

"Eh, not as dangerous as Fiona and Harriss."

"Who are they?"

His grin spreads. "You're in for a treat when you meet them. Fiona is a berserker, and Harriss is her djinn lover boy."

"What do they do that's so dangerous?"

"She ties him to a board, blindfolds herself, then throws daggers at him. With Kleo and I, we can at least dematerialize out of the way, but her—"

"Dematerialize?"

In a blink, he disappears. I stop moving and turn in a slow circle.

"Dematerialize."

I whirl on a grinning Brad as he leans against the wall behind me. "That is awesome."

"Never met a fae before?"

"Not one who could do that."

He shrugs. "We're full-blooded fae."

Most of the fae I've crossed paths with have been hybrids. Either part human or some other supernatural. "Can I ask what brought you here?"

"Can I ask you the same thing?"

"Needed a place to stay while I get my life together," I reply. It's not entirely untrue even if I left out the abusive fiancé and power abuse.

"Fair enough. Well, Kleo and I have been here for nearly two decades. She was sleeping with a member of our old House, and it turned violent. I got her out of there, brought her here, and we haven't looked back."

"I— I'm sorry."

"It is what it is. We all have our stories. Some are tragic, some merely opportunity. But everyone here in the circus has their reasons."

"And now you throw sharp things at your sister."

He chuckles. "Kleo is a tough personality. Spend some time with her and you'd probably like to throw sharp things at her, too."

"What about you? Rumor has it you're multi-talented. Lyra and silks."

"Rumor, huh?"

"If you're going to live here, you might as well accept it now. Rumors are part of the territory."

"Fair enough. Yeah, silks are my jam, but I can do lyra too." Now it's my turn to glance at him. "That doesn't make you feel threatened, does it?"

He laughs. "Well, you're just a get-right-to-the-point kind of girl, aren't you?"

I shrug. "Beating around the bush is a waste of time."

"So true." He smiles. "Not a threat at all. Unless you're a whiz with a blade."

"Nope, knives are most definitely not my thing." I shudder.

"Whew, job security," he declares, and I shrug off the darkness and smile at him. "In that case, Helen-of-multiple-talents, I think you're going to fit right in here."

"Thanks," I tell him.

"Thank *you*. I get to go back to my normal routine."

We turn a corner and step through an opening that I realize all at once is the Big Top. I stop short, taking it all in.

The area is huge with several different stations set up for practice. Cones and platforms offer sectioned areas—one for each act of the show. Overhead, a large canopy blocks out the harsh sunlight. The sides are open to the fresh air, allowing a light wind to sweep through the space.

From large speakers, energetic music cuts through the hum of voices or grunts of physical exertion. The energy is electric, and it's not even showtime.

"Wow," I breathe.

When I turn to look, I see Brad watching me with amusement. "First time on this side of the ring?" he asks.

"Is it that obvious?"

He grins.

"This is incredible," I say.

"And there it is," he says.

"What?"

"You've just been bitten by the circus bug. There's no going back now. Come on. I'll show you where you can set up."

I follow him straight down the center aisle, past a section reserved for a team of acrobats who are currently flipping and flying through the air in a choreographed routine. Past them is a butterfly shifter with wings more gorgeous than anything I've ever seen. She flits through the air—and then straight through the center of a flaming hoop.

I gasp, my stomach lurching as I watch to make sure the flames haven't caught the tips of her wings. But she flits effortlessly through, untouched, and then hovers above me. Her gaze finds mine, and she smiles, offering a friendly wave.

I wave back.

Someone whistles, and I look over, only to realize Brad's left me behind. He stands at the far end of the tent, waiting. I hurry over to where he stands beside a woman who looks so much like him they could be twins. Hell, maybe they are. Her blonde hair is cut short, even shorter than his on top. The brightly colored body-suit she wears is covered in glitter that matches the dusting on her high cheekbones. She's beautiful. When I reach them, she cocks her head to the side.

"Helen, this is my sister, Kleo," Brad says. "She's almost as good with a blade as I am."

"Fucker." Kleo punches him.

"Hi," I say, "so nice to meet you."

"And you," she replies. "It's nice to put a face to the name."

I don't know what to say to that. It's another hint at the rumors Brad mentioned, but I'm not quite ready to offer up whatever confirmation they might want about my story. Instead, I shift my attention back to Brad.

"Liv said you guys could get me set up."

"Of course. Lyra's there." Brad points, and I look up and to my right, spotting the metal ring hanging high above our heads.

"Access?" I ask.

"There." Kleo points to a metal ladder hanging just behind her. The bottom of it grazes the mat flooring. My stomach sinks as I imagine the strength I'll expend from the climb alone. I'm not so naïve to think Adaya was wrong. There's only so much gas in the tank, and I'll use it all if I have to make that climb.

I look up again, tracking the other options. My eyes land on the long stretch of silks hanging on the opposite side of the center aisle.

"Are those available?" I ask them, pointing at the bright red gauzy material hanging behind them.

"They are," Kleo says.

"Do you mind if I use them for a moment?" I ask.

"Not at all. I'm ready to never touch those damn things again." She and Brad gesture for me to go ahead.

I walk to the silks, suddenly aware of all the eyes on me. I don't have to look back to know Brad and Kleo are watching, but it's more than just them. The hum of voices has gone silent, and I know every single performer in this tent has stopped to see what I'll do. My neck prickles with the sensation, and it's all I can do to keep moving beneath their scrutiny.

Fine.

They want a show; I'll give it to them.

Peeling off the oversized shirt, I let it fall to the floor near my feet. The fabric is too much against the gauzy material above me. I need bared skin for what I'm about to do.

The red silk dangles from an impossibly high ceiling, stopping just out of my reach. I stretch my fingers as high as they'll go above my head, but even then, the tips only graze the fabric.

I lift onto my toes, and my hands find purchase.

From the speakers, the music changes. The song slows into a dark and sexy ballad. The bass is deep enough that I feel it in my chest. Perfect.

I shut my eyes, syncing myself to the song and blocking out everything else. Slipping into my own mind, I reach for that space where nothing else matters but the movement of my own body. It's been way too long since I let myself go, but the moment I find myself here, it all just clicks.

Here we go.

With a deep breath, I grip the silks in both hands and swing my body upward.

The music drives my movements as I swing my legs up above my head, wrapping the silks around my ankles and wrists; once, twice, three times. Then I begin twisting and writhing my body so that the silk wraps around my torso too. After that, I swing hard, using my own momentum forward and back, forward and back, until I can wrap myself straight up into the air.

A cocoon.

Now, I'm the butterfly.

The song feels like a sexy dance with a lover. And my partner is the silk pressed against me.

Swinging, twisting, flying—it's freedom like I haven't known in months.

Freedom like I might never know again if the Ringmaster doesn't deem me worthy of his Big Top.

Too soon, I can feel my energy flagging.

I don't push too hard because a mistake up here could mean an injury far worse than I just recovered from. My movements slow. I begin to unravel myself, heading for the ground beneath me.

The song ends.

Instead of another one starting, the speakers go silent.

All I can hear is my own heavy breathing.

When my feet point at the floor, the sound of applause jars me. I release my grip on the silks and fall the last two feet. My knees buckle, and I crumple to the floor. Mild pain lances through my ankle. I hiss through my teeth, and wisps of hair fall into my eyes as I lean over to cup my hands around my foot.

"Whoa, you okay?" Brad and Kleo are suddenly there, pulling me gently to my feet.

"I'm good," I assure them quickly through labored breaths.

"Your ankle?"

"It's fine. I landed wrong like an idiot," I add sheepishly.

"It's these assholes' fault," Kleo says, nodding at the small crowd of performers. Their applause dies off, and they begin to return, one at a time, to their own practices.

"They shouldn't have startled you," Brad agrees. "I'll kick their asses for it."

"No." My response is too sharp, and Brad frowns. "I mean, don't cause trouble on my behalf. Not the first impression I'm going for, you know?"

"Oh, honey," Kleo says, "Your first impression was just made. And trouble is not the word they're going to use to describe it either."

Pain shoots through my leg as I straighten. Then my gaze lands on the furious pierced man moving into the ring. Killian is a sight to behold, but even as my insides warm at the sight of him and the memory of his lips on mine, fear ices straight through that attraction.

Because he is clearly gunning for the performers who applauded. His hands are fisted at his sides, and his mouth is set in a grim, determined line as he stalks toward the closest of the bystanders. It's a posture I've seen before, except this time, it's aimed at others instead of at me. Men and women completely unaware that they have a pissed-off lion shifter ready to make meals of them.

Chapter 8

Hot rage pummels my veins as I leave D behind and close the distance between me and those fuckers who just caused Sway to fall onto the ground.

"Killian," Liv calls to me, but I ignore her. She hurries off, probably to find Duncan or Bracken. Or worse, chase down D and tell him to get his ass back here after he just left. The fact that he was in the Big Top at all during rehearsals is out of the norm, but when he heard Sway was up and about, he snuck in at the last minute to watch her impromptu performance. She hadn't been up there two fucking minutes before he said, "Tell her she's in."

I hadn't been able to summon words to acknowledge him, such was my awe at watching her move up there.

Now, having watched her perfect performance, and

then her dangerous fall, thanks to these assholes, I'm speechless for a different reason. Logically, I know it was an accident, but something in me snapped when I saw it, and now, I don't care. There is no logic eating through the anger, just the desire to destroy those who caused her pain.

"Killian!"

Her voice stops me in my tracks moments before a slender hand grips my arm. Her touch is warm—no, scalding—on my flesh. Sway swims into view, her panicked eyes the only thing that cuts through my anger.

"They caused you to fall."

"No. My own weakness caused me to fall. I'm still a bit worn out, and I misjudged."

I narrow my gaze on her face. Her pulse quickens, an easy tell of the lie. They did cause her to fall with their jarring applause, but her fear for them is also evident in the paleness of her face and the way she's gripping my arm as though she can keep me rooted where I am.

"Misjudged?" I question.

"Yes. Can you help me up to my room? My ankle is a bit weak, and I don't want to try to make it alone."

More like you don't want me bashing skulls the moment you leave the practice arena. "Fine." Without asking for permission, I scoop Sway up into my arms.

"What? No. I can walk." She squirms.

"I know you can. But you're not going to." I start

walking, glaring at the performers who clearly don't realize just how fucking close they came to death.

The only ones who do seem to realize it are Brad and Kleo. And they know better than to say a fucking word against me.

The only people who will be touching Sway besides me are Duncan and Bracken.

Sway remains silent as I carry her up the stairs to the second floor. I stop once we reach her door then set her down as she reaches into her bra and withdraws her key. My need stirs at the sight of it. Never, in my entire fucking life, have I wanted to be an inanimate object more than I do right now.

"That's where you're keeping your key?" I ask.

"Do I look like I have pockets in these things?" she tosses back, and my gaze flicks to her tight shorts that couldn't cling more if the fuckers were painted on. My dick hardens as I study the curve of her ass in that thin material.

Sway's too busy sliding the key into the lock to notice, so I tuck my erection as best I can while I wait. After unlocking the door, she opens it and limps inside. I follow, my anger stirred all over again at the sight of her injury.

"Let me see your ankle."

Her brow furrows. "Not necessary. I'll be fine."

"I'm not asking." I shut the door with more force than necessary, and Sway flinches.

Shit. The fear I saw in her downstairs is back, and my anger dissolves instantly at the sight of it.

"You don't have to be afraid," I say.

"I'm not."

Lie.

"You tried to protect them. Even though they caused you to get hurt."

"It was an accident. They don't deserve—"

I cross to where she stands in the center of the room. She doesn't move away, but I can feel the tension in her, and in this moment, I want nothing more than to ease it for her. I am willing to do whatever it takes, be whoever she needs. It should terrify me, but it doesn't. "I would never hurt you, Sway. I'm not like whoever did this to you."

She looks up at me, her soft gaze threatening to swallow me whole. "I know that."

"Not yet, you don't. But you will." I nod at the chair. "Let me see your ankle," I repeat, gently this time.

Surprise registers in her and she crosses to a chair.

She takes a seat then offers up the ankle in question. "I can put on a robe first--"

I kneel at her feet then grin up at her. "Come on now, love, I've seen you in less."

Sway's cheeks turn red, and I chuckle before turning my attention back to her ankle. When I press my fingers to the already swollen limb, she hisses. "Ugh. This is the last damned thing I need."

I touch her other leg then slide both of my hands up to grip her calves. I squeeze gently, massaging the muscles there as I look up to meet her gaze. Sway's eyes are on me, her lips parted, cheeks pink. Fuck, I want to drown in her.

"It's just a light sprain from the look and feel of it," I say. "No swelling even. What are you worried about?"

"I still need to audition for the Ringmaster. Adaya warned me not to take things too quickly, and I didn't listen."

"You already auditioned," I tell her.

"Excuse me? No, I didn't."

"The Ringmaster was watching your performance earlier. You're in."

She gapes at me. "Are you serious?"

"Yes."

Sway squeals in excitement and throws herself onto me. We topple backward, my upper body hitting the floor with a thud—her on top of me. "Shit! I'm sorry, I—" She starts to move, but I band my arms around her body, pinning her to me.

"Don't apologize, love. I've been dreaming about having you on top of me for days now."

The color in her cheeks deepens. "I—we—ugh. You assholes fluster me."

I chuckle. "Glad to hear it."

She props herself up with both hands on either side of my head so her dark hair hangs in a curtain around us. My cock tightens at the sight and feel of her against me. "It's not a good thing."

"Why not?" I ask as I reach up and brush some of her hair behind her ear.

"Because. You all keep moving in on me. Well, except for Duncan. So really, it's just you and Bracken."

"Give Duncan some time. He's always been more cautious."

Sway snorts and shakes her head. "Give him more time? So, you're saying that he's going to move in on me, too? What the hell is this? Some kind of game to toy with the new girl?"

I flip her over, pinning her to the ground beneath my body but careful not to hurt her with my sudden movement. Gripping her wrist, I pin one above her head, my thumb caressing her hammering pulse. I'm delighted that I don't sense fear from her. Just desire. Leaning down, I brush my lips to her jaw. "We don't play games, love."

"No?" she asks, breathless. "Because it sure as hell seems like a game from where I'm standing."

"You're not standing at all right now," I remind as I look down at her.

Her gaze drops to my lips, so I lean in a little closer, my own pulse hammering like a damned drum. I want her—more than I've ever wanted anyone. And that want —that desire—calls to me, not just as a man but to my beast.

He wants to possess her.

I want to bury myself inside her.

"Screw it." Sway arches off the ground and presses her lips to mine.

Her forwardness catches me off guard, and for a second, I let her take what she wants, tasting me, testing her own boundaries. But the moment her tongue brushes across the seam of my lips, all bets are fucking off. I tighten my hold on her wrist, deepening the kiss as I press against her heat. She wraps her legs around me, and I growl in response to the closeness.

Fuck, she tastes like sunshine.

Like pure fucking light.

Sway moans against my mouth, and my cock goes rock fucking hard. I grind into her, and the throaty moan I am rewarded with once more pushes my desire straight toward the ceiling.

Then someone bangs on the door.

"Son of a bitch." I push off of her, pulling Sway to her feet as I go. Her lips are swollen, her eyes glossy, and the desire to kill whoever is on the other side of that door is strong as shit. I cross over and rip the door open to find both Duncan and Bracken on the other side.

My brothers growl when they see me, so I flash a big-ass motherfucking grin. "Boys. What can I do for you?"

"Brad said you brought Sway up after she fell,"

Duncan says, his tone all business even though I can sense his jealousy.

It makes me smile. We share willing women—it's what we do. But he's so damned determined to keep Sway at arm's length, and it's killing him to know Bracken and I are doing the exact opposite. "Yes."

"Is she okay?" Bracken asks.

"I'm fine." Sway limps over and grabs the door from me, opening it wider.

Duncan and Bracken look her up and down then shift their gaze toward me. Their moods shift, and they switch to communicating through our bond instead of out loud. *"Three men are approaching from the woods. They'll be here any minute."*

"Why the fuck did you wait so long to say something?" I turn toward Sway. "Love, we have some business to tend to. But I'd love to pick up where we left off sometime soon." I press a quick kiss to her forehead, sidestepping her attempt to push me away before I can. With a grin, I step out into the hall.

The three of us begin walking, and I hear the door shut softly behind us.

"What the fuck were you doing in there?" Bracken demands.

"She kissed me." I all but puff out my chest like an asshole because I know it'll drive him crazy.

"As in, she initiated?" he asks suspiciously.

"Absolutely. Tackled me when she threw herself out of the chair toward me."

"You're fucking lying," Bracken accuses.

"Can you assholes chill out?" Duncan says wearily. "We have bigger problems."

"Any clue who they are?" I ask.

"Nope." Duncan shoves open the door that takes us to the Big Top. We move through it quickly, adrenaline singing in my blood.

I fucking hope it's the asshole that hurt her.

So I can rip his cock off and choke him with it.

We reach the front steps of the circus at the same time as our uninvited guests do. Three men—all wearing dark jeans and black leather jackets like they color coordinated or some shit. I try to sense them, to make out what type of supernaturals they are, and while I can pin two of them for shifters of some kind, I'm unable to sense the third.

It's the mystery asshole who smiles at me. Dark hair curls down over his ears, and his narrowed eyes give away the monster lurking beneath the surface. This guy is a killer.

There's no doubt about it.

"We're not open," Bracken says.

"I'm actually looking for someone." He reaches into his back pocket and pulls out a picture of Sway. She's smiling for the camera, wearing a white sundress with a low-cut front that falls in a deep V nearly to her belly button.

"And you expect us to have seen her?" I glance down at his hand, looking for a house ring and really fucking hoping he doesn't have one. If he doesn't, then there's no protection for him. No war that could take place when I inevitably rip his spine out through his fucking throat.

Unfortunately, I see it—an emerald encased in silver —the stone glinting green in the sunlight above. House of Earth and Emerald. *Son of a bitch.*

House of Earth and Emerald isn't as uptight as some of the others, but they'll still lose their shit if we outright kill one of their own for simply walking onto our grounds.

"Your boss has a reputation for keeping people against their will," he says, and my muscles flex with the need to smash this guy straight into the fucking ground.

"You come onto our property and accuse our boss of kidnapping?" Bracken looks from him to me and Duncan, then back to him again. "You must have balls of fucking steel between your legs."

The asshole grins. "Your boss's reputation is one I imagine is well-earned."

Duncan snarls at that. "We don't abduct people," he retorts. "We take in the houseless and give them some-where safe."

"The girl I'm looking for isn't houseless," he says. "She went missing, and I'm trying to return her home. People are worried about her."

"What people?" I ask, crossing my arms.

"Her fiancé and his family," he replies smoothly.

The blood in my veins ices, and every muscle in my body goes rigid.

"Easy, brothers," Duncan says through our bond. It snaps me back enough to notice that Bracken has clenched his hands into fists. "We haven't seen her. So, get the fuck off our property before my brothers and I make you leave."

The man doesn't look even the least bit threatened. He chuckles and reaches into his jacket pocket, withdrawing a simple white business card with a phone number. "If you see her, give me a call." As he reaches forward, the sleeve of his jacket comes up, revealing a tattoo that matches the last fucker's: a dagger with a drop of blood at the point of the blade.

For fuck's sake.

What the hell could the people she's running from want with her so badly that they'd nearly beat her to death then send multiple Crimson Hunters after her?

Duncan takes the card, and the three men turn and move away, disappearing back into the trees.

As soon as we're back in the Big Top, Duncan stops and offers me the card. "Find out what you can make of this."

"If he's lying, you mean," I say.

Duncan sighs. "Just say it."

"That asshole says she has a fiancé," I nearly shout.

"Easy." Duncan glares at me. I know he wants me to calm down, but I'm barely holding it the fuck together right now.

"She's spoken for," I say through clenched teeth.

"She was a prisoner," Bracken corrects.

"Bracken's right," Duncan says. "I asked her if she had anyone who would miss her, and she said no. That tells me this fiancé might just be the fucker who hurt her, so chill out, and get ahold of your shit."

I force myself to take a deep breath and do as he's asking. He's right. I need to stop jumping to conclusions. Still… "If her fiancé is the one who hurt her, he deserves so much worse than death," I say. "No wonder she can't trust anyone."

"No wonder she can't trust men," Duncan adds, and I frown.

"What do you mean?"

"It's not just a fiancé. It's all these Crimson Hunter assholes coming for her too," Duncan points out.

"Yeah, these hunters spell bad news," Bracken comments.

"We should have just fucking killed them," I snarl.

"And risk bringing a war to our doorstep?" Duncan questions. "I won't let them get their hands on her again, either, but if we can avoid a war, then that's what we need to do." He shakes his head. "We need to hide her better, and I have an idea. Let's go to D."

I nod in agreement, but as I study the card in my hand, I can't help but wonder if perhaps the dominos have already started to fall—pushing us directly into the line of fire.

Chapter 9

What the hell am I thinking? Letting Killian and Bracken steal kisses from me is one thing, but I started it this time. And if I'm being honest, I'd do it again too.

Ugh.

I came to the circus for refuge, not … *sex*. But the longer I'm left alone to relive that kiss between me and Killian earlier, the more I'm forced to admit that I don't regret it. Not with Killian and not with Bracken either.

In fact, I'm mostly left wondering what kind of kisser Duncan is now too. Would he be passionate? Gentle? I reach up and gently touch my lips. Honestly, he strikes me as the type of man who remains so buttoned up during the day that, when he finally does snap—it's gloriously passionate.

Warmth swirls in my belly at the mere thought of

him, and then there's the comments that both Killian and Bracken have made that make it seem like they want me to play this game with all of them. Shouldn't they be jealous of one another? Instead, they're acting like they hope I find out just what Duncan is capable of behind closed doors. All while continuing … whatever this is with them.

Robert wanted me to himself. So much so that he'd imprisoned me out of reach of anyone else. But Killian and Bracken seem oddly all right with sharing me.

If their kiss-a-thon competition is any indication, anyway.

Three hot-as-hell lions.

All of them protecting me.

All of them wanting me.

Well, I haven't seen any evidence of Duncan's interest, but Killian and Bracken act like it's only a matter of time before he makes a move, too.

Just the idea being with the three of them—at once —sends a thrill of excitement pulsing through me. It's not something I've ever considered, but with them, I can't seem to stop the mental images once they've started.

Shaking the thought away, I force myself to focus elsewhere. Like my performance. If Killian was telling the truth, then the Ringmaster has deemed me good enough to stay. I won't be able to relax until I confirm that, but I have a feeling marching down to the Ring-master's office myself isn't the best move.

The minutes tick by, and Killian doesn't return. None of them do. Not that I expected them to, but, well, apparently, I've grown used to them checking in on me every ten seconds.

Finally, I give in to my growling stomach and go in search of food. My ankle is still tender but nothing serious. If I'm careful, it should be back to normal in the next day or two. It was a stupid mistake on my part, anyway. If I'm going to perform here, I'll need to get used to the noise of a crowd. Besides, stupid ankle pain aside, the thrill of having people watch me up there is something I'll never forget. I can't wait to experience the thrill of a packed house, all of them watching me.

I'm just exiting the stairwell when I nearly run into someone.

"Oh, sorry!"

Liv smiles as I jump out of the way, avoiding a collision with her very pregnant belly.

"Hey," she says, "I heard your performance was a slam dunk earlier."

"I guess so."

"You guess so? D says you're a natural."

My brows shoot up instantly. "The Ringmaster said that?"

"He's not as mean as he looks," she says in a

conspiratorial whisper. "But don't tell the others. He doesn't want to lose his street cred."

I grin at that, and she links her arm through mine. "Come on. I was just coming to find you. Hungry?"

"Starved," I admit.

"I know just the place."

Liv gives me a quick tour as we walk, pointing out the amenities as well as introducing me to the other performers we come across.

"Nice aerials," Lex, a shapeshifter, tells me.

"Stop hitting on her," a woman snaps, glaring at him as she pushes past and offers her hand to me.

"I wasn't," Lex protests.

The girl rolls her eyes. "Dude, it sounded like you said nice areolas."

Lex stutters, but the girl just shakes her head and holds out her hand to me. "I'm Fiona."

The berserker. I shake her hand. "Helen."

"I've heard. You're the new Liv."

"Um, I don't think anyone can be Liv," I say.

"Relax, I'm fucking with you. And her." She gives Liv a sideways smile. "How's the baking going?"

"Just fine." Liv rubs her belly affectionately, and despite Fiona's no-bullshit demeanor, I can tell she really cares. It's sweet, and I can't help but feel a tad jealous of the connection these two women share. For years, I longed for a friend. But when you fear being used, it's impossible to trust.

"You two eat yet?" Fiona asks.

"On our way now," Liv tells her.

"I'll join you." She falls into step with us, but we don't get far before we're stopped again.

"There you are." Duncan strides toward us, his long legs eating up the ground. My stomach flutters at the sight of him looking so serious and intent—on me. My gaze drops to his mouth, to full lips I can easily imagine on my skin.

"We're on our way to lunch," Liv tells him. "Want to join us?"

"Can't. I need to talk to Helen."

Before I can respond, he takes my elbow and steers me back the way I came. My heart thuds as I realize his neutral expression is only a mask. The tension coming off him in waves tells a different story. He's pissed. The question is *why*? What did I do?

Fear curls in my gut.

"What's going on?" I ask, letting Duncan lead me down the hall and through a back access door I've never noticed before.

The next hall is shorter with only a single door already hanging open just ahead. Duncan pulls me inside and then shuts the door behind us with a loud thud.

I suck in a sharp breath at the sight of Killian and Bracken already waiting for me inside what looks like a central living room, complete with two couches

and a kitchenette-dining area along with three separate master suites splitting off in different directions.
The space smells like a combination of all three of
them.

Their private quarters, I realize. But my reaction to
that is short-lived as I hone in on their faces.

"What's wrong?" I ask, noting every one of their
expressions is set in the same hard look.

My heart thuds louder, and I catch myself backing
toward the door.

"We just came from the front entrance," Duncan
says quietly, placing his hand at my lower back to keep
me from moving away.

I change course, putting a few feet between us.

His voice is calm. Too calm. My pulse speeds.

"Three men came looking for you," he adds.

Every muscle in my body turns to ice—freezing
solid as the blood in my veins runs cold. He knows
where I am. Not that I should be surprised, I suppose,
since they'd tracked me this far the night I managed to
slip away. But fear holds me paralyzed now. If Robert
comes for me, will the Ringmaster honor my deal? Or
will he hand me over?

"What did you tell them?'

Duncan glares at me. "Fucking nothing."

"I'm sure he promised you something for my return.
Power? Status?"

Duncan crosses the distance between us and grips

me by the arms. "Do you really think any of us fucking care about that?"

I swallow hard, refusing to let his words seep past my defenses. "I've never met a man without a price."

"When it comes to you? There is no reward large enough," he replies.

Our gazes hold as I scramble to form some kind of rational thought that doesn't involve wanting to be fucked senseless by all three of these powerful men. Then I can forget about my past and about the monster still tracking me.

Duncan releases me and steps back.

"WE WOULD NEVER BETRAY YOU," KILLIAN TELLS ME, coming to stand right in front of me. His eyes are blazing with conviction. He means it. He's also furious, but unlike this morning, that fury doesn't scare me. It endears me to him for it.

And with that realization, my fear that the other two will hurt me dissipates as well. They might be angry, but it's not the same type of fury Robert portrayed on so many different occasions. These men, as ferocious as they are, would never hurt me.

"Thank you," I tell him. Glancing at the others, I add, "All of you. I appreciate your discretion."

"As a member of the troupe, you get our loyalty and protection," Bracken says.

"You also owe us an explanation," Duncan cuts in, crossing his arms. "You want to tell us why you'd run from your fiancé?"

Shit. I look away, trying to formulate some answer that won't get me thrown out on my ass. Of course, whoever came looking for me would tell them about him. I should have expected it.

"He's not my fiancé," I say finally. "Not anymore."

"That's what you have to say to the news we learned you're engaged?" Killian demands.

"Shut up, Kill," Bracken says.

Before I can answer, Duncan says, "Funny because fiancé is exactly the term the hunters who are being paid to find you used." Like before, his tone is flat. Neutral even. But when I drag my gaze to his, the look in his bright eyes is anything but neutral.

He's furious.

At the men who tried to find me. At my fiancé.

The realization warms me.

"Is he the one who hurt you?" Killian demands.

He's still standing close, but now he crosses his arms, closing himself off. It's for the best. I can't let my fantasies distract me from what matters, and that's making sure I never get sent back to that monster.

"Sway," Bracken's tone is gentle. He walks over and wedges himself between me and Killian, his gaze intent but encouraging. "You can talk to us. We're trying to protect you. But we need to know what we're up against."

Killian's rage; Duncan's control. I could have stayed strong against either, but Bracken's gentleness breaks down my willpower like nothing else.

"It's not what you think, okay? He doesn't love me. I don't think he's capable of it, really. All he wants is power. And to own me. Like a possession. No, like a weapon. He's not well-liked, but he's well-connected, and he uses those connections and resources like weapons too. He won't stop coming for me but only because he can't stand to lose. You should know that, at least."

"What's his name?" Duncan asks.

When I don't answer, he shoves his way into the circle we've created so that I'm facing all three of them, close enough to touch now.

"Tell me his name," Duncan says, "And we'll stop him."

I'm tempted, but in the end, I shake my head. "No."

Killian snarls at that. "Why are you making this so difficult? One name and we'll end it for you."

"That's why I'm saying no. If you go after him, you'll bring his entire House down on you for it. I won't let you get killed because of me."

"She's right, you know," Bracken says on a sigh. "I don't fucking like it, but she's right."

"Fuck being right," Killian growls, but it sounds more like a pout than a threat.

Duncan studies me. "Why does he want you? What kind of weapon do you possess?"

I meet his gaze with a hard look of my own. "The kind I won't allow to be used—by anyone."

Killian shakes his head. "She doesn't trust us. Even after everything."

I don't answer. I can't. Not about this. Because the truth is that I *do* trust them. It's *me* that I can't risk hurting them. My power corrupted the man Robert was. The last thing I'll let it do is tear down these three men.

"The hunters looking for you today wore a ring from Earth and Emerald," Duncan says. "Are you a member of that House too?"

"No. My family is gone. I have no House." Emotion clogs my throat as I think of my parents, but I blink it away. Now's not the time.

They all share a look.

"Well, love," Killian says, "there's some good news in all of this."

"What's that?" I ask warily.

"You've just bought yourself three full-time, round-the-clock babysitters." He grins, gesturing at himself and the others.

"What do you...?" I look back and forth between them as his meaning dawns. "You can't be serious."

"Dead fucking serious," he says cheerfully.

"The hunters that showed up today made it clear they suspect you're here," Bracken says. "They aren't going to stop trying to get to you, as you said."

"And your solution is to attach yourselves to me?" I demand, ignoring the images my words conjure. "How is that good news?"

Killian simply winks.

Bracken smirks.

Duncan opens his mouth to say something, but a knock at the door cuts him off. He answers it and then steps back to let the visitor enter. The Ringmaster steps into the room, and I force myself not to take a step back in surprise. The man has a presence like some kind of leviathan.

"There you are." His sharp gaze zeroes in on me.

"Did you need me?" I ask, noting the way Bracken and Killian have each turned to flank me.

"I'm assuming Killian told you I caught your practice session earlier."

"He did."

He produces a scroll of paper that he tosses onto the counter. "Your signature goes at the bottom."

I blink as he holds out a pen. When I don't move, Duncan walks over and unrolls the paper, laying it flat. Someone else shoves me toward it, and I make my way over to stare down at the words Performance Contract printed across the top. The words beneath it jumble together, too complicated and heavily worded for me to understand.

"This part says you agree to perform five days a week, barring physical injury," Duncan explains quietly, pointing to the first paragraph. "And this one says what you get in exchange. See?"

He points lower where I catch the words "room and board" along with a number for payment.

"I get paid?" I can't help but ask in surprise.

Duncan chuckles.

"Hell yeah, you get paid," Killian pipes up from behind me.

The Ringmaster simply waits while Duncan takes me through the rest, including my expiration date three months from now. I swallow hard and then take the pen and scrawl my name along the line at the bottom.

"All set," Duncan says as he rolls the paper back up and hands it over to the Ringmaster. "We good to bring Isaac in now?"

"Isaac? Who the hell is—"

"Yes," D replies, interrupting me. "Make it quick, and be quiet about it."

"Thanks, boss."

"Thank me when it works." He turns to me. "Your first show is Friday evening," the Ringmaster tells me. "Let Liv know if there's anything you need in order to be ready."

He turns to leave, but I step forward in surprise.

"Friday? That's in three days."

He turns back. "Is there a problem?"

"No," I say, my mind whirling with possibilities for a routine. Then there's makeup and costume and—

"Your wardrobe is being seen to as we speak," he adds. "The first batch will be delivered in the morning. The men here can inform you of the practice schedule."

He doesn't wait for my response before showing himself out.

After he's gone, all three guys turn back to me.

"I don't have time for this right now." I start to shove past them, heading for the Big Top so I can start working on a routine.

"Whoa." Duncan blocks my path with the other two crowding in beside him. "Where do you think you're going?"

"I need to see the layout of the Big Top again so I can start creating a routine."

They share a look that has me rethinking my excitement about being "attached" to them in any way. Before I can tell them to back off, Killian and Bracken move aside.

"Where are you two going?" Duncan asks as they head for the door.

"You take first watch," Bracken tells him, something passing between him and Killian that I don't quite catch. "Kill and I will call the vamp then do a perimeter run."

"It's my turn to patrol," Duncan says. He's clearly confused too, but he looks more pissed about it.

"We know," Killian says, putting up a hand to stop Duncan from following them. "But it's also your turn to ...well, you know."

He nods at me, and Duncan scowls as Killian and Bracken walk out.

Suddenly, the apartment feels way too small. Duncan stays where he is, watching me with an unread-able look in his bottomless blue eyes.

"Your turn to what?" I demand when the silence stretches.

"Babysit," he says on a sigh.

I start for the door, my temper flaring at the way he clearly doesn't want to be with me. "Whatever. You don't have to come with me. I know the way. Go deal with the vampire or whoever it is you need to call."

I pull the door open, but Duncan's suddenly right behind me, shoving it closed again.

"What are you—"

I turn around and find Duncan standing way too close. I stare up at him, forgetting to breathe for a second as his piercing blue eyes stab right through my defenses. His carefully constructed mask is still in place, but his stormy gaze tells me there's far more going on beneath the surface than he lets on.

"I need to work on my routine," I say, breathless at our closeness.

My thrumming pulse is near deafening.

My gaze drops to his full mouth, and I wonder again what it would be like to kiss him. He's wound so tight. What would it be like to see him lose control? To stop holding me at arm's length and touch me instead? And why the hell do I care?

Mere days ago, I was beaten to within an inch of my life by a man.

Shouldn't I be wary of the entire gender? But these men don't scare me. They make me feel things I never thought I'd feel for anyone.

"Killian and Bracken think you're interested in them."

It's the last thing I expect him to say, so it takes me a moment to find my voice. "Excuse me?"

"Are you?" he presses.

"That's none of your business."

For some reason I can't fathom, he leans closer. "Everything that happens in this place is my business. But especially you, Sway. You've been my business since you first stumbled onto our property."

The way he says it sends a shudder through me.

"You have a funny way of showing it," I shoot back.

His eyes narrow. "What is that supposed to mean?"

"You act like I'm some annoying project to you. And when we're alone, you can't seem to get away from me fast enough."

He moves in and braces his arms on either side of

my head, dipping so that our noses are almost brushing. Eye to eye with me, he says, "I'm not running now."

His mouth. Right there...

I blink, my temper outweighing my very theatrical fantasies. "No, but you're testing me."

I shove him away, and maybe out of surprise, he backs off. But he doesn't argue. And that speaks volumes.

"I'm done playing whatever game this is," I tell him. "You can tell Bracken and Killian that, if this is how you treat all of the people you promise to protect, I don't want it."

Temper flashes in his eyes. "My promise to protect you has nothing to do with this."

"I don't even know what this is," I toss back.

"Do you love him?"

"Who?"

"Your fiancé. Do you love him?"

"I told you, I'm nothing to him."

"You said that. But you didn't say what you feel for him."

"Why does that matter?"

"Because I'm going to kill him, Sway. When I find him—and I will find him—he will suffer. There will be pain. And torture. And he'll beg for death before I give it. So, I need to know, do you love him? Are you going to blame me for all the horrible things I intend to do to the monster who hurt you?"

"No," I tell him, a little awed by the smoothness of the mask he wears as he paints a picture of torture and death. What must he have seen and gone through to become this? Suddenly, his crafted exterior makes so much sense. It's his control. When he can't control anyone else, he can control himself. His emotions. And what he lets everyone else see of him.

Realizing it softens me. My temper drains away.

"Duncan." I step closer, lifting my hand and pressing it to his cheek. "I don't love him. I never have. And I will not blame you for anything you do to him. I'll thank you for putting an end to the monster who has tormented me for far too long."

Chapter 10

Duncan

Sway swings on the lyra high above the ground, moving her body to a beat slow enough that her movements are sharp but sexy enough that my entire body is rigid merely watching her. Thankfully, no one else is here.

It's a purposeful move on my part. After watching her become startled by their applause this morning, I made sure to wait until the others had all quit for the day before bringing her back here to practice. It gave me more time with Sway—insisting we eat alone together in the apartment and dragging it out as long as possible.

Now, there's no one else to witness her olive skin beaded with sweat, her toned stomach bare, thanks to the low shorts and crop top she wears. No one else to watch me imagine the way those long legs would feel wrapped around my waist.

I clear my throat and lean back against the wall, folding my arms in front of me to hopefully hide the massive bulge in my pants should anyone walk in.

My thoughts drift to the way she'd looked staring up at me in my apartment earlier. To the fear that faded into something I don't dare imagine was lust. When I'd promised to kill her fiancé, Sway had looked up at me like I had the answer to her nightmares.

As though I am the hero she's been seeking.

If only she knew I was no fucking hero.

"How's our girl doing?" Liv steps from the shadows and comes to stand beside me, hand on her swollen belly. It wasn't long ago that she was abducted by her own past nightmare, and we'd nearly shredded all of No Man's Land to get her back.

Women.

They drive us to kill like nothing else.

"Good. Seems to be doing well despite her ankle."

"When you're up there, it's easy to forget the pain that waits as soon as your feet touch the ground."

I can hear what she's saying between the words, so I wrap an arm around her shoulders, and she leans against me. Liv is the little sister I never got to have. A woman who captured the heart of the hardest man I've ever known. I would give my life to protect her.

Something I used to only be able to say for D, Killian, and Bracken.

I look up at Sway. Now, I have another name on that list.

"You find out anything else? D said she has a fiancé looking for her?"

"That's all we know so far. She won't give up his name. Too scared of him still."

Liv shivers.

"You all right?"

"Yeah," she says with a soft chuckle. "I just know all too well how she must feel."

"Your nightmare is in the ground now," I remind her.

"And hers will be soon, too?"

I look down into Liv's pale gaze. The fact that she doesn't shy away from doing the hard thing if it means protecting those she cares about is a strength I admire in her. The fact that she already cares that much for Sway speaks volumes. "Absolutely. And I'm going to enjoy putting him there."

"Just don't get killed doing it." She touches her rounded belly. "This little one is going to need his Uncle Duncan around."

My heart warms, and I smile. "Uncle, huh? You sure know how to make a guy feel important."

"You are important. *And* worthy of what it is you desire most." Before I can ask what she means, Liv squeezes my arm gently and pulls away. As soon as she leaves the room, both Killian and Bracken come in.

"Fuck me. Why does she have to be so damned gorgeous?" Killian's gaze is already glued to Sway.

"She looks at peace up there," Bracken adds, also watching her intently. "Don't you think?"

"Did you find anything on patrol?" I demand, desperate to change the subject because talking about Sway with them—knowing where they stand with her—makes it even more difficult to refuse what it is I want: her. The promise I made to myself to stay away from her is getting harder and harder to keep.

"Nope. If the bastards are lurking, they're remaining upwind. We couldn't even catch their scent."

"They'll be here Friday," I tell them. "You can fucking count on it."

"Then we make sure they don't recognize her."

"How do we do that?" I ask Killian.

"Liv used to perform in a mask. We get her one."

The idea has merit, but even with that mask, Liv's attackers knew just where to find her. It's a risk, one I wish I could avoid by putting this asshole in the ground before she takes the spotlight for the first time. "It's a good start," I say as I shift my gaze back to Sway. "You make the call?"

"He's on his way as we speak."

"Good. That should help. If they've been tracking her, then with his cloak, they may believe she left."

"You really think so?" Killian questions.

"We can only hope," I reply as I focus in on Sway.

She's so in tune with her body, twisting it in perfect tandem with the slow, romantic beat that's playing from the speakers. From the rafters, a single spotlight shines down on her.

"So?" Killian prompts.

"So, what?" I ask, already knowing damn well what he means.

"How'd it go with her earlier?" Bracken bumps my arm with his. "Did you make it three for three with a kiss?"

"No."

They share a look at my clipped response.

"Fuck, man. Why are you holding back?" Killian asks. "We can tell you want her as much as we do."

"That's exactly why I won't have her," I say.

"What the fuck does that mean?" Bracken asks.

"Maybe the best way to protect her is to keep sex out of it," I say, "Did you ever think of that?"

They both look at me with varying expressions of disgust.

"That's the dumbest thing I've ever heard you say," Killian announces.

"And we've heard you say a lot of dumb shit, dude." Bracken shakes his head.

"Fuck you both," I mutter.

"No, thanks. We have our eye on something better." Killian's grin makes me want to punch it off him. Assholes.

"I'm going to make my move on her," Bracken announces.

I turn to look at him. Killian's grin is wide as he says, "Same." He turns to me. "You'd better make your choice soon, Dunc. Because we already have."

⸻

BY THE TIME SWAY COMES DOWN FROM THE LYRA, BOTH Killian and Bracken have been gone nearly an hour already. Knowing that they plan to make her theirs eats away at me.

Mixing business with pleasure is messy, but this is more than that. Sway is more than mere pleasure. And that's what scares me.

Granted, she'll be gone in three months, anyway. So that something more doesn't actually matter, does it? My gut churns, and that truth hits me head-on. I'm reluctant because moving in on her means losing her. All three of us might be left wanting more when Sway's time here is over.

What the hell are we going to do then?

When she's back on the ground, her slight limp is the only evidence of her still-aching ankle. Cheeks flushed, her expression is joyful as she crosses over toward me. Every step she takes eats away at my resolve. Killian's voice rings in my ear. *Make your move soon because we already have.*

"That was exhilarating." She grins. "Did I look—"

I don't let her finish. I grip the back of her neck and spin her, pressing her back into the wall as I slam my mouth to hers. Her hands grip my arms as mine pin her to me. I expect her to pull away. To shove me off of her, but her submission is instant.

She opens beneath me, and her soft moan is music to my fucking ears.

I drive my tongue into her mouth, sliding it against hers. She tastes like a fucking daydream. Like nothing I've ever had before. Like redemption. I arch into her, my cock far harder than it's ever been as I press into her.

My hands glide down her body, and I grip her ass, lifting her so those gorgeous fucking legs are wrapped around my waist. I kiss her until I'm drunk on what she has to offer.

Until the rest of the world fades away.

Her body fits perfectly against mine, as though she were made for me. For my brothers.

To fuck.

To possess.

To love.

And it's that last one that cuts me deeper than anything else. This woman will mean more to us than any other has. She will have the power to destroy us

Still, I don't pull away because Sway's arms come around my neck. Her full breasts press against my chest, her sweat-slicked skin pinned to me. I release her mouth, and she tips her chin up like a good fucking girl as I drag my tongue down the side of her neck. Her skin is tangy beneath my tongue, and the animal in me surges to the surface.

He craves her, too.

"Well, fuck me, Bracken, looks like he's made his choice."

Panting and dazed, I lift my head and look over at my brothers, who are both grinning widely at me. Again, I expect Sway to pull away but she doesn't. I look down and find her staring up at me, eyes wide and glossy with lust. I kiss her again one last time, pressing my lips to hers gently as I let her body slide slowly down mine.

And when her feet finally hit the ground, I step back. This wouldn't have been my first choice for how to ask her about the three of us, but it's too late to stop them now. All I can do is hope she'll hear us out.

"Choice?" Sway questions as she looks from me to them. "What choice?"

Bracken smiles. "On whether or not he was in, too."

"In on what?" Her brows draw together, and she crosses her arms. "What the fuck is going on?"

"Easy, love." Killian chuckles. "We've merely decided that we want you. Is that not clear?"

"We're a pride," Bracken says. "And because of that, we share everything."

"Everything," Sway repeats, her gaze narrowing on him before she shifts it to me. "As in—"

"Women," I tell her softly.

Her swollen lips part as she looks up at me. "I'm sorry, come again?"

"I'd like to," Killian jokes with a wink.

"We all care about you," I say because I realize just how badly we're fucking this up. Normally, sharing is not this hard. Normally, the women want all of us—together. But Sway clearly has never experienced something like that. "And we all want to show you just how much."

"You *all* want to sleep with me?"

"Now you're getting it." Killian winks again.

Sway's eyes narrow as she tells him, "I told you I'm not a toy to be played with."

I step in closer, panic gnawing at my gut because I can see her dismissal written on her face, and if she turns away from me after I've had a taste—I'm not sure how I'll handle that. "We don't play with toys," I tell her. "But we will give you more pleasure than you've ever known." I reach forward and run the pad of my thumb over her swollen lips. "You just have to give us a chance."

Sway swallows hard and takes a step back. "I—I can't do this. You don't understand."

"We know you're in danger. We'll keep you safe," Bracken insists.

"No." She takes a deep breath. "I have to protect myself from you, too. From what—" She shakes her head. "I need time. Give me time."

She turns and leaves, not sparing another glance back at us.

I run a hand through my hair. "That went really fucking well, didn't it?"

"She'll come around," Killian says then turns to me. "That was some damned kiss."

"Yeah," I reply, a bleak sort of fear settling in my gut at the idea that she might not come around. "She's potent."

"I fucking told you." He grins. "*She matters,*" he adds through our bond.

"*That's what I'm worried about,*" I reply as my mind begins concocting all the ways this could go horribly fucking wrong.

She could decide she only wants one of us.

She could decide she wants none of us.

Fuck, after what we just told her, she might just run away.

My lion surges beneath my skin, desperate to be free. To run off some steam. "You're on guard duty," I tell Killian. "Bracken, let's go find us some fucking hunters."

Chapter 11

Sway

I sleep like shit, mostly because I'm too busy wondering whether one of the guys is stationed outside my room, still babysitting me like they promised. It's tempting to crack open the door and check to see if one of them is out there, but that feels too much like taking back my answer earlier. Once the shock wore off—in what world do three attractive, caring males ask to date me?—I'm left only with my own heartache.

I can't give them what they want from me. Even if I wanted to trust them, being with me is just as dangerous for them as it is for me, and I won't put them at risk. Not even if it means losing out on my own happiness.

So, I stay in bed, tossing and turning until dawn.

In the soft light, I dress in an outfit nearly identical to the one from yesterday; short shorts that won't get in the way of the friction I need up on the equipment and an oversized tee layered over a sports bra. Then, I toss my hair up in a high bun and square my shoulders for the outside.

I'm going to have to face them eventually. Best to get it over with. Like ripping off a Band-Aid. But when I open the apartment door, Liv and Bracken are huddled together just outside.

"Oh." I stop, startled at the sight of them.

They break apart with Bracken giving me a look I can't bring myself to meet. Instead, I focus on Liv. She smiles at me.

"Good morning, Helen. We were just coming to see you." They move into the apartment, and Bracken shuts the door behind them.

"Morning," I murmur, already wishing I'd stayed in my bed. Awkward doesn't even begin to cover it. "I was just..."

A knock on the door has me trailing off. Bracken pulls it open to reveal Killian, D, Duncan, and a man I don't recognize. His sandy brown hair falls in loose waves to his shoulders, and when his gaze lands on me, he smiles a cocky, sideways grin. "You must be Helen."

I swallow hard. He's handsome, and even without using my abilities, I can sense that what he desires most is vengeance. Against who or what, I don't know. But a thirst for blood rarely ends well. "And you are?" I ask.

"Your White Knight." He bows. "Also known as Isaac."

"Shut the fuck up and get this over with," Duncan snaps.

"Threatened?" he asks.

"Hardly. We just have shit to do."

Isaac chuckles and moves into the room. I take a step back. "What exactly are we getting over with?" I demand.

"We're going to hide you." Killian crosses his arms. "So that what happened yesterday doesn't happen again."

"The men looking for me."

"Precisely," Isaac replies. "Let me do this, and I'll make sure no one ever finds you again."

For the first time since I laid eyes on him, fear twists into hope. "Will it work even when I leave here?"

"For as long as we both shall live," he replies with a wink.

"What do you need from me?"

"Your hand and a drop of blood."

I hold it out without further hesitation. "Do it."

Isaac closes the distance between us and takes my hand then reaches into his pocket and withdraws something. One click of a button reveals a blade. My heart pounds as he presses the tip to my palm. A tinge of pain is followed by drops of crimson welling up onto the surface. He smears it with the knife then locks his gaze with mine as he licks it from the blade.

A low growl fills the room, and my gaze lifts to find Duncan watching, his teeth bared. I swallow hard and consider flashing a smile. But somehow, I think that would only make things worse.

Magic prickles along my skin as Isaac closes his eyes. Seconds pass in complete silence until he releases me and tucks his blade back into his pocket. "All done."

"That's it?" Duncan snaps.

"It may not look like much," Isaac replies, "But I assure you it worked."

"Thank you," I tell him, feeling lighter than I have since I first arrived. This means freedom. It means being able to leave and not be tracked.

"Anytime." He steps back from me and turns to D. "I'll be sure to ring when I need that favor, big guy."

"I'm sure you will," he replies. "Now get the fuck off my property."

Isaac chuckles and leaves the room, D, Duncan, and Killian all following. As soon as the door shuts behind them, I let out a breath. "What favor?"

"Don't worry about it," Bracken says. "And now I better get going. As soon as Isaac leaves, we have a security brief, and Duncan will have my balls if I'm late."

He nods at Liv and closes the distance between us so

he can drop a kiss on my forehead. "See you soon, gorgeous."

He's gone before I can figure out how to make my mouth work.

Liv watches me with an amused glint in her eye. "You okay?"

"All good," I force out.

"Hungry?" she asks.

"Yeah," I say.

In more ways than one.

"Good. I love to eat these days, and I don't want to do it alone. Come on."

She leads me out of the apartment, down the hall, and into the cafeteria. The aroma of food fills my lungs and makes my stomach growl. Liv grabs a tray then hands me one. She piles hers high with fruit cups, eggs, bacon, and muffins. When I do the same, she actually high-fives me.

"What's that for?" I ask.

"Eating should be a team sport, that's all." She grabs her tray and heads for a table by the window. "Come on."

I laugh and follow her over. "I'm surprised you're down here. I figured you ate breakfast with the Ringmaster."

She waves her hand dismissively. "He's at that

boring security briefing this morning." Reaching for the butter, she smirks at me, adding, "Besides, I already had the appetizer before I came down."

I nearly choke on my orange juice but manage to swallow it down. "Oh."

"Well, I'm pregnant, not dead," she says with a laugh.

"Fair point." I return her grin, and together, we dig into our food.

It's actually really good. Much better than I expected for cafeteria-style. Apparently, the Ringmaster takes care of his people. It's a direct contradiction to his hard reputation, but the more time I spend with Liv, the less his kindness surprises me. She clearly softens him. Instead, I wonder what he was like before they met. I bet that's a hell of a story.

"Whoa, you have that look in your eye." Liv's words call me back, and I blink, refocusing on the strawberries and yogurt in front of me. "Like you were a million miles away just then. Everything okay?"

"Yeah, it is." She looks unconvinced. "I swear, I'm just settling in and still figuring everyone out."

"Uh-huh. And does everyone include three hot lion shifters?"

Well, shit. She's not going to hold anything back. I lean back in my chair and meet her gaze. "Actually, I was wondering about you and the Ringmaster. He doesn't seem like the paternal type, and yet..."

She holds up her hand. "Fair enough. My question was nosy as hell. But I hope you're not offended. I guess I'm rusty at making friends. And the truth is, I like you. I actually see a lot of myself in you."

The words themselves sound a bit cliché, but the shadow that passes behind her normally sunny gaze is not.

"You showed up bloody and beaten on their doorstep too?" I can't help but ask.

"Sort of."

"Seriously?" I gape at her. "I didn't actually mean—"

"Oh, I know." She waves me off. "You'd never know it to meet me now, but my past was not an easy one. My power was a bit of a sore spot, and, in the end, my parents pushed me away because of it. I found myself tied to a man who only wanted me because I was easy to control. He abused me and would have ultimately killed me if I'd stayed there. So I ran. D found me damn near dead in an alleyway. He offered me a safe haven in exchange for service then killed everyone who was after me. This place is where I found freedom. And then love." She gently touches her rounded belly.

My throat tightens as I listen to her story. A story that sounds eerily familiar to my own. The difference is that she was saved by her attachment to the people here. That isn't in the cards for me.

"I'm so sorry," I say quietly.

"Don't be. I'm not that girl anymore. And I wouldn't trade my past for anything because it brought me here. It is the reason I get to be a mom to this little one." She rubs her hand over her belly, and I can feel the love emanating from her now.

It's beautiful—even as it reminds me of everything I can never have.

"I don't think my ending will be as happy as yours," I tell her. "But I'm so glad you got away."

"You got away too," she points out.

"That doesn't mean I'm safe."

She looks ready to say more, but I don't think I can talk about this without crying, so I stand up, grabbing my tray. "Thanks for breakfast," I say. "I need to get going."

I start to walk away, but Liv stops me when she calls out, "It's hard to see that you're safe when mentally you're still wrapped in the nightmare. Sometimes our worst enemy is our own inability to let go and move forward."

Tears blur my eyes.

Without turning, I nod, no longer trusting my voice, and hurry out.

Somehow, I manage to find the trash and tray return. In the hallway, I take a sharp right, beelining for the stairs. So much for practice. Now, it's all I can do to make it back to my room before I completely lose it.

I yank the door wide, exiting the stairwell nearly at a

run as I rush toward my apartment door. A figure pushes off from the hallway wall near my apartment. Through my tears, I see Bracken, concern etched into his handsome face.

Shit.

Now he wants to show up?

"Sway," he says, coming forward to meet me. "What's wrong? What happened?"

"Nothing," I say, trying to shove past him as I dig for the key I stashed in my bra earlier.

"You're upset."

"I'm fine."

Fumbling, I nearly drop the key. Bracken grabs it from me. "Here. Let me."

His voice is gentle, which only makes it worse. Before he's even turned the key in the lock, the floodgates open, and tears stream in thick tracks down my cheeks. I duck my face to hide it. He unlocks the door and pushes it open for me. When I try pushing past him, he follows me in.

"Tell me what's wrong," he says, his voice almost pleading.

"I don't want to talk about it," I say, my voice catching.

Bracken's reaction is instant.

In a single flash of movement, he's across the space and folding me into his arms. "Whoa," he says softly. "What's all this?"

His gentleness is the last straw. I sniffle as more tears come, most of them landing on his shirt now. But he doesn't even notice as he lifts me completely off the ground and carries me to the bed. Then, he sits, settling me in his lap and rubbing my back.

It's so unexpected and sweet that my heart flutters.

"Why do you have to be so fucking nice?" I groan against his shoulder.

"Excuse me?" There's amusement in his tone, but he doesn't stop rubbing my back.

Ugh.

"I'm trying to resist you, and you're making it really damn difficult," I say.

"I see. Well, I'd apologize, but then there's the whole *wanting you* thing, so making it easy for you to resist me is not really in my best interest, is it?"

His shoulders are hard with the muscle he carries, but underneath that, he's soft. And inviting. A comfort —when I so desperately need some. I can't remember the last time someone held me like this. And for some reason, that fact makes me angry enough to want this now. To have something for myself even if it's just a shoulder to cry on. A very sexy, very tempting shoulder.

"Did Liv say something to upset you?"

The question startles me enough that I sit up and look at him. "What? No, of course not. Liv is great."

His eyes are soft on mine. Understanding. "I'm glad you think so. She's like a sister to me."

"She was trying to fish for information about us as soon as you left," I admit.

He wiggles his brows. "And did she get any?"

I scowl.

He grins.

It's an innocent smile, but it makes me ache all over again.

"Bracken..."

His smile disappears. He cups my cheek with a calloused hand and peers at me intently, his concern touching me in a way nothing has in so long. Beneath the gentleness is a fierce aura of outright violence; a willingness to kill if needed. "Please tell me who hurt you."

I hesitate, fully planning to dodge the question. Ignore it. Lie. Pretend. Anything but the truth. But something about Bracken's vulnerability changes my mind.

"Is it too dramatic if I say everyone I've ever known?" I whisper.

"Not dramatic," he says. "But that's a long list of people I'm going to have to kill."

"Not my parents. Nature already did it for you."

"Shit, Sway. I'm sorry. Is that why you don't talk about them? They hurt you?"

"No. My parents were pretty great. But they were from two different houses whose families never stopped feuding. I was nine when they died in a car accident.

After that, no one ever fully agreed on who should get custody of me, so no one really did. I stayed with aunts and my grandmother for a few years, but because of their custody battle, I was never allowed to join either House."

"That's why you have no House."

I shrug. "I don't care about that, but that means no protection either."

He tucks a loose strand of hair behind my ear. "Who do you need protection from, gorgeous?"

I hesitate, already shocked at how much I've just told him. It's more than I've shared with anyone. But instead of feeling exposed, one look at Bracken's face, and I feel safer than I ever have.

"I met him at a party. He was older than me. Successful. Important to his House. He bought me gifts, made me feel special. I didn't see the red flags for what they were." I take a deep breath and press on. "Six months later, my apartment was broken into, so he convinced me to move in with him. He said if I married him, I would get to remain House of Earth and Emerald forever. I would be protected. I needed to feel safe, so I agreed. But the moment I moved into his place, things changed. I began to see the real him. His temper grew worse and worse. His requests became orders. I wasn't allowed to leave the house alone. My refusals didn't matter anymore. I—" I blow out a breath and meet Bracken's eyes. "If he finds me..."

I don't finish, but Bracken's gaze has gone dark and feral. The beast inside him is closer to the surface than I've ever seen on any of them. But there's nothing scary about it—not for me.

"I'm going to kill him, Sway. Rip him limb from limb. It won't be quick. And even then, it won't satisfy me because you deserve more than that. I can't go back and stop it, but I can give you this. I can swear to protect you from him, whatever it takes."

"Bracken."

He cups my cheek again, the gentle yet murderous look he wears cutting straight to my core. It's a turn-on, which probably says something about me, but I have to squeeze my thighs together to meet his eyes without giving in to the urge to strip and give myself over to him right here and now. If the sex didn't mean anything else, maybe I would. But he and the others have made it clear this is not that simple.

"Gorgeous," he murmurs.

I pull away from his touch. "I can't ask you to protect me when I'm not able to give you what you want in return."

"Is that how you think this works?"

"Isn't it?"

He looks at me intently, the distance between us so close I can feel his breath. "You've been hurt by too many people to know this yet, but things are different for you now. We're different. Me and my brothers. We swear to protect you, so that's what we'll do. That protection is separate from our desire to have you in our beds. One doesn't determine the other. Do you believe me?"

I bite my lip, hesitating. Not because I don't believe him. But because I do.

He leans closer as if testing me. When I don't pull away, he kisses my jaw then my cheek then my temple.

"I don't want a transaction. I want to worship you like you deserve to be worshipped."

Using the hand he's hooked around my neck, he tips my head down to kiss my forehead then back up again to kiss the corner of my mouth.

"When you come to my bed, Sway, it will be because you want me as much as I want you."

Chapter 12

Bracken

The stands are packed tonight. Supernaturals from all over Portland—some even farther—have traveled to view the show. They fill the seats surrounding three sides of the Big Top. Men, women, and children who laugh and cheer with each new act designed to shock and entertain.

I fucking hate it.

The crowds remind me of the fighting ring I was forced into back in my old House.

They remind me of pain.

Blood.

Death.

I cross my arms and remain in the shadows on the outside of the outer ring. Watching, waiting. For anyone who is here to cause fucking problems. Duncan is on the opposite side of the Big Top with Killian lingering near the entrance. Before the show, I told them what Sway shared about her fiancé and the way he trapped her with lies and fake promises of protection. They both nearly lost it with bloodlust, and I can't blame them. The more I hear about this piece of shit, the more I feel compelled to hunt his ass down and end him, but now it's time to fucking focus.

On Duncan's order, I scan the hands of the guests for the telltale ring of their houses. House of Earth and Emerald headquarters is far enough away from Portland that there aren't many visitors wearing their symbol of protection, but I make special note of them, watching their every move as the show progresses. Normally, I feel like the three of us are plenty of protection, given what we're capable of.

But with Sway here and about to be on display, I've never felt so inadequate.

Already, the crowd cheered along with Fiona as she threw daggers at her Djinn lover, Harriss. They gasped and laughed at Brad and Kleo's rope-walking antics where the rope became a weapon in the end, and now they watch in complete silence as the spotlight remains empty while Sway climbs up the metal ladder toward the lyra waiting for her.

My heart hammers as soon as the music begins.

A low, torturous melody that seduces as it builds, it's a song for love-making, a perfect rendition of how I feel for her. How my brothers feel. For days now, we've behaved like gentlemen, but the tension of being near her and not having her has built toward something I know we can all feel coming to a head.

If she doesn't choose us soon, I don't know how we'll keep sane.

Seconds tick by until Sway comes into view. Suddenly, the spotlight sweeps up to center on her, and the crowd murmurs their oohs and ahhs. She sits on her lyra like it's a swing, gripping the top of it with gloved hands meant for gripping. She wears a red bodysuit complete with gold embellishments and a small, black top hat that is secured to her dark hair with an obsidian ribbon. Her face is painted completely white, her lips a startling red.

Eyelids covered in golden glitter, she looks like a living doll. Something that was done on purpose to shield her from anyone in the audience who might be here searching for her. It's why we didn't advertise a new performer on the lineup.

No, from the outside in—it's business as usual at No Man's Circus.

The last few days have been quiet. No more visitors lurking or asking about her. But that's only left me more on edge.

The lyra comes to a stop halfway between the ceiling and the ground. Then, the tempo increases, and Sway opens her eyes. She drops down, and my heart seizes. Her hands grip the bottom of the lyra, and she moves her legs slowly, dancing in thin air.

I'm captivated by the sight of her, ensnared by feelings I never thought I'd have.

"Fuck, she looks good," Killian sends through our bond.

"She does," Duncan agrees.

Meanwhile, I'm completely and utterly speechless. She's broken, something you'd never know by watching her now. But I've seen the fissures in her heart—her soul. Cracks that I long to soothe.

"Fuck," Killian growls, and my adrenaline surges.

I turn, scanning the crowd. *"What is it?"*

"More Crimson Hunters," Duncan replies. *"Third row, middle. I saw his tattoo, but there are three more beside him I'm fairly certain are here with him."*

It takes me mere seconds to see the fuckers. They are staring at Sway as though she's the next thing on the menu. A low growl emits from me, and I clench my hands into fists. *"We need to get them out of the audience."*

"We do that and they'll know something is up."

"Do you see the way they're watching her?" Killian demands. *"They already fucking know."*

"Killian's right," Duncan says. *"We get them before they leave. Bracken, head toward the exit with Killian. I'll stay here and keep an eye on them."*

"On it," I reply as I begin moving toward the exit.

Killian doesn't even look my way when I come to stand on the opposite side of the door. Light from the lantern beside him glints off the piercings in his face, making him look even more sinister than normal.

The crowd gasps, and my attention immediately shifts to Sway. She dangles from the lyra with one hand, her other down at her side, both legs dangling below as it turns slowly. Then—she lets go and plummets.

My heart falls with her.

Until she lands on the back of a large bear—Lex, the shapeshifter, having chosen his next form. He runs in a circle around the ring as Sway straddles him, waving and grinning as the crowd goes wild. Jealousy comes out of nowhere, making my blood run hot.

It should be me she's wrapped her legs around.

Or Duncan.

Or Killian.

Not this fucker.

"Movement," Duncan warns.

We all shift our gazes to the hunters as they stand and start making their way toward the ground. I ready for them, as does Killian, but the fuckers slip beneath the stands instead.

"Go," Killian tells me. *"I'll remain here for now."*

I move along the outside of the Big Top, strategically making my way to the stands where the fuckers disappeared. Grabbing the canvas flap and lifting it up, I move beneath it and then immediately duck as a fist swings toward my head. I throw out an elbow and slam it into the gut of a hunter who snuck up behind me then spin and catch the tip of a dagger against the side of my throat for my trouble.

"Get over here," I say through the bond. *"I can't shift, or I risk bringing the stands and all these people down!"*

"Coming," Both Duncan and Killian say at the same time.

"You're not so fucking scary now, are you, *animal?*" the hunter in front of me says.

"Let's go somewhere private, and I'll show you animal," I snarl back, my hands clenched into fists.

"I heard you were quite a fighter in your time." He rolls his shoulders. "Should we find out?"

His words startle me. *The fuck?* This asshole knows about my past. That means these clowns are doing their homework, and that's even more troubling than some random meatheads following orders to kidnap.

"Fuck yes." I ready myself for his attack, but the scent of another fills my lungs. Someone behind me approaching fast. I drop down and swing my leg out, taking a hunter to the ground as I do. I jump down on top of him, heart racing, and snap his fucking neck like a twig.

It cracks, and he falls still.

Duncan and Killian rush in, Killian wielding knives in both hands.

I stand and glance behind me, pissed the fuck off that the other three hunters are gone. "They couldn't have gone far."

The stands above us erupt with cheers.

"I'll get to Helen," Duncan says, using her fake name just in case anyone's listening. "You two track them down."

"With fucking pleasure," Killian snarls.

We rush beneath the stands, ducking beneath brace boards until we reach the end. A large square has been sliced open along the bottom of the Big Top's canvas wall, so we slip out and into the darkness. In the distance, the carnival awaits, its bright lights giving the rest of the area a soft glow.

Killian and I shift in tandem, shredding our clothes as we do. Four paws on the ground, I sprint over the grass while I track the scent of them. It disappears into the trees just before the carnival, so we do, too.

<hr>

Two hours later, we're walking into D's office at the back of the Big Top, naked, dirty, tired, and pissed the fuck off.

D sits behind his desk, arms crossed, while Liv is seated on the couch, hands resting on her belly. Duncan and Sway are nowhere to be seen.

"Pants," D orders, gesturing to two pairs beside the

door. Liv chuckles and rolls her eyes, but both Killian and I tug them on.

"Did you catch them?" the Ringmaster asks.

"No. Lost their scent in the trees. Fuckers are professional." Killian is furious, angrier than I've ever seen him.

"So are you," D reminds him. His copper gaze shifts to mine. "Any more news on who is hunting her?"

"All we know is his House," I tell him. "Earth and Emerald. Beyond that, she won't talk.

"And the hunters haven't given you anything else?"

"Nothing that makes up the bigger picture as to just what is so terrifying about this asshole," Killian grumbles.

"He's being careful," D says, "sending all these Crimson Hunters instead of coming himself."

"The man is a fucking coward sending them instead of coming himself."

"We keep killing his little soldiers, he'll come," Killian says smugly. "It's only a matter of time."

D blows out a breath. "Crimson Hunters are one thing. They're hired mercenaries. They know what they're signing up for when they come here. Whoever this asshole is that's really after her might not be in the same category. And I don't want this shit to start a war, so until we clarify that, we can't just attack one of their citizens."

"With all due respect, D," Killian starts, "the only

way we get this asshole to stop coming for her is to put him down. Same way you did Ernesto."

D's gaze hardens. "Ernesto had no House," he replies. "This asshole does, which means we need to do what we can to reach a diplomatic solution. Otherwise, we risk an all-out war. One we won't win."

I bite back a retort. D has his own secrets to keep hidden, secrets that would have both him and Liv hunted to the ends of the world should they come out. Same with their unborn child. I won't risk them, which means I need to at least try to control myself here. "And if it comes down to killing him? If Earth and Emerald won't hear us out? What then?" I ask.

D shakes his head. "We'll find a way."

I can feel the stress radiating off of him. Something his mate can also sense. She stands and crosses over to put her hands on his shoulders. D relaxes beneath her touch.

"The hunter I killed? He have a House ring?" I ask.

"No. And he's been dealt with. Duncan already took care of him." His gaze narrows on my face. "But you should have checked before you killed him."

I ignore the warning. "Where is Duncan now?"

"With Sway," Liv offers. "She is not aware that there was any danger against her life tonight." Her words are laced with a silent order. "And she doesn't need to find out. She's been through enough."

"Understood," Killian and I both reply at the same time.

"In the meantime, the wards protecting the employee quarters have been strengthened; we'll know if someone tries anything," D says. "You're dismissed."

I offer both him and Liv a nod then turn and follow Killian out into the hall.

"You okay?" he asks.

"No," I reply, my mind racing back to the words that fucking hunter said to me. "He knew who I was."

Killian stops and turns to me. "What the hell do you mean?"

"He knew about the fights. About my past. Talked shit to me about it."

Killian's gaze darkens. "And how the fuck did he know that?"

"I don't know," I reply. "But whoever we're dealing with cannot be underestimated. There's no telling what else these assholes have figured out."

"You didn't tell D," he points out.

I sigh. "No."

"You want to explain to me why not?"

"Because D has politics to worry about," I say. "And we have Sway."

Kill grunts an agreement. "We need help if we're going to keep constant watch."

And if we want to convince her to be with the three

of us, we need to spend some time together as a group. We both think it though neither one says it out loud.

"See if Brad, Lex, and Fiona want to pitch in for some overtime," I say. "It's in the budget. D won't care."

"Will do," he says aloud. And then through the bond, *"Tell Duncan what you told me."*

"Tell me what?" Duncan replies immediately.

We exchange a glance, and then he peels off to get it done. Through the bond, I tell Duncan everything I just told Killian.

When I'm done, Duncan doesn't argue with my decision about keeping it from D. If anything, he sounds relieved. He's calm as fuck too, which only means he's strategizing with more determination than ever. When Dunc goes quiet, that's when the world should watch its back.

What we don't say out loud—or even through our bond—is that, by not telling D about those fuckers looking into our pasts, we've just made a choice to put someone else before him. I have no idea when or how it happened, but in this moment, Sway is more important to all three of us than anyone else. Even D—who has our undying loyalty. I feel the significance of our deci-sion like a weight on my chest, but I can't bring myself to feel guilty. All that matters now is her. And all that's left is to convince her to let us love her.

I pace my room like a caged animal, blood pumping, heart racing, and adrenaline sending me soaring. My thoughts race a mile a minute as I try to breathe and calm down. But it's a useless attempt. I have to move, to work off the excess energy. Being in the spotlight, knowing how many people watched me perform tonight—it's like a drug.

A high I never want to end.

Unable to remain inside this room, I march to my apartment door and fling it open, no real destination in mind. Immediately, I stop short at the sight of Duncan leaning against the opposite wall.

He looks up from his phone, and our eyes lock.

A zing of electricity crackles between us.

"What's wrong?" he asks, shoving his phone away.

"Wrong?" I look back at him, wondering for the

millionth time what would have happened between us the other day if his brothers hadn't interrupted. "Nothing is wrong," I assure him, breathless with how much I mean that statement. For once. Nothing is wrong.

"Then what—?"

"Tonight was incredible," I tell him. "I don't think I can stay in this room, though. I'm so freaking wired." I start for the stairs.

"Whoa, where are you going?" His boots padding against the carpet tell me he's following. Not that I needed the sound to do that for me. I can *feel* his presence. Just as I can sense when Killian and Bracken are near. Energy pours from these men.

Raw.

Carnal.

Delicious.

"I heard the other performers say they were headed to the carnival after," I say, stopping so I can face him.

Hesitation flickers in his sharp eyes. He glances down at the rest of my body. "The carnival's dress code is a bit more casual than that."

I look down and realize I'm still wearing my costume.

"Whoops." I grin up at him and then head back into my room, grabbing a sweatshirt and leggings. "I'll just be a minute," I call out before hurrying into the bathroom.

I have no idea when they managed it, but someone's

already repaired the door so it latches now. For some reason, that makes me smile.

I change and wash the rest of my makeup off then pull my hair out of the tight bun from before. It falls in tangled waves, but I don't care. I feel free. When I'm finished, I re-emerge and find Duncan waiting inside my apartment. He looks serious, but then he always looks like that, so I brush it aside, determined not to let him ruin my mood.

"Ready?" he asks, sliding his phone away again.

"You don't have to come," I tell him. "I can find my way alone."

His brow lifts.

"Right. Babysitters," I remember. "You don't mind?"

"I'm happy to be wherever you are." His words are quiet and serious. I can feel how much he means them, too. But it's the look in his eye that has me shuddering with the intensity of him.

Perhaps I'm not the only caged animal in this room.

"Me too," I tell him honestly.

A moment of silence passes between us. Then it's him breaking the spell and reaching for the door. I follow him out, heart thudding. And, for the first time in a long time, my magic stirs.

I ignore it, focusing on my breath as Duncan leads me down the stairs and out the doors to the adjacent lot where the carnival is going strong. We're just reaching the entrance when Bracken appears from the direction of the Big Top.

"Hey," I call as he falls into step with me.

"Hey, gorgeous," he says. "You looked amazing up there tonight. Like you were born for it."

"Thank you." My smile is wide. And I straighten, proud of my performance and happy as hell he witnessed it. "I felt amazing doing it."

"So, circus life agrees with you, huh?"

"I think I'm officially addicted."

He laughs. "Feeling good?"

"I feel like I could conquer the damn world right now," I tell him. "Or at least this carnival."

He grins and slings an arm around my shoulders. "Come on. You can win me a stuffed rabbit or something."

I smile up at him. "Deal."

Duncan trails behind us as Bracken and I walk the aisles of games and attractions. The atmosphere is chaotic but fun. The music from all the different booths overlaps with one another, each competing for attention. Even the lights are designed to distract and lure. It's a perfect fit for my mood.

"Where's Killian?" I ask.

"Running an errand," Bracken says. "He'll find us later."

"Good. I think I want to beat each of you at a carnival game tonight." I clap my hands together, excitement thrumming through my veins.

His brow lifts. "You realize we've had years to perfect our carnival game skills, right?"

"Maybe *you* have," I admit. "But something tells me Killian and Duncan aren't exactly out here throwing darts at balloons every night."

"You're not wrong," he says wryly. "Come on then. Let's see what you've got."

While we walk, I recognize a few of the performers milling around the crowded aisles too. I spot Fiona still in her costume and armed with her knives, and before I can reach her to say hello, one of the guests stops her and asks if she'll throw a knife at an apple on his head. She enthusiastically agrees.

I turn away, not sure that's my particular thrill ride.

Bracken chuckles at my expression. "Not in the mood for roulette?"

"No, I think ring toss is more my style." I stop in front of an old-school ring toss game, and the male attendant nods at us.

"How many?" he asks.

"Duncan?" I turn to see him scanning the crowd rather than paying attention to me and Bracken. "Do you want to play?" I ask.

"I'm good," he says, glancing at me and then back to the others.

I shrug it off but can't help feeling dismissed. Then

again, isn't that what I did to them when I turned down their offer?

An offer I haven't stopped thinking about every waking moment since.

"Two please," Bracken tells the attendant as he takes the offered rings then grins back at me.

"You're going down, gorgeous."

"Is that what you think?" I take my rings, holding them lightly as we both face the targets: a sea of empty glass bottles.

The attendant moves aside, and I focus, blocking out Bracken. Again, my magic stirs, but I don't let it influence me. Or him. I want to do this all on my own. And besides, my magic is the last thing I want ruining this night.

My first ring misses, bouncing off the side of a bottle and falling onto the ground. Bracken's first ring hooks, and I turn to glare at him.

"Two more to go," he says, grinning deviously.

"You can't use your supernatural senses. That's cheating."

"We're both capable of—"

"Nope," I say. "Not me."

He frowns. "It's not like I can turn it off."

"Try," I say dryly.

My second ring misses, but so does Bracken's. I square my shoulders, focusing on the third and final ring. Bracken goes first—and misses. I eye him, wondering if he's done it on purpose, but he gives nothing away. Duncan has backed off and stands at the corner of the stall, watching us with arms crossed.

I ignore him too because his distant attitude is starting to bring me down.

I concentrate and toss the final ring.

It hooks a bottle, and I let out a whoop.

"Woo!" I do a little dance, and Bracken laughs, grabbing my hand and twirling me.

"You do know a tie isn't a win, right?" he asks when I come to a stop.

"It's not a loss, though," I point out, refusing to come down off my high tonight. I don't get enough good days, so I refuse to let it be anything else.

"We don't get a stuffed bunny for a tie," he adds.

"Well, damn." I pout, eyeing the stuffed animal prizes hanging above our heads. "We could go again."

"I have a better idea. We need a tiebreaker," he says.

"What do you have in mind?"

"Come on." He grabs my hand and leads me through the aisles, past a dart board full of water balloons and a dunk tank where Kleo currently sits in the hot seat. I offer her a small wave and swear Duncan growls behind me. But a glance back at him gives away nothing.

Bracken stops in front of a climbing wall made of rope.

"Seriously?" I ask.

"Too hard?" he asks.

"Too easy. I'll smoke you."

He wiggles his brows. "Guess we'll find out. You ready?"

Before I can answer, Duncan rushes toward me and picks me up clear off my feet, hustling us into the alley and around the corner of the game stall.

"What are you—"

He doesn't set me down again until we're behind the stall and I'm pressed between the exterior wall and him.

"What the hell," I demand.

But the minute I catch sight of his expression, my anger melts away. There's concern in his usually sharp eyes. No, worse. There's fear.

"Duncan," I say, pressing my hands to his cheeks. "What's wrong?"

"Nothing, I… Fuck, I thought I saw something…"

From close beside me, Bracken snarls. "What the fuck, Duncan? You scared the shit out of her, man."

"I'm sorry. It was nothing. I just—Some asshole had a dagger tattoo but it wasn't— Dammit. That's my bad. We can go back."

He starts to move away, but I grab his shirt in my fist, holding him against me. He looks at me in surprise, but underneath that surprise is the same desire I feel. And before I can remember all the reasons why I shouldn't, I kiss him.

My lips crash against his, surprising us both.

Duncan makes a noise—a grunt of shock, I think—

but then he crowds in closer, deepening the kiss until I can't breathe in without inhaling him too. My hand curls around his shirt and then relaxes, sliding up his shoulder to the back of his neck.

His tongue coaxes my lips open, his hand reaching for my hip and pulling me forward so our bodies meet in every place they can.

There's a sound of movement, and I realize Bracken is backing away, giving us space.

I break the kiss with Duncan long enough to reach out and grab Bracken's arm. He looks up at me with the same surprise and then narrows his eyes in a flash of heat. "You sure about this, gorgeous?" he asks in a low voice.

I keep one arm firmly planted on Duncan's shoulder. With the other hand, I pull Bracken in close.

"I'm sure," I say.

The two of them share a look, and then Bracken moves in until they're both pressing me back against the wall. "Tell us what you want," Bracken says. "We need to hear you say it."

"I want you to kiss me," I say, my voice hoarse as I realize I'm not going to back out. Not for all the logical, sane reasons in the entire fucking world. Not when I want this more than I've ever wanted anything or anyone in my entire life. "Both of you."

Bracken looses a growl and then slams his mouth against mine. His hand threads through my hair as he takes everything he can from my offer. His tongue claims my mouth, and I feel the heat of desire pooling between my thighs more intensely than I ever have.

On my other side, Duncan presses a kiss to my throat just below my ear. The sensation of both of them touching me sends me spinning higher than the lyra ever could. All we're missing is—

"Looks like I'm late to the party, love."

I gasp, pulling away from Bracken to see Killian standing on my other side.

He gives me a crooked smile that anyone else might find threatening, but I only feel the thrill of anticipation. "May I?" he asks.

I nod, and he wastes no time swooping in and claiming a kiss of his own. Where Duncan and Bracken are holding me possessively, though, Killian's fingers trail lightly down the center of my torso, between my breasts, and then to the hem of my sweatshirt before sliding inside to trace soft lines across my abdomen.

My body is on fire, blazing with heat beyond anything I've ever known.

"Fuck, you taste good," Killian murmurs as his mouth releases mine, and Duncan replaces him. Hands roam my body, touching my skin, exploring me in a way that makes me crave them even more. Then, Duncan's easing back again, and Bracken's there, teasing me, licking me, biting me.

I drink in the taste of each of them. Their scent, their

touch. Each of them explores my body in different ways, claims my mouth with different force and skill. A hand finds its way to my aching core, fingers brushing over the fabric of my pants, igniting me even through the layer of clothing standing in our way.

It's erotic being out here where anyone can see us, but I don't stop them. Hell, I don't think I could even if I wanted to. Instead, I arch and squirm, aching for more.

Another hand finds its way beneath my sweatshirt.

"You're not wearing a bra," Duncan growls.

I smirk. "No, I'm not."

Fingers brush my bare nipple, squeezing lightly as pleasure explodes inside me.

My head swims with it, but despite the overwhelm and strangeness of it all, I feel only safety and certainty. These three men have each made me feel safe, protected, and cared for—individually and together. They want me. Just the way I am. Yet, they always give me space when I need it. There's no manipulation here. And while they each captivate me in their own way, I've never felt more in control. It doesn't matter, all the reasons why we shouldn't be together, not anymore. It's about so much more than protection now. It's about claiming. From this moment on, these men are mine. And I am theirs. Fully and completely.

Chapter 14

Killian

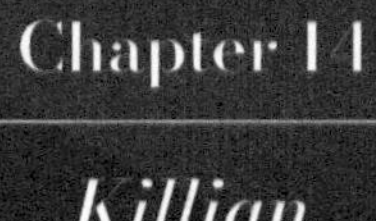

Pulling away from Sway is the hardest fucking thing I've done in a long time, but I do it anyway. We all do because we all know this isn't something we can act on. Not tonight.

Under the moonlight's glow, Sway looks up at me with swollen lips and pure sex in her hungry eyes, and something stirs inside me I once thought had vanished forever. Something I thought I didn't deserve to ever have in the first place.

"What's wrong?" she asks, breathless.

The others don't respond, and I know they're doing their best to lock down their own need right now. Taking Sway right here isn't something I'm morally against in general. Hell, I've fucked plenty of women behind carnival stalls over the years. But it's also not fair to her for her first time with three men to be behind a shed.

Especially not when she's still being hunted. Just because I didn't find anything while I was patrolling doesn't mean they aren't still out there.

"Nothing," I assure her.

"Then what—?"

"I don't give a fuck if the perimeter is clear. I'm not letting our guards down like this out here." Duncan's freaking the fuck out through the bond.

I do my best to remain calm in front of Sway, but the asshole's paranoid as hell since those hunters slipped through our fingers earlier tonight.

"We should get back inside," I tell Sway.

"Oh. Ohhh." Her eyes widen, and the scent of sex coming off her only increases.

I groan. "That's not what I meant, love."

Disappointment registers in her beautiful gaze, and I want to kick myself for putting it there. "I don't under-stand," she says.

"As fun as this is, the crowd's starting to thin out. We can't blend in much longer, not with all four of us standing together." Bracken's got a good point.

"Well, I'm not walking away from her right now," I tell them. *"It'll hurt her feelings."*

"Fuck," Duncan snaps.

"We need to go," Duncan urges out loud. "We're too vulnerable here," he adds, and Sway's eyes narrow immediately. She doesn't miss the warning in his tone. Dammit. He couldn't just use the bond to say that?

"What the fuck, bro?" Bracken hisses.

"Now you've fucking done it," I tell him.

"Just tell her you have blue balls or something," I snap at him.

But it's too late. Sway's glaring at him then Bracken then me.

We're so busted.

"What the hell is going on?" she demands. "And don't say nothing. Duncan's been acting weird all night, and you all look guilty of something."

I hesitate, debating how to handle this and mostly urging Duncan to answer for us since he's the dumbass who let her know there was something else going on. But Dunc remains quiet as a mouse. Fucking coward. He'll kill a man while looking him right in the eye, but admitting to Sway there's something wrong has already broken him.

"We'll tell you inside," Bracken says, earning a dirty look from Duncan.

These two assholes are hopeless.

"Fine," she says stiffly, pushing her way out from between Bracken and Duncan.

She takes a second to straighten her clothing. In the moonlight, I glimpse the smooth, toned sight of her stomach before she pulls her sweatshirt into place. Just a quick flash of skin and then it's gone, but it's enough to harden my cock all over again. Fuck. This woman is going to be the death of me.

"Well," she says pointedly when none of us moves. Mostly because we're all staring at her like fucking idiots. "Let's go."

Sway heads out from behind the stall and emerges into the wide aisle still crowded with people.

"You've done it now," I say to Bracken as we all fall into step behind her.

"I heard that," she calls back.

Of course she did.

The three of us trail after her through the carnival aisles, and I can't help but feel like we're doing some sort of walk of shame. Not about the kiss. That was fucking epic, and I know none of us regret it for a single second. But Bracken's just promised her an explanation that we all promised each other *not* to offer her just yet.

And now we're stuck.

Because my brothers and I are willing to do a lot of bad shit—especially for good reasons—but we're not going to lie to her.

One kiss and my lion is already as loyal to her as he would be to his—

Shit.

I stop walking so abruptly that Duncan bumps into me.

"The fuck," he grumbles, stepping out from around me. "What's wrong with you?"

"Nothing," I manage, slightly dazed as the shock washes over me.

We fall into step together. I can feel him studying me, trying to figure out what the hell just happened.

"Did you sense something out there?" he asks, suddenly on high alert as he scans our surroundings.

"No, nothing like that." But now that I've stopped putting all my energy into sensing threats lurking, I notice the strange tug inside me. Like an invisible rope with one end attached to my chest and the other end firmly planted in Sway's heart.

Like a mate bond.

It's the last thing I ever expected to feel. With a past like mine, landing here at the circus, meeting my brothers, and D… It was enough. It always would have been enough. But now, I'm not sure it'll ever be enough again.

Not unless I can have her too.

I can't quite wrap my head around it, so I focus on putting one foot in front of the other and getting my ass back inside. There will be time to figure this shit out later. Right now, we have an explanation to give as to why we're all acting like paranoid pricks tonight and, undoubtedly, an earful to get for our trouble.

Chapter 15

Sway

Irritation along with cooling lust flushes my skin with warmth as the guys follow me upstairs. I expect them to take me to my apartment, but instead, they usher me into theirs and lock the door.

Bracken stands with his back to it, leaning against the frame. His greenish-brown gaze is trained on me as he crosses both muscled arms. Duncan and Killian move farther into the room, though, standing on either side of me—a triangle trapping me at the epicenter.

None of them speaks, and their silence pisses me off. "Who's planning on starting?" I demand, looking pointedly at each of them.

Killian clears his throat and runs an inked hand over the back of his neck. "Dunc, you decided to open this can of worms."

Duncan glares at him in silence.

"Duncan?" I prompt.

"Fucking ass," he snarls at Killian before shifting his gaze to mine. "There have been—incidents."

"Incidents," I repeat warily.

"Involving your fiancé and those he's hired to hunt you."

My heart skips at his words. I'd expected nothing less from that monster, but hearing it out loud, from Duncan no less, throws me off balance. "Ex-fiancé," I correct, unsure why the hell it matters to do so. "And what do you mean incidents? More than what you've already told me? What happened?"

"We caught a hunter in the woods right after you arrived," Duncan admits quietly.

"I see," I say, reading between the lines. "Did you... question him?"

"He declined to answer," Duncan says, and something about the politeness of his explanation makes it all more sinister.

"What else?" I demand.

Duncan frowns, but he goes on. "A few days after that, three more hunters showed up on our doorstep, asking if we'd seen you."

"You already told me about them." I cross my arms.

"More hunters showed up again tonight," Bracken says.

I whirl on him. "At the carnival?"

"At your show," Killian finishes. "They saw you perform."

"I don't understand. Isaac was supposed to cloak me, right?"

"We're not sure how they knew," he says, eyes flashing. "Maybe it was a lucky fucking break. But now they've seen you."

I take a deep breath and close my eyes. Panic claws at my chest, though. It tears me apart from the inside out. "Did you catch them?"

"Only one," Bracken replies. It's then I notice a bit of dried blood on the side of his throat. I rush over and reach up to touch it.

"They hurt you."

"Just a scratch." He grabs my hand and gives it a reassuring squeeze. "Already healed. Honestly, I'd forgotten it was there."

Stepping back, I let my mind race over what needs to happen next. I'd always known staying in one place was dangerous—but I'd hoped Robert would be long gone by now. Returned home with the others who'd been visiting the embassy the night I managed to get out.

My stomach churns. I'd foolishly believed Robert would only try to hurt me. I never imagined my running would put others in the line of fire. It's something that I clearly misjudged, and seeing Bracken's injury, however small, makes me feel guilty. "I need to leave. Now." I start toward the door, but Bracken refuses to move. "You don't understand. I have to go. He can't find me."

"We will protect you," Bracken says.

"It's too much of a risk. If he knows I'm here, I need to leave."

"You're not going any-damn-where," Killian growls. "So, get that out of your fucking mind right now, Sway."

I whirl on him, tears burning in my eyes. "You have no idea what he's capable of. He'll do anything to get me back."

"Why is that?" Duncan questions. "Because he loves you?"

The laughter that bubbles from my chest lacks any and all humor. "Hardly."

"Then what is it, Sway? Why is he so hell-bent on getting you back?" Killian questions.

I could tell them everything. Come clean and spill my soul right here where they can see it. But even that comes with risks. What if I tell them and they choose to use me just as Robert is planning to? What if they tell the Ringmaster? A man like that craves power, and I'm the ultimate bartering chip.

The safer move is to keep it to myself.

To remain hidden.

But when I look up at Bracken then turn to Killian and Duncan, I can't bring myself to lie anymore. I'm tired of it. Exhausted. And I know in my heart, they're different. Or I desperately want them to be.

"Robert is hungry for power," I say, shoulders sagging as the truth escapes—finally.

"You already told us that." Bracken scowls.

"What I haven't told you is that it's my fault."

"And how the fuck is it your fault?" Killian snaps.

"I twisted him to want it, and I give him the ability to take it."

"Sway," Killian says in a warning tone. "You're not making any fucking sense."

I close my eyes then take a deep breath. "He seemed like a great guy when we met. But after I moved in and we started spending more time together, his goals changed. He's set his sights on ruling and has spent all this time quietly moving up the ranks of politics and leadership within his House. But his slick manipulations will only take him so far. As much as he hates to admit it, he needs help. That's where I come in. With me, he can finally make his move to take over Earth and Emerald."

Killian snorts. "That's fucking suicide. He'd need an army."

"Not if he doesn't plan to fight with weapons," I tell Killian.

"I don't understand."

"If he has a way of influencing an election or altering the minds of those in charge, then he'd have it in the bag. No army necessary. All he'd have to do is sow seeds of doubt—then watch them blossom into a full-on coup. The people would fight his battle for him."

"And how the fuck would he do all that?" Bracken questions.

"He wouldn't," I reply. "I would."

"You would? What the hell does that mean?" Killian questions.

"My power seeks out the seeds of desire and intention and influences them. My magic is a very specific kind of manipulation, and Robert craves it for himself. With me at his side, the entire future of Earth and Emerald could be shifted as easily as walking into a room."

Tears burn in my eyes as I wait for greed or horror to be reflected in their handsome gazes. But honestly? They look confused as shit. All three men stare back at me like I'm speaking in tongues.

So, I continue. "I'm a muse. A being capable of inspiring or destroying the strongest of men. I can change outcomes, alter entire timelines and dynasties by simply latching onto what is already in a person's mind and amplifying it."

"A muse?" Killian asks. "As in a guiding inspiration?"

"Yes," I reply.

"I thought muses were extinct," Duncan says.

"I'm the only one I know of in existence," I tell him, the words rubbing at the old wound of losing my parents.

"Do you have any physical abilities?" Bracken questions. It's clear he's unimpressed.

I glare at him. "You don't have to brute force your way into power if you can alter the way someone sees the world," I snap. Of all the reactions I expected, dismissing my power is not even close to what I'd pictured. "Why do you think you lost at ring toss tonight?"

He straightens. "What?"

"I told you to mute your senses; you said you couldn't. But it got you thinking about doing just that, and my power made it happen."

His gaze widens. "You *cheated?*"

I chew on my bottom lip. "Not on purpose. It just happened, and then by the time I realized what I'd done —I'm sorry. It's what happened with Robert, too. I didn't do any of it on purpose. It just happened because I can't mute myself all the time."

Duncan shakes his head. "Making Bracken suck ass at ring toss is completely different than shifting an entire House's fucking power dynamic."

I gape at them. They don't believe me.

That pisses me off.

I shift my attention to Bracken, letting my magic seep out of my body and latch onto him. His cheeks flush, and he pushes off from the doorframe, his body swaying like he can't hold still. His gaze lands on Killian, and he bites his lower lip.

Killian side-eyes him though most of his focus is on me.

Picking out the thread of lust for me that's still alive inside him, I urge Bracken to take things further, and he removes his shirt.

"What the fuck are you doing?" Duncan demands.

"I—" Bracken turns away from Killian and walks up to Duncan instead. He reaches out and caresses Duncan's jaw, so Duncan jumps back.

"The fuck, man?" Duncan asks.

"I don't know. I think I want you, dude. Ugh. What the hell is happening to me?" Bracken demands.

I turn it off.

Bracken whirls on me. *"You!"*

"I'm the catalyst that can alter the course of history," I say.

"Fucking shit," Bracken breathes. Then he looks at Duncan sheepishly. "Sorry, bro."

"That was fucking weird," Duncan comments.

"Can someone fill me in?" Killian demands, looking back and forth between his brothers.

"Go ahead, Bracken, fill him in," I reply sweetly as I

cross both arms. "Tell them about how turned on their presence made you just now."

His eyes widen, and he looks at both of them.

"I sensed your lust from earlier," I tell Bracken, "And I used it to make you want that same thing from both of them."

Duncan and Killian look stunned, and if I weren't so afraid for my already bleak future, I might have laughed.

"*That* is what I am capable of," I reply. "Only, the man hunting me wants me to influence an entire House to oust their current leader."

"What else have you used your powers for since arriving here?" Duncan demands. I can see the anger on his face, and that leads me to understand just where his mind has gone. My temper flares at his insinuation.

"I never wanted to sleep with any of you, so if you think for a second I used my power to make you, you're a damned moron." I wipe the tears from my cheeks. "Besides, my power won't work unless there's already a seed planted. I can't conjure doubt or inspire an idea when there's nothing there to latch onto."

Killian grins at Bracken. "So, my presence turns you on?"

Bracken growls. "Not a fucking chance."

The inked shifter shrugs. "Says you. Sway says otherwise."

"It can be minuscule," I reply quickly, hoping to

save Bracken at least a bit of embarrassment. "Likely because he associates you all with sex since you enjoy sharing women."

Duncan shakes his head. "If you were this fucking powerful, you should have told us. Keeping shit like that to yourself makes you untrustworthy—which makes you dangerous."

"Dangerous." I nearly laugh at the word. "That's an understatement. I broke Robert. It's the only reason I stayed as long as I did because I felt—" I close my eyes as tears roll down my face. "I *feel* guilty."

"Robert is a pissant," Killian snaps. "And you wouldn't have been able to make him an asshole unless a part of him was, right?"

"I made it so much worse."

Bracken shakes his head. "Did you ever think that he might have targeted you because of what you are?"

"No one knew," I tell him. "My parents—"

"How did they die?" Duncan questions. "Tell us how your parents died, Sway."

"An accident. They were—" And then it hits me. "They lost control of their car and drove into a tree. It never made sense at the time. My dad was a great driver. He drove for dignitaries and politicians."

His eyes narrow at my words. "Did you ever suspect foul play?"

"No, I—" Horror twists like a blade in my heart, and

I cover my mouth. "No. I didn't even know Robert then."

Duncan moves in closer. "Maybe not, but I'd be willing to bet he fucking knew you. If he had anything to do with your parents' deaths, then you've been a target since day one."

The image of my parents' bodies—broken and bloodied—fills my mind for mere seconds before they twist, morphing into the bodies of the three men before me. "I need to leave. I have to go now so he can't—"

"If you think for a second we're letting you leave, you've lost your fucking mind." Bracken turns to Duncan. "We need to let D know."

"What? No. You can't—"

"He won't use you," Bracken snaps. "But he does need to be aware that there is an even larger threat. He can warn Earth and Emerald that they have a snake in their midst."

Duncan nods. "Agreed. Sharing that kind of information will help our cause."

"This can't be happening." I groan and cover my face with both hands. Tonight had such promise. I'd felt more alive than I have in years—yet I'd been in danger the entire fucking time. How did I not see the hunters? How did I think I could be lucky enough that they wouldn't find me tucked away in this circus?

"Let's go." Bracken takes my hand, and despite the

danger I've found myself in, my body heats even with his simple touch.

These men—these lions—have gotten under my skin.

"Where are we going?"

"Your apartment."

"But Duncan said—"

"Fuck what he said. You need sleep."

Chapter 16

Sway

By the time we reach my apartment, sleep is the last thing on my mind. Imagining Robert having a hand in my parents' deaths and then picturing his hired hunters in the crowd tonight is wreaking havoc on my mind, sending my heart racing in a potentially uncontrollable panic.

I *barely* escaped him the last time. In fact, I only got away because he'd been so busy with political matters that took him away from the room we were staying in. If it hadn't been an emergency... I don't want to think about where I'd be now. He so rarely left me alone that running from the embassy had been my only real chance.

How the hell am I supposed to do it again? How can I outsmart professional bounty hunters who have spent their lives training to track down those who do not wish to be found?

"What's going on in your mind?"

I shift my gaze to Bracken, who has just shut my door behind us. "I'm worried," I reply honestly. No sense in hiding anything now.

"We'll keep you safe. As long as you let us." He narrows his gaze on me.

"You're worried I'm going to run."

"You didn't exactly put our minds at ease with your talk about leaving."

"Knee-jerk reaction," I assure him.

"You've changed your mind?"

"I'm saying it might not matter. I won't survive if I run. Shit. I might not survive if I stay here, but at least, here—"

Bracken is across the room in the blink of an eye. He towers over me, staring down. "You *will* survive here. We won't let anything happen to you, Sway."

"You sure there's a *we* anymore?" I ask. "Duncan seemed pretty pissed at me."

"Duncan just wants you to trust us," he assures me. "He'll cool off, just give him some time."

"Look, I know you'll protect me," I reply. "But who's going to protect you? The man hunting me is dangerous, Bracken. He has contacts and hunters deep in his pockets. Any one of them could—"

Bracken cups the side of my face and pulls me

toward him. "We're resilient," he says softly. "There's not a man alive that I fear."

"Just because you don't fear something doesn't mean it's not dangerous." I can't help the slight tremble at the memory of just how true my words are.

"What did he do to you, Sway?" he questions softly as he runs the pad of his thumb over my cheek.

I close my eyes against the onslaught of imagery I wish I could forget. "Too much," I manage.

"Tell me."

I pull away from him and put a few steps between us. "He beat me. But you already knew that."

Bracken lets loose a low growl.

"He used and manipulated me. Pressured and forced me into doing things I didn't want to..." I trail off then take a deep breath. "But as much as he tried, he didn't break me."

"No," he agrees. "He didn't."

All the mental and physical abuse. Being gaslit and told I wasn't worthy of love but he was going to give it to me anyway. I dealt with all of it, and he came close to breaking me. Hell, maybe he would have succeeded if I hadn't found myself here.

These three men. These powerful shifters.

They believe I'm worth something.

They want me.

I meet Bracken's gaze. "Bracken, I—"

He closes the distance between us for a second time

tonight, gripping the back of my neck. The look in his eye is wild with a need I feel just as strongly. "Are you doing this to me?" he whispers. "Making me desperate to have you?"

"No," I reply honestly.

"I didn't fucking think so." Bracken slams his mouth down onto mine. A tangle of teeth and tongues, he assaults my mouth with fire. I grip his arms, letting him take what he wants from me.

Because I want it too.

No, I *crave* it.

And if I'm going to be hunted either way, I'm done denying myself what I want most.

Bracken's hands slide down my body, and he grips my ass, lifting as I wrap both legs around his waist. He presses me back against the wall then takes my hands and pins them above my head with one of his.

It's then he pulls back and stares down at me.

I'm at his mercy. Trapped between his hard body and the wall.

"If you're going to say no again, you'd better fucking do it now."

"I'm not."

"No?" he questions as he uses his free hand to trace my jaw.

"No. I want you. All of you. And I'm tired of fighting it."

He leans in and scrapes the stubble coating his sharp

jaw against my cheek. Goosebumps flare to life along my flesh even as my insides turn molten. "Tonight, you'll just get me," he whispers. "That still okay with you, muse?" He thrusts his hips against me, pressing his hard length against my center.

"Yes," I breathe. "Please."

"Please what, Sway?"

"You. Me," I whisper. He's barely begun, and already I can hardly formulate a single word.

"Tell me what you want, Sway."

"You inside of me," I reply. "Now. Please."

Bracken chuckles and, keeping me pinned to his body, pulls away from the wall and crosses toward my bed. "I'm taking my time with you, gorgeous. There's not a damn thing we have to rush. Not tonight."

He sets me on my feet then pulls back and stares down at me. I can see fire in his gaze. Passion I'm desperate to taste. "Take your clothes off," he orders as he backs away and crosses his arms. "I want to watch you."

My pulse hammers as I reach down and tug my sweatshirt over my head. Since I wear nothing beneath it, Bracken's sharp intake of breath is music to my ears. I look up at him before turning so he can see my back as I kick out of my shoes. Then, slowly bending at the waist, I lower my leggings to the ground.

Bracken growls low and deep, and if I weren't already drenched with desire, that sound alone would have done it. "You have the most perfect fucking ass. Don't move," he orders.

I remain bent over as Bracken comes to stand behind me. He palms my ass with both hands and squeezes. A moan slips from my lips as he slides those hands to the insides of my thighs. But as I wish he'd keep touching me, Bracken moves away.

"Stand up and face me."

I do as he orders, turning to face him. My gaze drops to the massive bulge in his pants, and my mouth waters. What will it feel like to have him inside of me? What would he do if I dropped to my knees and opened my mouth for him?

"Fuck, Sway. Killian deserves a fucking medal."

"For what?"

"Keeping his hands off of you after seeing you naked. You are breathtaking."

My cheeks heat.

Bracken peels his shirt over his head, and I nearly choke on my own desire. *Fuck.* Broad-chested and muscled, he has the body of a fighter. I step closer and reach out to press the tips of my fingers to a massive scar that runs from one pectoral muscle down to his side. As I look closer, I see dozens more smaller ones just like it. I inhale sharply as I realize scars mar nearly every inch of his chest.

"I used to lose fights on purpose," he replies, and I

recall him telling me his House used to force him to fight.

"Why?" I ask.

"Because they would fix fights in order to win the bets placed on the fighters, and I refused to play their game. They'd whip me for it, but I didn't stop."

"Fucking assholes," I breathe as I trace them.

"We all have our scars," he replies as he gently brushes his fingertips over my collarbone.

"We do," I reply then take a step back. "Now, you're wearing too many clothes, Bracken."

He flashes a wicked grin and then undoes the belt on his jeans. Kneeling, he unties the laces of his boots and kicks them off then shoves his pants down. His cock springs free, and every muscle in my body tenses when I see the sheer size of it.

"Oh my."

"Intimidated?" He smirks.

"I mean—"

"Don't worry, sweet, it'll fit." Bracken crosses over toward me then tips up my face and kisses me deeply. All of that concern vanishes when his lips touch mine. Bracken backs me up toward my bed then lays me back on it, all while his mouth claims mine.

He pulls back and kneels at the edge of the bed but pulls me closer so my ass is barely on the mattress. "I've dreamt of tasting you. Of burying my tongue in this sweet pussy."

"Then do it," I say as I spread my legs further. I've never been afraid to ask for what I want in the bedroom, but being with Robert made me fearful to make any kind of suggestion.

Bracken, though? He's eating it up.

Literally.

He dives between my legs, and I cry out as I arch my back in pleasure. He draws my clit into his mouth, sucking, tasting, wet heat obliterating every concern I'd ever had about sharing my bed with him or the others.

If this is what passion feels like—I come undone, the orgasm simultaneously tearing me apart and putting me back together. I've never felt so alive. So sexy.

"Yes," I gasp as he continues fucking me with his tongue. He draws out every inch of pleasure, every moment of bliss, until my muscles turn to liquid. Then, Bracken slides up my body and covers my mouth with his.

The taste of my release dances on my tongue as he kisses me.

And then Bracken fills me.

I cry out, a lightning bolt of pain shooting through me from the size of him pressing into my body. Bracken continues kissing me, gripping my breast with one of his large hands. He pinches my nipple, rolling the pebbled peak between his thumb and forefinger while he stills inside of me.

I breathe him in then wrap my legs around his waist as pleasure builds.

"You're so fucking tight," he growls against my mouth. "Hot. Wet. Fuck, Sway."

He draws out then thrusts back in, languid strokes that push me past the pain and straight into the fact that he's hitting spots I only ever managed to hit when using a vibrator.

"That feel good?" he asks.

"Yes. So fucking good," I say. "Please—more, Bracken." I grip his back, fingertips digging into his muscles as he picks up the pace.

He pulls out and slams back into me.

Over and over again.

Fucking me until all concerns over my safety are gone. Because if he can fight half as good as he fucks—

"Yes! Faster!" I cling to him as another orgasm builds. The muscles of my abdomen clench—then release.

"Yes, baby, come on my cock. Come for me, Sway."

Stars explode in my vision all while lightning snaps through my veins. The second orgasm is even more intense than the first one, and it's all I can do to cling to him as I come undone.

Bracken stiffens as he comes, going still as a statue as his dick pulses inside of me. "Fuck." He looks down and grins at me. "You're magnificent."

I grin back at him. "Not nearly as amazing as you are."

He kisses me again then slips out of my body and lies back on the bed beside me. He reaches over and takes my hand, holding it as we lie together in complete silence, our combined breathing ragged.

"That was fantastic."

Releasing my hand, Bracken rolls to face me then props up on his elbow. "It was," he agrees. "Does this mean you've given our proposal more thought?" He reaches out and traces my nipple with the tip of a finger.

Pleasure warms me.

"I have," I reply.

"And?"

Swallowing hard, I meet his gaze. It's terrifying to think of three men taking pleasure with me. But I realize now that I'd been looking at it all wrong. It won't be them taking their pleasure; it's a give and take.

And I have no doubt they'll give even more than they take from me.

"I want to know what it's like."

Bracken grins. "To have the three of us worship you like you deserve?" He presses a kiss to my lips. "Because you deserve to be worshipped, Sway. To come so many fucking times you'll hardly be able to walk." Another kiss.

"That sounds—amazing."

Bracken grins. "We're going to treat you right, Sway. I promise."

Chapter 17

Killian

toss and turn as Bracken's pleasure seeps in through our pride bond. Fucker. He's not even trying to hide his feelings. Then again, I wouldn't either. In fact, my inner predator is ready to shout its choice of mate to the world—and that's not something I'm ready to share. Bracken might be in deep enough to handle the news, but Duncan is still being a moody bitch about the whole thing.

And that's not even considering how Sway will take the news. Shit, she'll probably freak the fuck out if she finds out I want more from her than just her delicious fucking body.

Dammit.

My connection with her is so much deeper than sex, and I haven't even brought her to orgasm yet.

One thing at a damn time, Kill.

Grumpy and blue-balled, I give up on sleep and decide to relieve Duncan early. If I can't fuck, maybe I can run off the need to. The moon hangs low and heavy as I exit the building into the darkness. By now, the carnival has shut down, and the only people out and about are me and Dunc.

Through the bond, I call to him. *"Dude, I can't fucking sleep with Bracken getting his rocks off,"* I tell him. *"Tell me there's a trespasser I can maim."*

"Sorry, it's quiet out here," Dunc returns.

"Location?"

"Here." He steps out of the shadows in human form, and I jump then glare as he grins back at me. "Gotcha."

"Fuck you," I tell him.

His grin turns to a chuckle. "Not me, but Bracken might."

Now, I can't help but chuckle with him. "That shit was priceless," I agree.

"And impressive as hell." His smile vanishes. Back to business already.

"She's powerful," I agree, leaning against the building and scanning the darkened tree line out of pure habit. My lion can sense as far as the circus property line, but I still like to keep an eye out.

"She's been used because of it," Duncan says, surprising me with the concern in his tone.

I give him a look. "She's under your skin, isn't she?"

He snorts. "I thought it was obvious by now. She's all I fucking think about anymore. And if that weren't enough, we're keeping secrets from D—for her."

"It's not just about sex, is it?"

He sighs.

"Why didn't you tell us?" I ask, forcing my lion to chill out. Now that he knows Duncan is in, my lion wants to claim her right this second.

He wants her for the three of us, though, and that's not something I can guarantee my brothers want too.

"She's dangerous," he says quietly.

"You're scared of her?" I can't keep the judgment out of my tone, but he shoots me an irritated glare.

"Not like that, dumbass." He looks out at the tree line again, both of us still alert despite our intense conversation. "I've never felt like this for anyone else."

"I'm glad to hear you admit it," I say.

"Shut up."

"I'm serious. I know you, Dunc, which means I can see you care about her. And I can see you fighting it."

"Old habits die hard."

"She's different," I tell him.

He eyes me. "That's the problem."

My mouth quirks at that because I know exactly what he means.

"Tell you what," I say, "why don't you go give her a wake-up call, and I'll finish your shift."

He shakes his head. "Nah. You go."

"Dunc, just give in already."

"I'm working on it," he says irritably. "I—"

We each pick up the scent at the same moment.

I go still, my lion assessing the intruder.

"One," I say, "North wall."

"I'm going in straight," he says, his body already shuddering with the oncoming shift. "You circle in from the west."

"Got it."

I shift a second behind him and take off at a run. My massive paws eat up the ground, and my mouth waters with anticipation of biting off whatever fucking head I find trying to worm its way into my world.

It takes me all of three seconds longer than Duncan to reach the asshole trying to sneak across our line. By then, Duncan has tackled him to the ground and elicited a yell that quickly becomes a moan of pain as Duncan's front paws slice his shirt and chest wide open.

"Dammit, that fucking hurts," the man moans.

Even in the darkness, I can see the Crimson Hunter tattoo printed on his arm.

I ignore his screams, scanning to make sure there aren't more of them out here.

"How many you got?" Duncan demands through our bond.

"Just this one," I tell him.

"Same. Don't let your guard down," he orders.

"Didn't plan on it."

I shift back to my human form and stroll over to where the hunter is still pinned by Duncan's front paws. "Who are you?" I ask.

The man cries out in pain.

"Why are you here?"

"I'm looking for some runaway whore," the man says. He's shaking now, and the scent of urine hits me.

Coward.

He would've done this and worse to Sway.

"Well, you found us instead, asshole. Aren't you lucky?"

TWO HOURS LATER, DUNCAN AND I HAVE CLEANED UP our mess, and I make my way wearily back upstairs. Through the bond, Bracken stirs, immediately demanding answers as he realizes something has happened while he slept.

Instead of going back to my apartment, I change directions and knock on Sway's door.

"Come in," Bracken calls immediately.

I walk in and am greeted by the sight of Sway still in bed, wrapped in nothing but her own bedsheet. Her hair is mussed, and the relaxation that exudes from her is a huge change from the stress she's been carrying around since she arrived. Despite the events of the last two hours, all I can do is stare at her, completely mesmerized by her beauty, inside and out.

"Well?" Bracken demands. "What the hell happened?"

I blink, refocusing on him but saying nothing.

"She already knows something went down," Bracken adds as if that's the reason for my silence. "And we promised to stop keeping secrets, remember? Besides, she said if we don't start telling her shit, she's going to bite my dick off."

I look back at Sway, who blinks at me innocently. Little devil…

"A hunter breached the north line a couple of hours ago," I say.

Sway's worried expression fills immediately with tension.

"He was alone, and we took him down quickly," I add, hating that look of fear in her eyes. "He's no longer a threat."

"Dammit," Bracken says. "Why didn't you wake me up? I should have been there to help you."

"Duncan and I both agree that, until this threat is dealt with, it's best if one of us is with her at all times," I say, my gaze fastened on Sway as I wait to see how she'll take this latest development. "No more posting up in the hallway, either. We need eyes on her."

I'm fully prepared for her to protest, but instead, she

looks resigned. And maybe even a little intrigued by the idea.

"Good call," Bracken agrees. "Where's Duncan?"

"Briefing D. He said for you to find him as soon as you're up."

"I'm going." Bracken sits on the edge of the bed and plants a kiss on Sway's full mouth. I watch as she kisses him back, fully fucking turned on by it. When Bracken pulls away, Sway's gaze darts uncertainly to me.

My dick springs to immediate attention the moment our eyes meet.

Bracken heads for the door. "I'll see you later, okay?" he tells Sway.

"Be careful," she says.

"Always, gorgeous." He nods at me, and then he's gone.

He doesn't have to tell me Sway changed her mind about the three of us, not with everything I felt from him through the bond last night, but I haven't heard it from Sway's mouth yet, so I remain where I am.

"Are you okay?" she asks.

"Yeah, love, I'm fine. Why?"

"Do you still...? I mean..." Her face flushes. "Bracken said you all still want to... if I want to."

I bite back a groan at how fucking cute it is that she's being shy about it.

"We all still want you, love, if that's what you mean."

She bites her lip. "Even after what I told you last night about what I can do?"

"Sway, there's not a damn thing in the world you could tell me to make me stop wanting you."

"And you don't want my power for anything?"

"We want you, love. Your body, your personality, your kind heart, your strength, and your bravery. We don't give two shits about your magic."

She looks relieved at that. "That means a lot. No one's ever wanted me for me, you know?"

I force myself to remain where I am even though all I want to do is hold her and wipe away the memories she's clearly still haunted by. Well, it's not all I want. Not if you count fucking her senseless. And then killing every last creature who's ever hurt her.

I watch her carefully, tucking away my murderous thoughts. I've already taken one life today and it's not even eight in the morning. "Does that mean you want us?"

Her gaze snaps back to mine. "I... yes." Her flushed cheeks turn even redder than before, and I consider it an achievement that I don't just blow my load right here in the sweatpants I'm wearing. She's the sexiest creature I've ever seen.

"But." She bites her lip. "If you want me, then why are you still standing all the way over there?"

Yeah, I am so fucked. "Because I buried a dead hunter not an hour ago," I say in a hoarse voice. "And

I've yet to shower, so I don't think you want me in your bed."

She brightens. "That's perfect because I happen to need a shower too."

The shyness is gone, and the look she gives me has me tossing caution to the damned wind. Not that I had much left to begin with. In less than a second, I'm across the room and scooping her up, bedsheet and all. She squeals, grabbing my neck and holding on for support as I lift her off the mattress and into my arms.

I look down at her, noting the flecks of gold in her amber eyes. "You are fucking killing me, woman, you know that?"

Before she can answer, I kiss the fuck out of her.

She opens for me immediately, kissing me back with a passion and need I didn't expect. But the moment she does, I stride for the bathroom, our lips still locked. She tastes delicious, and my already hardened cock aches to be inside her. Maybe even inside that mouth of hers, too.

All I know is I've wanted her since the moment she showed up on our doorstep, and nothing is standing in the way of this fucking moment.

Inside the bathroom, I set her on her feet and back her against the wall, still kissing her like it's our love language. Sway sighs, her palms landing against my bare chest. The moment her skin touches mine, heat ignites.

Mine, my animal growls.

This time, I don't even try to deny it.

My hands slip around the top edge of the sheet, and I yank it free. It falls to the floor at her feet, and I step back so I can admire the perfection of her naked body.

I let my eyes scan slowly over her breasts and down her abdomen.

"What are you doing?" she asks, face flushed, lips already swollen.

"This time, you're not lying injured on the floor," I tell her, "So looking is fair game."

"It's only fair if I can look too," she says.

With a single movement, I shove my sweatpants down to the floor and step out of them. Sway's eyes widen as if she hadn't expected me to comply. But she doesn't realize I've been dying for this exact moment for days now.

Her gaze scans my body, and I watch her expression as she catches sight of my nipple piercings. She bites her lip, scanning lower. When she sees my already hard cock, her eyes widen.

"You're pierced...there?" she asks.

I wink. "You'll thank me later."

Without missing a beat, I reach over and turn the shower on.

Turning back to her, I smirk as I edge closer to where she stands. "Your shy act doesn't fool me, you know."

"No?" she whispers, eyes twinkling.

"No. You know exactly what you want and exactly what the fuck you're doing."

Her lips curve in a devious smile. "Yeah," she admits. "I do."

She reaches up, winding her hands around my neck so she can pull me down to kiss her again. Her tongue darts out, licking my bottom lip, and surprised pleasure shudders through me.

"That's it." I grab her hips, lifting her clear off her feet, and carry her into the shower, setting her down again directly under the stream of hot water.

She shrieks, but all it does is turn me on that much more. I back her against the tile wall, and this time when our mouths meet, I let her feel my hunger in the way I claim her mouth. Her hands run up over my chest, the hot water streaming down between us. I growl as she grazes her fingers over the metal in my nipples before trailing lower to grab my cock in her fist. She runs her thumb lightly over the piercing on my dick, and I groan.

"Like I said, you know," I tell her, pulling back just enough to trap her gaze with my own.

She meets my eyes. "I know I want you," she says, breathless and smelling like lust.

"That's a good damn thing," I tell her. "Because I want you too, love, so fucking bad."

I crush my lips to hers then grab her thigh and hook her leg around my waist; one then the other until her ankles are locked behind me and her thighs are squeezing my hips. Reaching around, I let my fingers slide over her wet skin and down between the globes of her ass, exploring her folds from behind.

She presses her tits against my chest, her hands tangling in my hair as she clings to me.

Slowly, I ease a finger inside her pussy. "Are you sore?" I ask.

"A little," she admits, already breathless. "But—please, Killian."

Her entire body is taut with need. Desire rolls her off her in waves even though she's admitted to being sore. It shouldn't turn me on—that she wants me still—but it really fucking does. After all, I'm no stranger to taking pleasure from a bit of pain.

It takes all my control to slowly ease that finger out again. "Please what?" I growl.

"Please, more," she pants.

"There's my girl," I tell her, easing the finger in again.

She whimpers, and I increase the pace ever so slightly.

"You feel so fucking good," I tell her. "Better than I imagined."

She moves to the rhythm I've set, panting against my mouth as I fuck her mouth with my tongue at the same speed as my finger in her pussy. My cock presses against her core as she rocks back and forth with me now.

I move faster, reveling in the way her body responds to me. A moment later, her legs tighten, and her hands grip me tight as she tips her head back, the orgasm flooding her body.

She moans, and I watch as she rides the wave of her own pleasure.

Then, I slip my finger out of her and lift her up, sliding her down on my cock.

"Oh." Her eyes widen, and I go still.

She's hot. Tight. And so fucking wet. "Am I hurting you, love?"

"No, well, maybe. I just need a minute. Your piercing is... I can feel it."

I give her a lazy smile, planning to take this as slow as I can. "You like it?"

"I do."

"Good, now stay with me because we've got all the time in the world."

She isn't patient though. As soon as I begin to move against her, she rocks her hips, meeting me stroke for stroke and urging me faster. Pressure builds, and my beast rises to the surface until I'm hanging onto my own control by a thread.

"Fuck," I groan as Sway's tight walls clench around my cock. "Yes," I hiss. "Come for me, love."

The moment she does, I let out a roar as my orgasm rips through me.

Sway clings to me, riding the wave alongside me

until we both float back down again. Her hands cup my face as I look into her eyes.

"You okay?" I ask her.

"I'm so far past okay," she says.

I chuckle. "Good."

She kisses me, and when she pulls away, her expression has changed.

"Mmm, you've got that look in your eye," I tell her, reaching up to tuck her hair away from her face.

"What look?" she asks.

"The worried one." With my thumb, I smooth the line out of her forehead.

"I was just thinking…"

"Tell me," I say.

"Well, I like you."

I grin. "That helps things, doesn't it?"

"I mean, I like all three of you. But that's confusing."

I lean in and press a kiss to the tip of her nose. "Not confusing at all," I tell her. "It's all part of the plan."

Sway

I'm not entirely sure how I haven't been split in two.

Between Bracken last night and Killian—twice—this morning, I'm completely and utterly spent. He sleeps beside me now, the light glinting off of the rings through each of his nipples. I never thought I could be so turned on by piercings, but fuck me if I didn't lick every single one of them less than two hours ago.

My body is sore even though my muscles are so relaxed they might as well be liquid. And even though I'd love nothing more than to stay right here and go round three with one of my sexy lions, I know I need to get up and start prepping for tonight's show.

It's going to be a doozy, given my nerves and lack of sleep.

Quietly, I roll out of bed, moving the covers back up as I go. On two feet, I stretch and roll my shoulders. Damn, I feel good. I smile, unable to help myself as I glance back down at the naked, sandy-haired man lying in my bed. He barely fits on the narrow mattress alone, much less with me by his side.

"Keep staring like that and I'm going to put you on your knees, love," Killian says as he opens his eyes and grins wickedly.

"Oh?" I question then stalk closer to the bed. "And what will you have me do on my knees?"

That grin spreads. "I'd tell you taunting a predator is a dangerous move, but we've established you know exactly what it is you're doing."

I chuckle. "That doesn't exactly answer my question."

Killian scoots up against the headboard. "I'd put you on your knees and fill that smart mouth with my cock," he replies. "Then, I'd have you fuck yourself with those delicate fingers as I fucked your mouth."

I swallow hard, wetness pooling between my legs.

Killian inhales. "Fuck, I can smell your desire from here."

Someone knocks on the door.

"Saved by Dunc," Killian replies with a wink as he hops out of bed and answers the door—still completely naked.

Duncan walks in, and his gaze levels on me. It's

only then I realize that I, too, am naked as the day I was born. I make a move to cover up but then remember that I don't have to. All three of these men want me.

And I intend to have them, too. Even if it can't be any longer than my stay here.

But the moment he sees me, Duncan turns around and shows me his back. The dismissal hurts worse than I care to admit, which is probably why I respond like I couldn't care less. "I'm going to get dressed for practice." I kiss Killian noisily on the cheek then rush into the bathroom.

By the time I've showered and dressed, both men are gone. I stand in my empty apartment, heart surprisingly heavy. How did I go from pushing them away to hating being alone so quickly? And what the hell is Duncan's problem? Didn't he tell me they all wanted me? Didn't he make a move, too?

He did, I remind myself. But that changed the minute I told them about my magic. Killian and Bracken assured me they were fine with it, but clearly, Duncan doesn't feel the same way.

Anger spreads through my system. So, desperate to burn some of it off, I slip into some shoes and yank my door open—only to walk right into Duncan, who'd been standing on the other side.

His masculine scent invades me. I hate that it warms me from the inside. That it turns me on and pisses me off all at once.

"I thought you left," I say in surprise.

"I thought you'd want privacy," he says as I pull the door closed behind me.

"You do seem to know exactly what I want, don't you?" I snap then push past him.

He falls into step behind me. Lurking just close enough that I can hear his muted bootsteps. He doesn't speak and makes no attempt to catch up to me even as I make my way downstairs and into the dining hall.

It's nearly empty though Liv is seated at a table by herself, scowling at a bowl of fruit. Dealing with her bad mood is ten times easier than dealing with Duncan's, so I leave him behind and head straight for her.

"What did those grapes ever do to you?" I joke as I sit across from her.

"Adaya claims I need to eat more fruit. But all I want is French fries. Like, all the time."

I laugh and pluck a grape from her bowl. "Fruit first then French fries."

"Fine." She picks a grape and eats it. Then she leans back in her chair and rubs a hand over her swollen belly. "How are you doing? I hear there was a close call."

"The guys managed to subdue them, but yeah. Apparently, I have hunters after me now."

Liv purses her lips. "How are *you*?"

"Managing. A little irritated this morning." I cast a

glance over my shoulder at Duncan, who remains near the door.

"Duncan piss you off?" Liv asks with a knowing smile.

"Something like that. How are you feeling?'

"Tired. Jealous you get to be in the air tonight when I can't even manage to lift my own ass out of the tub these days."

I laugh. "You're growing life, Liv. That is much more impressive than me on the lyra."

"I saw your performance," Liv replies. "You have skills."

"Thanks, but my best medium is still silks."

"Then why aren't you performing on those?"

"I don't know. The Ringmaster said he needed the lyra filled in your absence."

She rolls her eyes. "He'd be fine with either, trust me. Do what you want."

"Thanks," I tell her. "It might be fun to do a routine that incorporates both."

"Ohh, that's brilliant. Hey, I think you should stay on even after I'm back. We'd make an epic team. They wouldn't be able to take their eyes off of us." She winks.

The idea intrigues me. I've never performed with a partner before. It could be fun.

"True." But even as I say it, something unfurls in my belly. Who the hell knows if I'll even be alive until Liv has her baby? With Robert sending hunters after me, there's no telling how long it'll be before one manages to slip through the cracks. It's not like they haven't gotten close before, and I've only been here a couple of weeks.

"What's on your mind?" Liv asks.

A lot. But since I don't feel like doing a deep dive into all the twisted reasons I'm pissed this morning, I push up from the table. "Nothing. I'm going to go get some practice in. Let me know if I can do anything to help."

"Unless your powers include the ability to speed up time, I'm afraid I have to just wait this one out."

I smile softly but leave without another word.

"You're not eating?" Duncan demands as I move into the hall.

"Lost my appetite." I continue moving past him, pissed off that the rage burning a hole in me is only tempered by the desire I feel in his presence.

"What happened?"

"Nothing," I snap. I cross over into the practice area, so glad to have it all to myself right now.

Duncan grabs my arm and spins me toward him. "What the hell is going on with you?"

"So, we're talking now?" I ask sweetly.

Duncan releases me and steps back, his bright hazel gaze darkening. "We were never not speaking."

"No? Because you've certainly made me feel

welcome in your presence since the moment you showed up in my apartment this morning."

"Why does my behavior bother you? Because I didn't bend you over and fuck you?"

My hand cracks across his cheek. "How *dare* you cheapen what I have with Bracken and Killian."

"Not cheapening it," he replies, his eyes flashing. "Merely stating a fact since that's why you seem to be pissed at me."

I gape at him, anger and embarrassment at war within me as I realize he's not far off. I'd wanted him to take me to bed, and when he hadn't, I took it as a rejection. "If you're so miserable around me, then why the hell didn't Killian stay? Or Bracken?"

"They had somewhere to be," he growls, a muscle in his jaw twitching. He's pissed, but so am I. "So, you're stuck with me."

"Which never would have bothered me before," I shoot back. "Why are you being such a fucking dickhead?"

Duncan leans in. "This is who I am, Sway."

"No," I reply. "It's not. I might not know you well, Duncan, but I know you're not this much of an insufferable asshole to anyone but me." I press both palms against his hard chest and shove. But he doesn't move. I might as well be pushing against a fucking wall. "Get out. I don't want you in here."

His glare darkens, and I wonder if he's not going to

refuse. Honestly, if he does, I might just march back up to my room until whatever stick is stuck up his asshole is gone. "Fine." He turns on his heel and marches out the door.

The moment I'm alone, I suck in a deep, steadying breath then angrily wipe away the tears that I wouldn't dare let fall in his presence. *Insufferable ass is an understatement.*

AN HOUR INTO MY PRACTICE, I'VE MANAGED TO WORK off my anger. Well, most of it, anyway. Duncan might be an ass, but I know he wants me. I can sense it—the pull that's there between us; a string that can be tugged.

Not that I would ever do that. Not in a million years would I ever influence Duncan to do what I know we both want. Stealing his choice like that is a cowardly move and not one I will wield against him.

"You look great up there."

I jolt and nearly lose my grip on the silks as I scan the area below me for the observer. A man I've only seen a handful of times smiles up at me. He's bare-chested and wearing loose pants. His white hair sticks straight up as though he stuck his finger into a light socket. Both brows match the same bright shade and are arched as I slide down the silks toward the ground. "Hey, sorry, didn't see you there."

"No worries. I came to get a workout in."

"You don't use the gym?"

He shrugs. "Us carnival performers are not typically welcome in the circus gym."

"Really? That's shitty." My feet hit the ground soundlessly.

Once again, he shrugs it off. "It is what it is. I'm Zaxby, by the way." He reaches a hand out. "Rooster shifter and the star of a carnival game where onlookers try to pelt me with fruit."

"That sounds awful."

He shrugs. "It's a job."

I shake his hand. "I'm Helen."

His grip is cold. "I know. You've made quite a bit of drama these days. On the run and everything." He winks.

"What makes you think I'm on the run?" Nerves settle like stones in my gut, and I cast a glance at the door. It's blocked with chairs that weren't there before.

I pretend not to notice, but inside, panic is blaring like a siren.

"Aren't we all?" he asks. "It is, after all, why we let the Ringmaster own us."

"Have you been here long?" I try to tug my hand free of his, but he only squeezes harder, refusing to let go.

"A few months," he replies. "Already exhausted with it, though."

"Sorry to hear that. Can you please let me go? I need to—"

"I can't do that. See, I need to get the money to buy out my contract. And you're the golden ticket I need." He rips me toward him.

"Dunc—!" I scream, but a hand banded over my mouth silences me. I slam my elbow back into his gut, and he groans, loosening his hold enough that I can break free.

Someone pushes against the door, but the chair wedged beneath the handle holds.

"Sway," Duncan roars.

"Help!" I try to run.

A hand closes around my ankle, and I fall forward, my hands barely preventing me from slamming face-first into the hard floor. He rips me backward, yanking me toward him and straddling me.

"You can't be dead," he says, already winded. "I made him a promise. But you can be unconscious." His gaze momentarily drops to my breasts barely covered by the sports bra I'm wearing. It's then I note the way his pupils expand, the way his lips part just a little.

And even though minutes ago I was swearing I'd never influence Duncan to want me, it's my only route here. I just have to hope Duncan gets through in time because, if I let this asshole drag me from this room, they'll never find me. Instead of fighting him, I go still.

"Are you sure you want to turn me in?" I question, letting my magic seep from every pore in my body.

Zaxby stills as my power infiltrates his mind. "What?"

"I can see that you find me attractive," I say seductively even as bile rises in my throat. "Don't you want just a taste, Zaxby? I won't tell. Go ahead."

"Sway," Duncan roars. He slams against the door, and it moves just a little.

My heart thuds wildly, but I force myself to appear calm. "Go ahead. Touch me."

His gaze rests on my breasts. And he releases me just long enough for me to rip my hand free and slam my fist into his jaw.

The door splinters, and a massive lion sprints into the ring. He leaps over me and growls at Zaxby, who's managed to get to his feet. Tail twitching, Duncan stalks forward. He pauses for a moment and shifts, standing before me as over six feet of glorious, naked man.

"Who the fuck hired you?" he snarls at Zaxby.

Zaxby stares at me then back to Duncan. "I—"

Duncan grabs him by the throat and picks him up, slamming him to the ground. Bone crunches, and Zaxby screams. "Tell me who the fuck hired you," Duncan growls again, "Or I'll rip you to shreds right the fuck here."

"Duncan—" I start, panic clawing at my chest.

Because if he answers, they will know *his* name. And if they go after him, they'll die. "Duncan!"

Performers rush in. The berserker and her djinn lover, Brad and Kleo, and—to my complete dismay—D. The Ringmaster says nothing as he crosses his arms and watches his head of security torture one of his performers.

"Who?" Duncan bellows, completely ignoring my pleas and the growing audience.

Zaxby says nothing. Duncan partially shifts his hand, exposing large claws that he slashes over Zaxby's chest. Blood spurts, and flesh tears as the rooster shifter screams in agony.

"I can keep this up all fucking day!" Duncan yells. "Who hired you?"

"R-r-r-robert Bardot," he stammers.

My blood runs cold.

Duncan turns and glares at me. "That him?"

I don't respond. Don't breathe. Afraid to confirm what I was desperate to keep from him in the first place.

"Tell him," D orders from right behind me.

I close my eyes, and tears slip free. I nod.

Zaxby screams, and I open my eyes just in time to see Duncan slash his claw over Zaxby's throat, damn near severing his head in the process. Bile rises in my gut, but I swallow it back down and cross both arms over myself.

"Get her upstairs," D orders Duncan. "Fiona, get a group and clean this fucking mess up."

"You got it." She rushes in, offering me a sympathetic smile as she passes, but heads straight for the body.

Duncan puts a hand on my shoulder and guides me out.

Somehow, someway, we make it upstairs. But he doesn't take me to my room. Instead, he guides me into his apartment. The scents of all three men hit me right in the gut, and my twisted soul embraces the desire I feel even in the midst of death.

"Drink," he orders as he offers me a glass of water.

I do as he says, my vision clearing even as panic claws its way through me like I'm made of wet tissue paper.

Duncan knows.

The Ringmaster knows.

Fuck, nearly everyone here heard his name. They heard *my* name.

Which means they're going to go after him, and he will kill them. Not only is Robert embedded deep in the House of Earth and Emerald, but he's a fucking monster. A killer who hides behind the smile of a gentleman. And even though he doesn't have the brute strength of a lion, he's powerful enough in his own right as a warlock.

I finish the water, and when my stomach begins to

settle, I turn just in time to see a freshly showered and partially clothed Duncan coming out of his room.

Where Bracken is scarred and Killian is pierced, Duncan is all hard muscle and smooth skin. He's built much in the same way they are—a force to be reckoned with. But Duncan's weapon isn't his muscle; it's his mind. My mouth goes dry at how much I want him.

"Are you okay?"

"Do you really care?" I snap without thinking, so I close my eyes and take a deep breath. "Look, I'm sorry. That was unfair. Even if you were—" I open my eyes, shocked to find Duncan standing mere inches from me.

"I am so fucking sorry," Duncan grinds out. "You have to understand—I never wanted this."

"What? Me to be attacked?"

"I could smell his desire for you," Duncan growls. "Just as easily as I could sense your fear."

"That was my magic," I say quickly. "I needed to distract him before he did what he threatened and knocked me out. I knew that if he managed to get me away, I'd end up back with—"

"Robert?" he finishes.

I nod.

"Why the fuck didn't you give us his name?"

"It won't do you any good. He's with the House of Earth and Emerald, and he's embedded like a vein in the highest levels of their leadership."

"Veins can be cut."

"Not this one," I tell him as I reach out and press a hand to his chest. "Please. Don't die for me."

"Who said anything about dying?"

"You have no idea what you're up against."

"I'm hard to kill," he retorts.

"Stubborn, too," I shoot back.

Duncan reaches out and traces a finger along my jaw. "You have *no idea* what went through my mind when I couldn't get to you."

A throbbing ache forms between my legs as my blood heats.

"I was prepared to tear the entire fucking circus apart. As long as I've lived, I've never felt that kind of bloodlust."

There's a haunted look in his eye, and it makes me want to chase it away. But I also need him to know I accept him for who he is—who he was. "You killed him quickly, but you haven't always," I say, and his gaze snaps to mine.

"No," he agrees, "I haven't."

"Tell me about your past, Duncan."

"It's ugly," he says.

"Nothing about you is ugly."

He stares at me so long I think he'll refuse. Finally, he says, "My father was a strategist for a covert unit that took orders from several high-level families. Problem was none of the families knew they weren't his exclusive client. He traveled a lot, so I didn't see him much growing up, but when I was eleven, my mom died. Instead of pawning me off on relatives, he brought me to work with him."

I stare at him, trying to imagine the things he saw. "That must have been hard."

"Actually, I fucking loved it. Mostly, we sat in conference rooms, playing war games. I was seventeen before he took me into the field, and by then, I was addicted. Not to the killing but to the psychological warfare of trapping my prey. I think my lion... well, I thrive on shit like that, I guess. Moved up in the ranks fairly quickly because of it too, and my old man was so fucking proud."

"Sounds nice to have that connection with your dad. Where is he now?"

"One of the families got wind of the organization's double-dipping. They felt like they'd been played, so they retaliated. He was hit by a sniper and died instantly."

"I'm so sorry."

"After that, the organization splintered. Half were put to death. The others went underground. Contract work. I began taking private jobs in order to gather intel about the sniper that took out my father. Took me five years of non-stop blood and death before I found him and put him in the ground."

He shakes his head. "I probably wouldn't have stopped either. I was in too far. Torturing and killing was all I knew. But then I met Killian." He looks at me, and some of the bleakness and grief lifts. "He gave me someone else to live for. Damn, that sounds sappy as shit. Don't tell him I said that."

I smile. "I won't."

He studies me. "I'm not the good guy, Sway. In fact, I've made a career out of being the bad guy. You should know that before we—Before I—"

"I know everything I need to know," I tell him softly. "And that is who you are and how big your heart is. You saved me. That first night when you scooped me off your doorstep. You didn't have to do that, but you protected me even when you didn't know me. That makes you the good guy in my book."

"What if it's not enough?" he asks.

"It's enough for me," I tell him. "And besides, earlier with Zaxby, you protected me. If you hadn't done that—"

"I don't even want to think about it," he grumbles. "I was such a fucking idiot for letting you go in alone." He drops his forehead to mine.

"I asked you to leave."

"I never should have listened." His hand snakes behind my head, and he buries his fingers in my hair, forcing my head back to expose my throat. Duncan lowers his head and caresses my hammering pulse with his lips. "I never should have let you leave your apartment this morning."

"I didn't want to be alone. I would have left—"

"You wouldn't have been alone," he replies. "You are so fucking gorgeous." He grips my hip with a large hand and pulls me toward him. "Seeing you standing there naked this morning, knowing both of my brothers had already tasted what I so desperately crave—it undid me."

And because I want to show him I want him too, even after everything he's shared about himself, I pull back and drop to my knees. Duncan stares down at me, lips parting. I reach up and trace my hands over his ridged abdominal muscles, caressing every inch of flesh I can reach as I make my way to the waistband of his sweats.

"Sway—"

"Shhh," I whisper.

His breathing turns ragged as I pull his sweats down and free his massive length. The throbbing inside me grows completely out of control, so I clench my legs together to ease the ache. "I can smell your arousal," he growls, and when I look up at him, those hazel eyes have turned a deep gold, his predator shining through.

I lean forward and take his dick into my mouth. The flesh is velvet steel, and I have to wrap a hand around his shaft because there's no way in hell he's fitting all the way in. Gripping, I pull back and slam my mouth back down onto him.

Duncan maintains control with his hand in my hair,

holding me to his cock as he begins to thrust against me. "Fuck, Sway. Fuck." Duncan leans back against the counter as I continue sucking him off, tightening my grasp on the base of his shaft as I move.

"I can't—" Duncan pulls me off of him and to my feet, crushing my mouth to his. His tongue plunges into my mouth, and I feel every hesitation melt away, his resolve finally fucking snapping. He pulls back and stares into my eyes. "I'm not gentle."

"I don't care."

"Sway—"

I cup his face in my palms. "No, Duncan. I want you. However I can have you."

"Once I start—"

"Don't. Stop," I reply.

He pulls me in close and grins, a carnal smile that sets my heart on fire. "Good girl." Duncan lifts and carries me toward the couch. He sets me down next to the arm of it and steps back a few steps.

"Take your clothes off," he orders—just like Bracken did. Except, unlike Bracken, I know this won't be gentle and easy to help me adjust. Duncan's vulnerability earlier only solidified what I already sensed about him. His need to dominate is part of who he is. Giving him control is the best gift I can offer to a man like that.

Thrill coursing through my veins, I slowly peel my sports bra off and toss it to the side. Duncan's gaze grows hungry. So I turn to show him my back as I push my shorts down, bending over and showing my ass as I let them hit the floor.

Duncan rushes forward and pushes me over the arm of the couch, propping my ass up like a fucking buffet. "This is how I've pictured you," he says as he grips my ass with both hands, kneading the muscle. "Bared for me. Crying out as you come. Gasping when I slip into this tight fucking ass."

I let out a soft moan as his hands slip between my thighs.

"Would you let me do that?" he asks huskily. "Fill you in every way possible?"

"I'll let you do whatever you want."

"But is it what *you* want, Sway?"

The very fact that he asks that, that he cares enough to make sure I'm not simply agreeing out of fear of losing him means the world to me. And I'm as surprised as he is when I reply, "Yes."

Duncan's hot breath fans over the insides of my thighs as he buries his face between my legs. I cry out when his tongue closes over my swollen clit. He sucks, pulling it into his mouth and gently nipping with his teeth.

"Yes! Oh my—yesss!" I cry out as my orgasm slams into me. I come hard, but Duncan doesn't let up. He slips a finger inside of me even as he continues stroking my clit with his tongue. He slides it in and out, the wet friction so damned delicious.

"That feel good, baby?" he asks as he slowly fucks me with his fingers.

"Yes."

"You're so fucking wet," he growls. "Do you want me? You want my cock?"

"Yes," I reply, breathless.

"Who are you thinking about right now?"

"You."

"Not my brothers?"

"No."

"Good. This is my time. You can think about all of us when we're all fucking you, baby, but my cock had better be the only one on your mind right now."

"It is," I promise. My pussy is throbbing, my release dripping down my legs. I don't know that I've ever been this wet because, while Duncan is the main one on my mind, I cannot help but picture all three of them doing what he is.

"You're ready for me," he says in a tone that's both a question and a command.

"Yes," I pant.

He withdraws his finger and picks me up, setting me on my knees on the cushion so my breasts are against the back of the couch. "Spread your legs."

I obey, sliding my legs further apart as he kneels on the couch behind me. He takes his dick and rubs it against my clit, stroking me with his hard length. Then, he slides into me from behind. I cry out, arching back into him as he fills me.

I'm so fucking turned on that any soreness I'd had is gone from my mind. Vanished as he slides out of me and back in, fucking me with measured control that I so desperately want him to let go of. Duncan grips my breast with one hand, pinching my nipple between his thumb and forefinger as the other hand slides down to my clit. He strokes it for a moment then pulls his hand back and slides his fingers between my ass cheeks.

I gasp when he presses against the tight hole, and when he slips a wet finger inside, I come undone.

"Fuck yes, baby. You like that, don't you?"

"Oh my—fuck yesss," I moan.

He removes his hand from my breast and shoves me into the back of the couch, pinning me there as he increases the pace, fucking me like it's our last day on earth. He keeps his finger in my ass, and the pressure there is far more delicious than I *ever* would have thought possible. The control in him is long gone now, and knowing he's finally let go with me sends me careening right off the edge of the cliff.

Duncan's entire body goes rigid, and he growls then leans down and bites my shoulder. Pain stings as another release tears through me.

"Yes! Duncan!" I cry out as his dick twitches inside of my body, his release filling me as he marks me both body and soul.

And even though I'm terrified about what my feelings for him, Bracken, and Killian mean, I embrace it now.

Fuck, I want to *drown* in the way they make me feel.

I only hope I'm not what gets them killed in the end.

Chapter 19

Duncan

Still asleep, Sway rolls onto her side. I watch her from the doorway of my bedroom, wanting nothing more than to climb back into the bed beside her and curl my body around her perfectly shaped ass. But after a night spent that way already, I can't afford to waste any more time.

We have a name.

Robert Bardot.

That asshole is a dead man.

His name combined with his House is more than enough for us to hunt him—and my beast won't rest until we do.

Killian and Bracken patrolled all night so I could stay with Sway. I'm still surprised she let me talk her out of performing last night—a suggestion that came from D himself once Zaxby's guts were cleaned off the floors. Maybe it had something to do with having my cock buried inside her when I asked her to stay with me instead. My balls tighten at the memory of the way she offered her body to me, letting me dominate her in the way I so badly needed. I'd gone in fully in control, and somewhere along the way, that control had snapped.

I wonder if Sway knows how much power she truly holds over me. I wonder if my brothers want her too? I've spent the entire night trying to figure out whether to tell them what I feel for her.

All I know is I'm done fighting it.

Sway is my mate—or she will be. I just have to figure out how to tell the guys and hope they feel the same. We've always talked about claiming the same mate—our lions crave that kind of stability and close-ness. A lioness to keep us connected as a pride—but now that it's happening, I'm terrified they won't feel the same for her.

Hell, I'm more nervous about that conversation than I am about whether or not we'll find Robert.

The door to the apartment opens behind me, and I quickly reach out and pull my bedroom door closed with a soft click. Then I turn to see Killian and Bracken filing in. They both shoot me a knowing look, but behind their smug smiles is relief.

"It's about time you dropped the tough guy act," Killian says.

"Who says it's an act?" I shoot back.

He rolls his eyes and continues into the kitchen where he grabs a water from the fridge and proceeds to chug. I glance at Bracken and notice the bags under his eyes. None of us have been sleeping well, and it's not going to get better until we deal with this asshole Sway's running from.

"Any issues last night?" I ask even though I already know the answer.

They would have alerted me if there had been.

"Nope, all quiet," Bracken says.

He crosses to the couch and sinks down heavily, tipping his head back. "She still sleeping?"

"Yeah," I say.

"Good." He exhales. "At least, one of us around here is getting rest."

"You get ahold of D?" I ask.

Bracken grunts a yes. "He'll be here in—"

There's a knock at the door.

I answer it and find D on the other side, scowling. "I'm pretty sure, as your boss, I'm supposed to do the summoning, not the other way around."

"You know we can't leave her alone," I say.

"Yeah, yeah." He waves me off as he strides past me into the room. "What's this request?"

"We need to talk about that name we got last night," I say, and he stops, his eyes narrowing instantly.

"Robert Bardot," he says. "I heard it. What about it?"

"We know his name and his House—"

"So now you want to hunt," he finishes.

I wait, already not liking the hard glint in his gaze.

"We've been over this. You know you can't do that in his territory," he begins.

"No, but we can do it in ours," I say.

He studies me, and my heart thuds because, if he shuts me down, friends or not, I'll have to go against him. So will Bracken and Killian. And none of us wants to have to choose, but we will. And it'll be Sway every fucking time.

"She's special to you," D says, glancing past me to Killian and then back to Bracken on the couch.

I hesitate because this is not how I wanted to out myself, but D needs to know what's at stake here. "She's my mate," I say quietly.

The room falls silent, and I cringe as I wait for my brothers to freak the fuck out.

"Mine too," Killian says, stepping up beside me and patting my back.

"Mine too," Bracken says, getting up from the couch and coming to stand with me and Killian.

I don't question them, but now my heart thuds double-time because—*seriously? When the hell were they going to tell me?*

"I see," D says. "In that case, we'll need to do this

carefully. I won't let you bring war to my doorstep. Not even for a mate."

"If our plan works, we won't have to," Killian says.

"What's your plan?" D asks.

"Remember that group who came by a few weeks back, looking for information?" Killian asks.

D rubs his jaw. "You want me to cash in on the favor they owe me." He frowns. "A favor isn't enough to get them to agree to murder one of their own."

"All we need is for you to set up a meeting with them," I tell him.

D's brow lifts. "You want me to make an appointment so you can walk in all civilized and ask them to sanction a killing?"

"Do you have a better idea?" Killian tosses at him.

"What's in it for them?" he shoots back. "Because, unless you can make it worth their while to say yes, even a favor owed isn't enough for what you're asking."

"How about, if they don't, they'll be inviting a coup," I say grimly.

"What are you talking about?"

"Sway's a muse," I say. D's eyes light with understanding.

"I thought muses were extinct."

"People think dragons are extinct," Killian says wryly.

"Fuck you," D mutters—and then to me, "What does that have to do with a coup?"

"Robert has been using her to gain traction in politics. If he gets her back, he'll force her to manipulate public opinion and oust the current leadership so he can take control."

"You really want to tell them what she's capable of?" he asks. "You'll be putting her at risk."

I sigh. "I've thought of that. But it's a risk either way."

D shakes his head. "Fine. I'll set it up, but I can't guarantee they'll go for it."

I nod, knowing he doesn't want to cash in a favor for something like this. But he'll do it because we're his family.

"Thanks," I tell him.

He heads for the door. "Don't thank me until we get that fucker." He turns back, his hand on the knob. "I know what it's like to have a mate threatened, and I wouldn't wish it on any of you. Let's finish this."

He leaves, closing the door behind him.

The minute we're alone, Killian rounds on me—just like I knew he would.

"What the fuck, Dunc? Tell me you weren't just pretending in order to get D on our side."

"I would never pretend about some shit like that," I say, irritated he would even assume.

"Well, when the fuck were you planning on telling us how you felt?" he demands.

"Keep your fucking voice down," Bracken warns, glancing toward the closed bedroom door.

Killian scowls. His chest is puffed up, but it's not anger rolling off him. It's excitement—and apprehension. He wants this to be real. One glance at Bracken and I know he feels the same.

"Look, I just realized it for sure last night," I say quietly. "So, I would have told you right about now had we not needed to meet with D as soon as fucking possible."

Killian huffs, but he doesn't argue. He knows hunting that asshole comes first.

"She's really the one?" Bracken asks.

Any other time, I'd give him shit for the cheesy look of raw hope he wears—like a fucking kid on Christmas—but not today. Not for this. We're all too damn scarred to make fun of something like hope.

Or love.

Even the word itself still feels strange.

"She's been the one since the moment I fucking laid eyes on her," Killian says with zero hesitation.

"It's the same for me," Bracken agrees.

They both turn to look at me.

"What are you looking at? I already told you how I feel."

"No, you told D," Killian says pointedly. "Now it's time to say it for us."

"Yeah, we need to hear the words."

"This is dumb," I mutter, rubbing the back of my neck.

"It's not dumb; you're just being a coward." Killian crosses his arms and eyes me with that smug look again.

Fucker.

"Fine. I'll say it. I want Sway for my mate. Our mate. She's it for me, which means there'll never be anyone else. Satisfied?"

"Oh, I'm not the one you need to be concerned with satisfying, brother." Killian winks, and I picture myself sucker-punching him, which will have to do since I don't want to wake Sway up just yet.

"I'm proud of you, Dunc." Bracken's serious tone cuts through Killian's humor. "You deserve happiness. We all do."

"The question is how to convince her to give three damaged shitheads like us a shot," Killian says.

We all grunt at that. He's not wrong. The three of us are a fucking mess with dark pasts and fast tempers. Convincing someone like Sway to actually choose us feels like a lost cause.

"Well, I'd say we're off to a good start." Bracken's fiendish smile gets a laugh from Killian, but it has me shaking my head already.

"Sex is one thing," I say, "but claiming her as a mate is a different story."

"No shit," Killian says, "I mean, we're good, but she's not easily swayed." He cackles at his own pun.

I roll my eyes.

Bracken stares back at me. "We have to woo her."

"Woo her?" Killian's brows go up.

"Yeah, woo her," Bracken repeats, still staring at me.

"Why the hell are you looking at me?" I ask.

"Because you're not exactly the wooing type," Killian answers dryly.

I scowl.

"Look, we have to win her, okay?" Bracken says, clearly warming up to his own idea. "Make her fall for us. And not just sex."

Killian nods, a little dubious. "You're right. Damn, I've never actually tried to get a girl to fall in love with me. Normally, it happens by accident."

I can't help but chuckle at that. "You're so fucking full of yourself."

Killian grins.

"Look," Bracken says, clearly annoyed we're not taking this seriously enough, "we need to do dinners, dates, romantic gestures, okay? Show her we can make her happy."

"Again, you don't have to look at me like that," I grumble.

Killian's raised brow says it all.

"Screw both of you," I mutter. "I can be romantic."

"There's a first time for everything," Killian says to Bracken.

"I'm going to throat punch both of you," I warn.

"Now, that's downright swoony," Killian says.

I growl, and this time, they both laugh.

Assholes.

"We're going to hunt down the bastard who hurt her and rip him limb from limb," I remind them, glaring at them both. "It doesn't get more romantic than that."

Chapter 20

I wake in Duncan's bed to a hand gently stroking my cheek. Smiling, I curl into the touch, enjoying every minute of the tender caress. Not to mention how every inhale smells like the three men whose apartment I'm currently staying in. It feels like a dream—or it would if my body didn't ache with the physical proof that last night with Duncan was indeed a reality.

I open my eyes and look up into Bracken's bright gaze. "Hey," I greet sleepily. Unrolling from the fetal position I'd been curled in, I stretch.

When I've sat up completely, I see Killian and Duncan are both in the room, too, standing on the opposite side of the bed.

And I'm completely naked.

Shouldn't I be uncomfortable?

But, I'm not. In fact, I don't know that I've ever felt

more at ease with my nakedness than I do right now. "Morning," I say as I smile at all of them.

"We wanted to bring you breakfast." Bracken reaches to his right and lifts a wooden tray with fresh fruit, a steaming cup of coffee, and a stack of pancakes slathered in maple syrup from the nightstand.

"And there's a change of clothes for you in the bathroom," Killian adds.

"This is wonderful." I raise my arms and let him set the tray on my lap. Then, I pop a grape into my mouth and groan as delicious, sweet liquid fills my mouth.

"Fuck, woman, you trying to kill us?" Killian questions with a wicked grin.

"Definitely not," I reply. "I'm nowhere near done with any of you."

Duncan smiles, one of the first real ones I've seen from him—and it's so damned breathtaking. Bracken reaches out and takes a grape from the tray then slips it into my mouth. I close my lips around his fingers, sucking the grape from them as I hold his gaze.

These men make me feel bold. Strong. As though there isn't a single thing in this world I couldn't conquer. Maybe it's because, before I met them, I wasn't even sure I was strong enough to survive the night.

Bracken groans, and Killian plops down on the bed beside me, his hands stroking over the bare flesh of my back. "Damn, love, you bring out the animal in us." He leans over and presses his lips to the side of my throat. I release Bracken's finger, and he trails his hand down to cup my breast.

Duncan watches, and I hold his gaze, remembering all the ways he touched me last night.

Someone knocks on the door.

Killian groans as he goes to answer it. "Talk about poor fucking timing." Bracken tugs the sheets back up to cover me. "It's Liv," Killian calls out. "For you, Sway."

"Tell her I'll be out in a second." I jump out of bed, and Bracken smacks me on the ass. Duncan chuckles, and I slip into the bathroom before either man can make a move toward me. Because, to be honest? I'd been seconds away from asking *all* of them to join me in bed.

Liv may have interrupted the inevitable, but at least, this way I'll have some more time to fully process what a request like that will bring me. Pleasure? Definitely. But I can't help the feeling that it'll be so much more than that.

After stepping into some shorts and pulling on a tank top, I make my way out to find all three men sprawled out on the couch, laughing at something Liv said. Her hand rests on her swollen belly, her expression one of pure joy.

I stop for a second, enjoying the way they watch her. The genuine joy they seem to bring her. How am I so lucky that fate gifted me to land on the doorstep of three such amazing and powerful men?

If only I could stay here forever. The dark thought creeps into the back of my mind, and I try to shove it down. I always knew it would be three months. Ninety days of security before I'm forced to leave this haven I've found.

"Hey, love, looking gorgeous."

My gaze meets Killian's, and he winks at me, so I force a smile. "Sorry to keep you waiting," I tell Liv.

"No apology necessary. I rather enjoy being around these brutes."

"Brutes?" Killian presses a hand to his heart. "And here I thought you loved us like brothers."

"I do love you like brothers," she replies with a laugh. "Three annoying, loving, and sometimes thick-headed older brothers."

"Killian's thickheaded," Duncan retorts. "Bracken and I are just stubborn."

"What's the fucking difference," Killian asks.

Liv rolls her eyes and tries to stand. When she falls back, Duncan is there, pulling her to her feet. "Thanks, Dunc."

"Anytime."

Liv turns to me. She's braided her nearly white hair over her shoulder, and someone pinned small flowers in the long tail. Her face is bare, her eyes bright. "You feel up for some fun?"

"Always," I reply, curious about what she has in mind.

"Great. Feel free to escort us down, boys, but you are not invited inside."

"Always a bridesmaid, never a bride," Killian says with a hand pressed to his heart.

Liv chuckles.

"Bridesmaid?" I question. "Where exactly are we going?"

"Not a wedding," she assures me. "Don't worry, I think you'll like it." She leans in and wraps an arm around my waist as we make our way out into the hall. It's empty—per usual—but with the three men walking behind us, the space feels much smaller than it should. "So, I take it things are going better?" she asks in a hushed tone.

I don't know why she bothers; I'm pretty sure they can still hear her. "Definitely," I reply.

"You'll have to fill me in once we don't have eaves-droppers."

Now it's my turn to laugh. "Sure enough."

"Way to crash the party," Killian calls out.

A few minutes later, we're pushing through the door and into the dining hall. Or, at least, what used to be a dining hall. Now, it's a party room full of balloons, streamers, and jars full of pacifiers. Performers litter the space, laughing and drinking, some dancing in the far corner with balloons shoved under their shirts.

I stare in a sort of muted shock. "Is this your baby shower?"

"It is." Liv grins. "Fiona put it together."

"I—you're inviting me to your baby shower?" Somehow, it feels oddly personal. Even though I've shared quite a bit with the fury, I guess I didn't think I would have made the list for any personal events. My eyes mist. I don't think she realizes just how much this gesture means to me.

I've never had any real friends. Everyone in my life up until this point has only been there because they desired what I had to offer. But I've not had to buy any of these relationships with twisted deals or corrupt promises.

Which makes my imminent departure that much more difficult to deal with.

"Actually, it was the performers' idea to invite you."

At her words, Fiona and Kleo appear before me. "Hello, *Sway*," Fiona says with a mischievous smile. "Glad you could make it."

"Hi," I say, face flushing at her use of my real name. I brace myself for accusations or anger.

"Relax," she says. "I get why you lied. Zaxby was an asshole from the beginning, but what he tried to do last night... let's just say he's lucky Duncan gave him a swift death."

Kleo murmurs her agreement.

"Yeah, that fucker got what was coming to him,"

Brad says, joining us.

"Thanks," I tell them.

"Besides, Sway is a way cooler name than Helen," Fiona adds.

"Fi," Kleo says, rolling her eyes.

"Well, it is," she insists.

Kleo shoves her. "Come on, let's get you a drink."

"Like that'll help," Fiona says, but she lets herself be guided toward the bar.

Liv laughs as they walk away. "As you can see, news travels fast here."

"So, everyone knows my real name?" I ask. "And they're not pissed about it."

"Relax. You think these people haven't used aliases to run from their pasts too?" She snorts. "Now, I *insist* you forget about all that and enjoy yourself today," Liv says. "You're my friend, and this is a place for friends."

Adaya, who I haven't seen since she pieced me back together, pushes through the crowd, a pink drink in her hand. "Good to see you on your feet," she says. Then her gaze raises to the three towering men behind me. "Boys," she greets.

"Adaya," Duncan replies.

"We'll be just outside," Bracken adds as his fingers graze my lower back.

The three of them leave, shutting the door behind them.

"How are you feeling?" Adaya questions as she

takes a drink.

"Good as new. Better, actually," I add with a smile.

"So I see." Liv elbows me gently in the arm. "I take it things with the boys have taken a turn?"

My cheeks heat. "Is it that obvious?"

"You're staying at their apartment; you needed time to compose yourself this morning…then there's the massive hard-on Killian was sporting when he answered the door."

I stare at her for a moment then, unable to help myself, throw my head back and laugh. "I guess it's safe to say we're busted."

"Girl, you've been busted since the night you arrived," Liv says with a laugh. "I saw how they looked at you. They were goners from that moment."

"Even I can attest to that," Adaya puts in.

Their words warm me. The idea that all three men— even Duncan—felt that way about me all this time makes me feel wanted in a way I never have before. "Yeah, I guess I'm the one who took a bit of convincing. But it's new for me."

"What, sex?" Liv raises a brow, but I laugh.

"Not just sex. I mean the fact that there's three of them and one of me."

"New is exciting," she says with a grin. "Besides, what woman wouldn't want to be ravished by three sexy men? "

I laugh. "Fair point. I guess since it's not the norm,

it's taken me some time to come around to it."

She snorts. "We're not the norm, honey, and that's a-okay." She guides me further into the room, her arm wrapped around my shoulders. "Now! Who wants to guess how big my belly is?"

TWO HOURS OF GREAT FOOD, DRINKS, AND AMAZING companionship later, I'm stepping out of the cafeteria and nearly running head-first into the Ringmaster, who has posted up just outside. I stiffen, staring up at him as fear dances in my belly.

He looks down at me with copper eyes that seem to see straight through to my soul, and I resist the urge to scramble out of his way.

"Shit. Sorry. I didn't mean—"

"Killian will be right back," he tells me. "He went to grab some food since he was getting a bit testy."

"Oh." I smile. "He should have just come inside."

The Ringmaster arches a brow. "And risk Fiona cutting off his favorite appendage? Nah. Killian has at least some self-preservation in him."

I chuckle, feeling more relaxed than I ever have in his presence.

"I'm glad you came down today," he says. "Liv likes you."

"I really like her. She's one of the most genuine

people I've ever met. Killian, Duncan, and Bracken aside."

His smile is all predator. "Am I not genuine?"

I pale. "I don't mean that way. I just—I'm here on a contract for you."

To my complete surprise, the Ringmaster laughs. "Easy," he says. "I assure you that I take no offense to what you said. I'll be the first to admit I don't do anything for free. Liv, however, gives her affection without a price."

"She does," I agree, already trying to figure out how to back my way out of this conversation before I say something stupid.

"My security team has become quite enamored with you." He crosses his arms. "More so than I've ever seen them."

"I feel the same about them," I assure him. "They're great men."

"They are." He narrows his gaze. "I hope you understand how far they'll go for those they care for. What they are willing to sacrifice when what they desire is placed in the crosshairs."

His words are ominous, the dark meaning behind them just as clear as it would have been if he'd spoken it instead. "I do understand. And I am no stranger to sacrifice. If it ever came down to my life or theirs, it wouldn't even be a choice. I would give myself over in a heartbeat."

The Ringmaster eyes me for a moment longer then nods appreciatively. Whatever test he'd just given me? I get the feeling I passed. "I am glad to hear that. Are you enjoying your time here so far?"

"Yes." The light question does nothing to ease my mind. Instead, it only makes my fears worse.

"Good. Should you ever have any concerns, please feel free to make them known. You are contracted to be here, but that doesn't mean you have to tolerate any type of unwanted behavior. I protect my own. And while you are under this roof, you belong to me."

Belong.

The word feels like the lock on a prison cell.

"Fine, but my magic does not," I blurt.

"Excuse me?"

"I know they must have told you what I can do," I say, fear squeezing my heart. "But I won't use my magic. Not for you. Not for anyone."

"I see. And you think I'd attempt to force you?"

I lift my chin in defiance. "You can try."

"Relax, Sway. I have no interest in forcing you to do anything."

I don't know how to take his words. A few weeks ago, I wouldn't have believed anyone who said those words. But now, I've learned not all men are the same. All I can do is hope the Ringmaster is as trustworthy as the men I've given my heart to.

Muted footsteps fill my ears, so I turn my gaze to

the left as Killian comes into view, an apple in hand. When he sees me, his expression lightens instantly. "Hey there, gorgeous."

"Killian," I greet, honestly relieved.

"Thank you for the chat," the Ringmaster says. "Killian."

"Thanks, boss."

The Ringmaster dips his head in a nod then heads down the hall toward the stairwell.

"You good?" Killian asks as he bites into the apple.

"Yeah. He's just intense."

Killian laughs. "Understatement. D's a beast all his own." He slings an arm around my shoulders and guides me down the hall. "Any plans for this evening? After your performance of course."

"None as of yet."

"Good. Don't make any."

My heart is already racing at what he might have in mind. "And just what are we doing?"

He winks down at me. "Don't you like surprises?"

"Not usually."

Killian stops walking and turns to spin me against the wall. He presses into me, so close I can smell the sweet apple on his breath. "You're going to like this one, love. It's going to be an experience to be remembered."

Chapter 21

Sway

Killian refuses to tell me what the surprise is about and insists I spend the rest of the afternoon "relaxing," which apparently involves me lying on the couch in their apartment, watching movies, while they all take turns bringing me whatever I want or need. When it's time to get ready for the show, I start to get up, but Bracken is there immediately, blocking my exit.

"Where are you going?" he asks.

"I need to get dressed," I tell him, "And all of my costumes are at my place."

"Not anymore," he says.

"What?"

"Come with me." He takes my hand, leading me to his bedroom.

It's the first time I've actually been fully inside it,

and I immediately take in all the earth tones that give off a sense of grounding and calm. My eyes land on the giant bed that takes up most of the space, but Bracken pulls me over to the closet and gestures to the sliding door.

"What is it?" I ask.

"Open the door, and find out."

I slide the door open, and my eyes widen. All of my costumes—no, all of my clothing, period—are now hanging in Bracken's closet. I turn to him, unsure of what this means.

"You moved my stuff to your closet," I say warily.

"I moved your stuff to my closet," he repeats, a shit-eating grin on his face.

"Are you guys trying to kidnap me and just hoping I develop Stockholm Syndrome so I don't care?" I joke.

His eyes glitter, and he drops my hand to cup the back of my neck instead. "Sweetheart, if you want me to tie you up, just say the word."

I shudder in pleasure as I picture him tying me to that enormous bed so the three of them can have me. "If anyone's tying anyone up, it'll be me tying you," I tease.

His grin is quick and sexy as hell. "I'm down for whatever you want."

I shake my head. "What is with you guys being so nice today?"

"We're always nice," he protests, but I roll my eyes.

"No way. Duncan is never nice. Killian is only nice when he has something up his sleeve. And you..."

"What about me?"

"Fine, you're nice. When it benefits you. But I still don't trust you."

His lips twitch. "Maybe that's why I'm being nice."

"So I'll trust you? Seriously?"

He shrugs. "Maybe we want you to feel safe."

My heart melts a little at that, but since I'm still not sure he's giving me the full story, I cross my arms. "And moving my clothes into your closet is your grand plan?"

"It's part of it." Bracken leans in, brushing his lips over mine. "Just wait, baby," he whispers. "We have so many more plans for you."

The promise—and dark pleasure—in his words only makes me more excited to know what all of those plans might be.

BRACKEN FINALLY LEAVES ME ALONE TO GET READY, promising to see me later. As he leaves, he wears the same glint in his eye Killian did earlier. Something about the promise behind it makes my stomach flutter all over again.

Maybe it's the fact that they spent all day not touching me, or maybe it's seeing my stuff in Bracken's room, but when it's time to get dressed, I choose a costume made entirely of black lace, knowing it's going to drive them crazy.

Or hoping, anyway.

In Bracken's attached bathroom, I take my time painting a look that covers my face better than any mask. The end result leaves me with dark, shadowy eyes and silver sequins—a makeup job that complements my outfit and will contrast my bright red silks perfectly. Liv said to choose which modality I wanted for performances, so tonight, that's what I'm doing.

I step out of the bedroom and then immediately stop short when a growl sounds.

Duncan's gaze locks on mine from where he stands near the couch.

"What's wrong?" I ask, trying to read what the danger might be.

He stalks toward me and stares into my eyes with a wildness that makes my breath catch. Then his gaze runs the length of me so intensely I can feel my skin tingle.

"You can't go out there like that," he says.

I exhale. "I have to wear this for the show," I tell him.

He frowns like he wants to argue. "It's too revealing."

"I've been wearing costumes like this since I started here."

His gaze captures mine again. "Yes, but I've been inside you since then," he says softly. "I know what your body feels like. What you look like when you come."

My blood heats. "I haven't forgotten. But I can't exactly wear sweatpants up there."

"I don't want a crowd of strangers seeing your body," he says, and beneath his words is that same growl. A possessive sound, I realize. One I can't help but feel turned on by.

"Duncan," I say, and his body tenses at the sound of his name. "I don't belong to them."

His eyes flash. "Are you saying you belong to me? To the three of us?"

"Yes."

His expression tightens like he's trying hard to keep control. "I want to hear you say it."

"I belong to you and Killian and Bracken," I say.

He steps closer, sliding his arm around my waist and pulling me against his chest.

"Not yet," he says in a low voice, leaning in to trail kisses along my throat. "But you will."

Heat pools inside me, but instead of stripping me down, he straightens and backs away.

I stare at him, a little shocked he's restrained himself. Just like the other two, I remind myself. They're holding back on purpose. I just don't know why.

"Okay, what kind of game are you playing?" I demand.

"I don't play games," he says, and I know Duncan well enough by now to know he means it.

"Then what's the deal today? You three have taken turns doing me favors all day, but when you have the chance to take me to bed, you act like I'm a hot potato and can't get away fast enough."

"First, I can promise you I've never thought of you as a hot potato." His lips twitch. "But if that's the kind of kinky nickname you want--"

I shove his shoulder. "Cut the shit, Dunc."

"Okay, okay. The truth is we want you to know we like you. Not just your body, either. We like you for you, and we're trying to show you in the only way we know how."

The awkwardness in his expression is the only thing that keeps me from teasing the shit out of him for what he just said.

"You like me," I repeat.

"Don't get cute," he says gruffly.

I press my lips together. "Wouldn't dream of it."

He narrows his eyes.

"I think it's sweet."

"Sweet," he repeats, his lip curling in distaste.

"What's wrong with sweet?"

"No one's ever called me that before."

I can't help the quick laugh that escapes. "I'm not surprised."

Now he fully glares, and I swallow the rest of my laughter.

"If it helps, I like you guys too."

His glare turns intense. "That does help."

"And I don't need you to win me over with favors or gentlemanly behavior. You've already done enough of that to prove you're gentlemen."

His gaze turns suddenly piercing. "Then what is it that you want, Sway?"

"I..." I hesitate. Ten seconds ago, we were being flippant and flirty, and I could have said any number of silly things, but the way he's looking at me now says he really wants to know the answer. So, I go with the truth. "I want my freedom."

His eyes glimmer—with promises that involve blood and death and somehow make me feel more loved and secure than any other look he could have given me. "Then that's what you'll have. I swear it."

TEN MINUTES LATER, DUNCAN WALKS ME TO THE BIG Top, and by the time we arrive, I can feel the broodiness he's worked himself into at watching me in this outfit. I smile to myself because it means I'm not the only one already wishing the show was over so we can go home and find out what all these plans and surprises are exactly. He catches my hand before I can begin my ascent into the rafters and pulls me back to him for a searing kiss.

"What was that for?" I ask, breathless, when he pulls away.

"For luck," he says, "and for later."

I smile, light on my feet as I let him go and begin my climb.

At the top, I get ready and use the opening acts to scan the crowd. It's a full house tonight, which is good for business, but even from here, the moment I spot Killian and Bracken, I can see their tension. They move seamlessly through the shadows, so invisible that the crowd doesn't seem to notice them at all. It strikes me that I probably shouldn't have been able to spot them either, but my gaze finds them easily as if some invisible force connects us.

It's the same with Duncan, and I watch as they take turns patrolling a section and then exchanging looks that convey whether it's all clear or there's a threat to investigate. I wonder how I can know what they're thinking. Maybe I'm just reading too much into things. With a shake of my head, I refocus, noting how the music is cueing me up to begin.

When it's my turn, the spotlight shifts, and I leap into motion, tossing myself into the air with only a curtain of silk to save me. It's a breathless thrill and then a sensual dance with myself in front of a tent full of onlookers. Somehow, the same way I knew the guys had deemed the tent safe from threats before, I know they're watching me now.

I can feel it.

Their eyes track me as if their hands are touching me. And for them, I dance and soar and spin. For them, my own desire builds with each twist and impossible contortion of my body.

When the song ends, I am burning from the inside out, pulse thrumming, passion rising. All I want is the three of them. All I can think about is giving my body over to their domination. Duncan's words from earlier ring in my head about belonging to him, and I realize I've never wanted anything more than to belong to Duncan, Bracken, and Killian.

Chapter 22

Sway

At the end of the night, Bracken is waiting for me. The tent emptied of its guests an hour ago, but I stayed behind to help reset the props and rigging. The extra work has worn me the hell down, but one look at Bracken standing there and my pulse thrums with a burst of energy.

He's like a blast of the world's strongest caffeine.

"Hey," I say.

"Don't *hey* me," he says. "What are you wearing?"

"My costume." I glance down at the black lace and then up at him. "Do you like it?"

He steps closer, lowering his voice despite the fact that we're alone in here. "You're obviously trying to kill me," he says in a low voice.

I smile. "Not kill, just torture."

He groans and slings his arm around my shoulders,

leading me toward the exit. "Come on. Let's get you home."

Home.

The word hits me like a punch in the gut, and I nearly lose my breath at the casual way he says it. It knocks me off-kilter, slowing me down a step or two as my heart tries to make a big deal out of a throwaway comment.

What would it be like if this were my home?

I can't even let myself think it.

"You okay?"

Bracken's sharp gaze is already assessing me when I glance up. Shit.

"Fine. Hey, where are the others?"

His gaze narrows, and I can see he doesn't believe me. Still, he doesn't press. "You'll see." We stop outside the apartment, and he adds, "It's time for one of those plans I mentioned."

He pushes open the door and steps back, allowing me to go first. I walk into the apartment and stop, staring at the sight before me. All of the furniture has been shoved against one wall, clearing space for the full silks setup that has been rigged from the ceiling in the center of the living room. The sheer black material swings lazily from its fasteners, and on either side, Duncan and Killian stand, watching me with scorching stares.

"What is this?" I ask, wandering closer.

"You wore that little number to torture us," Duncan says.

"And it fucking worked," Killian added. His gaze is hungry now, roaming over me, and my skin heats where his eyes linger.

"Now, you can do what that costume was meant for," Bracken says, coming up behind me. "Give us a performance of our own."

"You want me to do a private performance," I say. "Right here for just you three." My pulse hammers, blood roaring in my ears. Being on display for a crowded Big Top is one thing…but a private performance for their eyes only? It turns me the hell on.

"We want you to let us look at you," Bracken says, brushing a kiss along my throat from where he still hovers behind me.

I shiver at the light touch.

"And touch you," Killian adds.

My skin prickles at the idea that they'll be close enough to do just that. And damn if I don't want them to. Badly.

"All right," I say, taking a step toward the silks.

"Without the makeup," Duncan adds.

I nod as he gestures to the bathroom.

"We'll wait," he adds.

I spin and hurry to the bathroom, washing my face and patting it dry. When I'm done, my cheeks are flushed, and I'm not sure if it's from scrubbing off the glitter or the fact that my blood is pumping with adrenaline and we haven't even started yet.

I stare at my reflection. It's crazy to think that I am the same person who crawled to their doorstep, seeking asylum. A woman who'd had no home, no love, no loyalty from anyone.

And now, I'm about to be completely and utterly ravished by three gorgeous men who claim to like me for more than what I have to offer them physically or magically.

It's a strange turn of events that has led me here.

But I wouldn't change it for the world.

With a deep breath, I turn away from the mirror and step back out into the living room. The lights have been dimmed, casting a soft glow over the room. Candles burn low along the counters and mantle, and one of the guys has begun playing a slow, seductive melody from speakers mounted just below their TV.

My gaze finds Bracken's first, and his lips curve at the sight of me. He's sitting now. They all are. In the time I was gone, they've rearranged the furniture into a loose circle around the silks, so they each have a chair and a clear vantage point—of me. And every one of them has stripped down to nothing but his boxers.

My mouth dries at the sight of them sitting there, looking like they were carved from fucking marble, for my pleasure only.

Shirtless, they all turn to watch me, but none of them get up.

Heart pounding, I walk to the silks and slide into the sling, the familiar feel of the fabric against my skin giving me courage. Then Killian hits a button, and the volume cranks up. I meet his eyes, nodding to thank him because it's exactly what I needed to drown out the nerves and give myself over to the movement of my own body.

So, I do.

Slowly, I begin to wrap myself up, using the silks themselves to climb a bit higher off the ground where I'll have room to move. A moment later, I'm secured and hanging with my legs out in full splits. I use that moment to pause and look up at my audience. My gaze collides with Killian's, and I suck in a sharp breath at the way he's watching me. His eyes are hooded, and the way he's slouched in the chair gives me a clear view of his erection bulging through his boxers.

When he catches me noticing it, he slowly reaches into his shorts and pulls his cock free, gripping it in his hand. Liquid heat pools at my core as he lazily strokes himself. Needing to relieve the pressure building inside me, I move again, twisting to the right until I can see Duncan. He's leaning back in his chair just like Killian, his hard length already gripped in his own large palm. His sharp eyes never leave mine despite the movement of my body and the performance I'm supposed to be giving him.

Electricity sparks between us, and my thighs ache with how badly I want one of them inside me. Or all of them. Fuck, I have no idea what is going to happen or where this is going. But I'm burning up at the mere thought of it already, and they haven't even touched me yet.

They might have put me on display, but I'm the one being teased here. If this is payback for my outfit earlier? Then sign me the fuck up for it every single night.

"Don't stop, love," Killian encourages.

I blink, forcing myself back into the performance they've asked for. My concentration is split, though, as I twist and turn for more glimpses of them stroking themselves as they watch me.

When I pause again, I'm facing Bracken.

He watches me intently, his erection obvious, but he doesn't touch himself. Instead, he gets up and walks over to me. He stops before me, his ridged ab muscles at my eye level. I'm in a V position now with my legs slightly parted, and Bracken comes to stand between my legs, watching me intently.

"You're beautiful, you know that?" he says.

Before I can answer, I hear the other two get up and come to stand behind me.

"She's fucking breathtaking," Killian agrees.

I don't answer, too caught up in their closeness. In what happens next. If they touch me now, like this, together, I might just explode.

"We're going to touch you," Bracken says as if reading my thoughts. "Do you want that?"

I can barely contain the "yes" that spills from my lips.

I want it so fucking badly.

Bracken reaches for me, sliding his palm out over my ribs and stomach. His fingers brush the bottom of my breast before trailing lower, and I arch up to meet him as he cups my heat. The heel of his palm rubs against my clit, and I strain toward him, pushing harder against his touch, wanting more. So much more.

"Bracken," I say, breathless for reasons that have nothing to do with the muscles I'm using to hold this open V. I'll hold it forever if it means I get to be with the three of them tonight.

But he doesn't answer except to continue stroking me lightly. Teasing. And building my pleasure in anticipation and need that threatens to drown me.

I gasp as another hand slides around from behind me. Killian leans in close to whisper, "You feel so fucking good, love." He cups my breast through the thin fabric, his thumb brushing over my nipple and sending urgency through me.

"Please," I whimper.

Then Duncan is there, leaning in close and kissing

me. But it's not light and teasing like the others. His mouth is commanding, reminding me that, even though I'm on the buffet, they're in charge of how this particular meal is going to be served. It only turns me on more to let them have me on their terms, and I moan as Duncan's tongue shoves its way past my lips, invading until he's taking everything he wants—everything I'm offering.

Lower, Bracken's hand slides along the hem of my costume, slipping inside the lace and tracing a line over my clit and through my folds.

"So wet," he murmurs.

Killian hisses, his fingers growing more insistent as he looks for a way past the lace covering my breasts. Suddenly, I hear a soft growl before his hands grab hold of the neckline of my leotard and rip it open.

I gasp, pulling away from Duncan's kiss in time to see the one-piece ripped clean off my body. All three men study me with a hunger that has need curling in my belly until I'm aching with it. My need is so consuming I can't ever remember *not* wanting them. Or not having them again and again.

Mine, something inside me declares.

"She's perfect," Bracken whispers, pulling me from the thought.

"Fucking right she is," Killian says.

"The picture of perfection," Duncan agrees.

In this moment, I can't help but look back at them,

shirtless, sculpted, and with expressions full of desire for me—and think they're absolutely perfect too.

"Tell us what you want, Sway," Duncan says.

"I want all of you," I say, trembling but not from nerves. From need.

"All three of us?" Killian asks.

"We need to hear you say it," Bracken puts in.

I look at the three of them, my veins on fire with how badly I want them to touch me now. But they wait, letting me know it has to be my choice.

"Yes," I say, "this is what I want. All three of you. Touching me. Inside me. Consuming me."

"Let's start with the first," Bracken says, his hooded eyes promising more teasing—and so much more pleasure.

"We'll get to the rest," Killian whispers against my ear. "Promise."

In answer, I spread my legs wider and reach for Duncan again, sealing his mouth to mine.

Duncan growls against me and threads his fingers into my hair, kissing me back with a vengeance. Bracken pushes a finger inside me then slowly out again, and I make a sound of pleasure against Duncan's mouth, arching to meet all of their touches.

Killian's thumb brushes my bared nipple, sending pleasure shooting through me, and then his mouth closes over the pebbled peak at the same moment Bracken's mouth closes around my clit. Their tongues are magic.

Pleasure explodes inside me.

My senses are pushed to their limits as Bracken fucks my pussy with his tongue the same way Duncan fucks my mouth with his. A moment later, Killian scrapes his teeth along my taut nipple, and I come undone.

My orgasm rocks me, suspending me in space in a way no silks ever could. The pleasure rocks me in waves that seem to have no end. And when I finally begin to come down again, Bracken moves aside, and Killian's there, sliding a finger inside me while he watches me with a possessive gleam.

"You're ours now, love," he tells me.

"Yours," I echo, arching to meet his strokes.

Duncan leans back, one hand cupping my throat and the other stroking himself as he watches me.

"Can I…?" I reach for Duncan's cock, but he grabs my hand, stopping me.

"Tonight," he says, "is about giving you what you need."

"What if that is what I need?"

"Woman's got a point," Bracken says.

Duncan lets go of my hand. I wrap my fingers around him and stroke slowly. He stands completely still, eyes locked on mine.

"Good girl," he tells me, and I respond by taking him all the way into my mouth until he brushes the back of my throat.

Duncan groans and tightens his grip on my hair, and I feel a surge of power at how easily I'm able to have him at my mercy.

Drawing back, I whisper, "More."

Bracken kisses my throat, his teeth scraping over my skin, and I close my eyes against the orgasm already building again.

"Eyes open, love." Killian's voice is silky smooth but commanding.

I open my eyes and meet his gaze.

"That's it," he says. "Don't stop sucking, but I want to watch you come for us."

Eyes still on mine, Killian leans down and presses a kiss to my thigh as he slips his finger out of me only to slide two back in. I rock my hips against his thrusts, sucking Duncan with the same rhythm. Then, Killian's mouth closes over my clit, his fingers still sliding in and out of me, and I come undone.

I utter Killian's name as I lose myself again, completely enraptured by the three of them consuming me this way.

Finally, Killian eases back, and I think he might walk away, but then he straightens and presses his hard length at my entrance. He pauses, his gaze asking me if it's what I want. "I know we said it was about you tonight. Tell me what you need right now. Tell me if it's too much."

"I need you," I whisper. "I need all of you."

He grabs my ass in both hands, lifting my hips to meet him.

"Yes," I gasp, overcome at the way he fills me and yet desperate for more of them.

I twist my body and lean over, covering Duncan's cock with my mouth again. He groans and steps closer, giving me better access, his hands threading into my hair as I move up and down the length of him.

Killian's hands grip my ass, holding me still as he thrusts. I pant with need, Duncan's cock filling my mouth until I can feel it pulsing against the back of my throat. Need threads through every vein in my body until I'm delirious with it. Even the silks feel like another iron grip on my limbs, like another lover joining the party.

Needing to feel them all at once, I use my free hand to reach for Bracken, sensing him behind me. My fingers brush his hip, and he moves closer, guiding my hand with his own to his hard cock. Wrapping my fingers around him, I grip him tightly, squeezing as Killian's thrusts continue to push me to heightened pleasure.

"That's it, love," Killian says. "Feel all three of us as you come."

The intensity of this moment, of the three of them all focused on me and our combined pleasure, is intoxicating. I give myself entirely to it, my senses on fire as my body responds to theirs. The fantasy of having them all at once is nothing compared to the real thing. This is the most erotic moment of my fucking life, and I am already looking forward to it happening again. And again.

Bracken's mouth is hot on my throat, his whispered words telling me to "Let go, gorgeous." Between my legs, Killian's breathing grows heavier, his eyes still on mine like he wants to make sure I remember his order from before. His thrusts are harder now, more insistent. My core clenches around him, and in my mouth, Duncan tenses. He's so close. We all are.

"That's the way," Bracken says, his hand closing over mine so that we're stroking him together now. His hands roam my body, and heat bathes me from all sides as we take each other closer and closer to the edge. Until finally, we tip right over it—as one.

Chapter 23

Bracken

D's office in the Big Top has never felt smaller than it does right now. I hate that I had to leave Sway sleeping upstairs. Hate that Duncan and I had to step away long enough to deal with this meeting, but Robert needs to be fucking handled.

Only then can we fully move on with the future we have planned with our mate.

Mate.

Not that we've told her as much. Knowing that she was essentially made for us would likely freak Sway the fuck out right now, and that's not what we're going for. Not when we finally have exactly what we've always wanted.

D sits behind his desk while Duncan and I stand on either side of him, waiting for the crystals to power a call that will allow us to see the head of Earth and Emerald as we ask for her blessing to slaughter a member of her House.

It seems like a big ask. Especially given the fact that the favor we're collecting on was in exchange for a simple name and location. Nerves churn in my stomach because I know that, even if this House leader refuses us, that bastard will not walk free.

But killing him without her blessing will more than likely mean war.

A steady buzzing fills the room, and D reaches down to tap the screen. It lights up, a woman coming into view. Nikki Ward is the Chancellor of House of Earth and Emerald, and her stance says she dares anyone to challenge it. Bronze skin and eyes so dark they're nearly black look back at us through the screen. Three men stand behind her, all of their stances telling more than words ever would.

These are her mates. The men who would burn the world down for her. I can only hope it's a point in our favor that this woman has three men who've claimed her—just like we hope to do with Sway.

"Ringmaster, good to see you again," the leader of Earth and Emerald states though her expression remains muted.

"Is it?" he quips.

"Hardly," she retorts, "But it seemed rude to tell you that I hoped you'd never call on that favor."

"My reputation is not that of a man who doesn't collect on debts. My reputation is that of a man who always collects on debts," D replies, his tone neutral. He stares back at her, commanding respect while also granting her what is owed.

"That is true," she says. "What can I do for you?"

"As I said in the message I sent, your time is up, and I'm collecting on what is owed."

"We fucking get it," the man on her left snaps. "Get on with it."

"A few weeks ago, a woman showed up on my doorstep. She'd been beaten to within an inch of her life, bloody, broken—you get the picture. Crimson Hunters chased her here with the intent to drag her back to her captor, and she requested asylum."

"And I'm sure you took her in with open arms," Nikki quips.

"More or less," he replies, not at all bothered by the insult laced in her words. D doesn't give two fucks what others think of him. In all the years I've known him, he never has. "Since her arrival, Crimson Hunters have been showing up at my circus, threatening my people, and trying to abduct her from my protection."

"And how are Crimson Hunters our problem?" Niall asks. White streaks his dark hair. He clasps a hand on the back of his mate's chair, territorial as any shifter would be. Especially a dragon.

"Because the hunters are being sent by someone in your fucking house," I snap.

D looks at me and arches a brow. Duncan clears his throat, but we both know he's biting his tongue too. We don't have the fucking time to beat around the bush. Every single moment that asshole draws breath is another moment Sway is in danger.

"Interesting." The woman leans back and crosses her arms. "Do you have a name?"

"Robert Bardot," Duncan says.

They exchange a look, which makes my pulse speed. They know him. By fucking name. I have no idea if that makes this harder or easier.

"And the woman?" she asks.

"I don't see how that's relevant," I snap.

"It is to me," she says. "What is her name?"

"Sway Verity," D replies. "She is here voluntarily and has no House ring or affiliation. She was a temporary guest of your House until she ended her relationship with Robert Bardot."

I growl at the way he says the words. Fucking bullshit. She didn't end the relationship so much as he tried to end her. Nikki's eyes zero in on my barely contained rage, and she studies me a moment.

"Sounds to me like you're saying she was held here against her will," Nikki replies. She leans back, and one of the men whispers something into her ear. Her expression shifts, going from a complete lack of interest to borderline fascination. "I saw her at your circus when we visited, but I couldn't place her face. Interesting. We were told Robert's fiancé is on an extended vacation to her family home."

"That is a lie," D replies coolly.

"I see. According to you, she left, and now Robert wants her back?"

"He is attempting to take her against her will. And he's put a bounty on her head to get her."

"For a mere human? If she's a worthless, houseless—"

"She is not worthless," Duncan snarls.

The woman shifts her gaze to him, a slow smile forming at the corners of her lips. "My question still stands. Why would he risk pissing off the great and powerful Ringmaster over a human woman?"

"Because she's not a human," D replies. "And he was planning to use her power to influence the election and put himself in your place. In fact, had Sway not run, you would not be sitting where you are right now."

The men all straighten enough for me to notice, but Nikki keeps her emotionless mask in place. "What type of magic can influence that way?"

"A muse," D replies.

Nikki's mates exchange a look.

"I thought they were extinct," Nikki says.

"Nearly. But I feel I need to remind you that she is

not a member of your House and is currently indentured to me."

Nikki grins. "We've no interest in your muse, Ringmaster. But Robert's access to her concerns me. Have you confirmed he is truly the one sending the Crimson Hunters after her?

"From multiple sources," Duncan says.

My temper flashes again as I remember that asshole Zaxby and what he tried to do to our girl. Somehow, I manage to keep my shit locked down though. The four members of Earth and Emerald remain quiet for a few moments, staring back at the screen, and I can't help but wonder if they aren't able to communicate through the mate bond. All of them in tune with one another. Jealousy burns hot inside of me. That's what I want with Sway. And Robert is an obstacle in our fucking way.

"What is it you request of us?" Nikki finally asks.

"Permission to eliminate a man who poses a threat to both of us," D says.

Gotta give it to him. He tosses the words out so casually that you'd think he's asking to borrow a cup of sugar.

Nikki merely sniffs. "I'm Chancellor for the next decade," she replies, "He doesn't pose a threat to me."

"He will," D argues. "One day. If you don't believe me, question him yourself. I am asking you for permission to solve a problem future you might not see coming."

She narrows her gaze. "You want to kill him?"

"Yes."

"And if I say no?"

"Don't," D retorts. "You owe me, and I'm collecting."

"A location for a life? Quite a bargain hunter you are."

"I agree. You are getting far more out of this deal than I am," D says. "Maintaining your control as head of your House is greater than the life of one."

A low growl emits from my throat.

"Easy, Bracken. He's merely playing a game." Duncan warns me.

"I don't fucking like it," I snap. *"Her life is far more important than any fucking house politics."*

"Agreed," Duncan replies. *"But we need them to think we're getting the shit end of this deal."*

"But it's not just one life, is it? Not if you're keeping a muse and taking a Councilman's life. Bargain hunter is an understatement," Adrian says though his grin alludes to a man who appreciates such an outlook. Then again, he was the prince of the fae syndicate before his mate chose to run for Chancellor of Earth and Emerald. Their hands are no cleaner than ours.

"Do we have a deal or not?"

Nikki contemplates, her expression remaining stoic as ever. It's no wonder the woman is head of Earth and

Emerald. Honestly, I get the impression that she's damn near as savage as the rest of us—maybe even more so.

"The murder of a member of my House on our side of the boundary would cause too much of an uproar," she finally says. "And I cannot hand out an execution without a fair trial. However, there are quite a few supernaturals who go missing in No Man's Land, are there not?"

The knot in my chest loosens.

"Happens all the time," D replies.

"Then take care of it on your side," she says. "We will chalk it up to a very unfortunate day for Robert. Wrong place, wrong time."

"What about Sway?" I ask. I need to know they won't be coming for her. That they won't target the woman I love because of the secrets divulged during this meeting.

"What about her?" Nikki questions. "As far as I'm concerned, she doesn't exist. The last thing I need is someone who can be used to manipulate the minds of so many others. Frankly, I'm surprised you all have let her live as long as you have. Seems a risky move, but I'm not one to tell others how to run their House. . . or circus."

"Sway does not use her magic for harm," Duncan interjects.

"Then count yourselves lucky," Nikki replies. "You

deal with him on your side of the line, Ringmaster. We're even after this."

"Agreed. Thank you."

She dips her head in a nod, and the screen goes blank.

I relax, as does Duncan.

"Next time, don't fucking interrupt me." D stands.

"She's our mate," I say.

"Which is why you couldn't take this meeting in person," he says. "They would have sensed your desperation and acted accordingly." He clasps a hand on my shoulder in a move that is more brother than boss. "I understand all too well the turmoil you three are facing with Sway's life on the line, but if we don't play it smart, we lose all leverage. Which we needed in order to get them to agree to our terms."

"Except, now we have to find a way to lure him here," Duncan says.

D turns toward him. "Bastards like him have a way of turning up. Sooner or later, he'll come to us. When he does, you three have my permission to put him the fuck in the ground."

Chapter 24

Sway

Killian is in the kitchen, frying up what smells like eggs and bacon, when I emerge from his bedroom wearing one of his t-shirts. It's big enough to be a nightgown on me, and when he looks up and sees me in it, he grins.

"Damn, you look good in my shit, love."

"Thanks, I still don't have a full wardrobe."

"At this rate, I'm never letting you get one, either." He looks up from the stove and winks. "You can have mine."

I smile. "Where are the others?"

"Meeting with D."

"Is everything okay?"

He hesitates, which only puts me on alert. "Killian."

He scowls. "All right, look, we never plan on lying

to you, but we also can't help but do anything necessary to protect you. Even if you don't like it."

"What won't I like?"

"For starters, a video conference with the Chancellor of House of Earth and Emerald where we trade in a favor owed for permission to eliminate that fuckface Robert."

I stare at him for a moment as his words sink in. "Seriously?"

"No lying," he reminds me.

"You're asking permission to kill someone?"

"Yeah. We're trying to be good boys this time."

I laugh. "This is you being good."

His smirk returns. "Trust me, I've never asked permission to make a kill before. Only for you, gorgeous."

That makes me laugh harder. "How romantic."

"Damn, Duncan said you would think so, and I didn't believe him." He slides a plate of eggs at me. "I hate when that fucker's right."

I take a bite of eggs, contemplating everything he said. "When you say you've never asked permission to kill before..."

He looks over, one brow arched. "Yes?" he prompts.

"Duncan told me he met you while he was a, um, contractor."

Killian chuckles. "That's one way to put it."

"I was just wondering if that's what you did too. As a career."

He stops moving dishes around and comes to stand in front of me on the other side of the bar. "Yeah, love, that's what I did."

He waits as if trying to see how I'll react. Just like with Duncan and Bracken, I can feel my heart squeezing at how sweet it feels to witness them letting their guard down with me. To be vulnerable.

"Will you tell me about it?"

"You really want to know?"

"I want to know everything about you," I tell him honestly.

His gaze softens as if he's just torn down another wall. "My parents were from two families who didn't get along. They fell in love anyway and ran away together."

"Sounds romantic. Romeo and Juliet."

"And just as fucked up." He sighs. "My grandfather hunted them. He tracked them to every village in their world until they snuck through a portal. Finally, they settled in No Man's Land. Growing up, my dad insisted I learn how to hunt and track and fight. He was from a line of warriors, and he wasn't the type to just wait around and be found out. We'd do intruder drills in the middle of the night. Hunting and tracking exercises on the weekends. It was fucked up, but I kind of loved it. Spending time with my dad and all that."

"Sounds like you guys bonded," I say.

"Yeah." His smile turns wistful. "My mom hated it, but she just liked to fuss over us is all."

"So, what happened?" I almost hate to ask it, but I have a feeling this story takes a turn.

"My dad made some friends in interesting places. He and I ended up joining an organization kind of like the Crimson Hunters where we could put our skills to use. I got more training. He started traveling a lot. We stopped seeing each other as often. Then, after one of my missions, I came home and found out my mother had been attacked. Home invasion. My dad and I hadn't been there to protect her."

His expression twists with pain, and he says, "I promised myself then and there I would never do that to my mate. If I was ever lucky enough to find her, I'd never leave her alone like that."

"Killian." I reach for his hand and squeeze it.

He stares down at it as he continues. "The hardest part was waiting for my dad to return so I could give him the news. When I did...it was fucking awful. He lost it. Quit working. Started drinking. He died six months later. I swear. I think the fucker died of a broken heart. Losing his mate was too much for him."

"I'm so sorry."

"I threw myself into work after that. It was the only thing I was good at."

"And that's how you met Duncan?"

He grins ruefully. "I got hired to take his ass out."

"What? You were supposed to kill him?"

"Something about him being on a revenge mission of his own. Whoever hired me was scared they were next. Some ex-sniper asshole. Anyway, it didn't take me long to find him, but then I realized he was a lion shifter like me. I'd never met another one, and I was curious, so I cornered him. Was ready to fight him with my bare hands—or claws—just to see what he was made of. You know, have some fun with him."

"Right. Because killing is fun."

He chuckled. "Didn't take more than a few minutes for us to realize neither one of us really wanted to kill the other. We've been friends ever since."

"That's incredible."

"Yeah, I think it made me start to believe in fate or something again. Like, when I lost my parents, I thought the whole Universe was a fucking asshole. But after I met Duncan, I realized maybe there was a bigger plan for me. Something that led me there." His eyes gleam with meaning, and he says, "And here. To find you."

I melt a little at his words. He stares at me with so much adoration and awe that I can feel it emanating from him. And I can't sit here without holding him any longer. Sliding out of my seat, I come around to stand in front of him and wrap my arms around his waist, tucking my head beneath his chin.

"What's this for?" he asks, hugging me back.

"For telling me who you are," I say.

"It doesn't scare you?" he asks.

"Nothing about you scares me, Killian."

He hugs me tighter after that. For once, it's not about sex or endless flirting. In the silent embrace we share, there is connection and acceptance that go far beyond the physical. And in this moment, I think I might love him—I think I might love them all.

THIRTY MINUTES LATER, I'M OUT OF THE SHOWER AND getting ready for rehearsal. Killian stands in the doorway, his gaze on me as I slip into a pair of shorts. The seriousness from earlier is gone, and in his eyes is the familiar gleam that I've come to recognize as dangerously horny. "It should be a fucking crime to cover up such perfect skin," he says.

I turn around to face him, noting the way his gaze drops to my still-bare breasts as he bites into an apple. His chest is bare, every inch of tattooed, pierced flesh on display, and the low-slung sweatpants he tugged on earlier are doing literally nothing to hide his growing erection as he watches me dress.

He takes a bite of the apple he's holding. Fuck, I want to be an apple. "And it should be a crime to look as good as you do, yet here we are."

"You think I look good?" he asks as he crosses into

the room, apple in his hand. He reaches me then leans down and presses his lips to mine. Sweetness from the fruit dances on my tongue as heat burns my flesh. "How good?" he whispers against me.

I lean in closer, brushing my pebbled nipples against his chest. Then, I slide down his body until I'm on my knees. I look up at him as he takes another bite of the apple then grip the waist of his sweats and tug them down to free his hard cock.

Killian's gaze darkens though he takes yet another bite out of the apple, and somehow the fact that he's eating it makes this feel even more erotic. I swirl my tongue around the head of his cock, licking up the drop of precum on his slit.

He moans.

I close my mouth around him and suck him in deep, feeling him all the way at the back of my throat and then still needing to wrap a hand around his shaft so I can make sure every inch of him is being pleasured.

"That's right, baby, don't stop. You hear me? Stop for fucking nothing."

Right as he says it, the door opens then closes.

I pause and then remember Killian's words about not stopping. Hesitantly, I stay where I am, anticipation building at being caught this way.

"Shit, we showed up at the right time," Bracken says just as he crouches behind me and I feel large hands go to my hips. "Hey, gorgeous. Are you already

ready for more?" he asks as he pulls my shorts down to my knees.

I look up at Killian, wanting to answer Bracken's question, but one glance at the gleam in Killian's stare tells me that I know I can't stop what my mouth is already doing.

"Mmm." I offer a hum of appreciation as consent, and Killian's head falls back in pleasure as the vibration of my throat massages his cock.

Bracken whispers, "You have no idea how badly I need this." He leans down and presses his lips to my ass as I continue sucking Killian's dick.

Then Duncan is there, his hand brushing over my breast as he leans in closer to my ear. "You take that cock like such a good fucking girl," he says. "I can still feel the way it felt to be so deep in your throat I thought you might choke on me."

The throbbing between my legs becomes nearly unbearable. Then Bracken runs the tip of his finger over my clit, and pleasure shoots through my body, igniting my blood like dynamite. "So wet," he says. I hear his zipper then the rattling of his belt as he shoves his pants down and grips my hips. The head of him rubs against my center, and I press back, desperate to have him inside of me.

It's empowering to know that these three men crave me the same way I desire them.

Their touch makes me crazy.

Their affection brings me more joy than I ever thought possible.

"You want this, baby?" he asks, tone gruff. "Want me inside of you, too?"

I hum a yes, my mouth still full of Killian. Bracken drives into me, and I whimper as he slides against the pillowy flesh deep inside of my body. Bracken fucks me like a man starved all while I give Killian the same affection with my mouth.

Duncan sticks his finger into his mouth then slides it down over my ass. He presses it at my entrance while Bracken fucks my pussy and Killian grips my hair. Then, with a smile, he slides it in.

I come undone, my body tightening around Bracken as the release slams into me at full force. My muscles shake, and seconds later, Killian's release fills my mouth. Salty liquid slips down my throat, and I come off of him with an audible *pop*.

"Fuck yes, baby," Killian coos as he kneels. "You like that?"

"Yes," I moan. Duncan works his cock with one hand, my ass with another. "I—oh shit." My vision wavers, stars dancing before me as they draw out every second of my release.

"We're going to fuck you here, Sway," Duncan tells me. "Are you going to be ready for that?"

"Yes. Fuck yes." I never thought I would be. Never

liked the idea of giving anyone that part of me, but if it feels half as good as this does—sign me up.

Bracken thrusts harder, harder, and then stills, his release filling my body. But I have only seconds to catch my breath before Duncan is there, right where he'd been, filling my body and setting me ablaze all over again.

He continues working my ass as he fucks me, slow, languid thrusts that push me to new heights.

"Look at me, Sway," Killian orders. "I want to see you when you come on him."

I meet his gaze as yet another release thrums to life deep within me. And then—I come undone, crying out and gripping Killian's shoulders.

"Fuck yes, love," he says. "You look so fucking sexy." Duncan withdraws his finger from my ass and grips my hips, slamming into me harder and faster with each passing moment. He stills, dick twitching as he comes. Marking me just as Killian and Bracken did.

For a moment, sadness pushes through me, momentarily eclipsing the joy. Because, one day soon, I am going to have to leave this all behind. How the hell am I supposed to move on with my life when I've found what I never knew I wanted?

SOMEONE POUNDS THEIR FIST ON THE APARTMENT DOOR, and I come awake with a jolt. I'm pressed to Bracken's chest, but both Duncan and Killian are already on their feet and sprinting toward the front door. I get up and fumble for a shirt as Bracken chases after them.

"What the fuck is it?" Duncan demands from the living room.

"Liv. She's in labor," I hear a male voice say, his breathing ragged. "D wants you three standing guard outside the door. And Liv is asking for the girl."

Fear and joy fight to take hold of me as I dress quickly and sprint toward the door. Harriss the djinn stands on the other side, his eyes wide and frantic. I push through and move past him, running down the hall without bothering to look back.

"Sway," I hear Bracken call out.

But I don't slow. Not until I reach the door to Liv's apartment. I've never been up here, but everyone knows exactly where the Ringmaster's private apartment is located. I knock quickly.

The door opens, and Fiona grabs my arm without a word, pulling me through the apartment and back to the bedroom.

Liv is lying in bed, her back propped on pillows, her knees bent, legs spread apart as Adaya kneels between them. Fiona rushes back to Liv's side, taking one of her hands and looking awfully pale for a berserker, who I imagine has taken more lives than I can count on both hands and feet. Liv's face is red and sweaty, her white hair slicked back from her face. Her crystal eyes are focused, her lips pursed.

D is on her other side, his hair a mess, chest bare, the skin on his left arm shimmers with scales, but I cannot tear my gaze from the beautiful shades of navy blue and purple his partial shift has revealed.

"She's asking for you," he says, tearing my attention back to reality.

"Liv," I say, concentrating on her.

"I'm so glad you're here," Liv says in a strained voice. "I think Adaya could use you."

I rush forward to Adaya, who is setting out several instruments on a towel on the dresser. "What do you need?" I ask.

"Help. The baby is breech, I've tried all other ways to turn it around, but nothing has worked. I need to do it manually, but it's going to be incredibly painful." She throws Liv a sad look.

"What do you need me to do?" I hate that Liv is going to suffer, and my fear for her and the baby grows tenfold.

"I need you to use your magic. Influence her joy to help alleviate the pain."

I gape at the water fae. "What?"

"It's okay," Liv chokes out. "You don't have to. I know you hate using—" She screams.

"Do it," Adaya orders, hurrying back to the bed with a pile of towels. "Get in here, boys!" she calls out.

Duncan, Bracken, and Killian rush into the room, all shirtless and wearing sweats. "What do we need to do?"

"Two of you, grab a leg; the other, stay by me. Sway," she says. "We need you."

I swallow hard and don't focus too much on the last time someone *needed* me. Instead, I don't think at all. I just do what needs to be done.

Rushing around the bed, I press a hand to Liv's forehead. "You're going to be okay," I tell her softly as I let the magic pour from my body. It rushes through me as if a dam has broken, and I hate that I find relief in finally being able to let it out after locking it up for so long. But there's no time for feeling any of that. Concentrating on Liv, I grasp onto her joy for this baby, onto the love she already feels, and enhance it. Liv's eyes flutter closed as Adaya presses two hands on her belly and uses all her strength to press against her, trying to turn the baby.

Liv's expression hardens, discomfort taking over, so I use even more power, helping her focus only on her joy. On what's to come and not what's currently happening. Liv's expression begins to relax, and I know I'm on the right track. She moans in what is obvious pain, but even through that, her eyes are clear and hopeful.

"There you go," I tell her. "Focus on your baby," I coo. I don't look at D or the others. Instead, I keep my gaze trained on Liv as I scan her face for any sign that my magic isn't doing what I need it to do. It's never failed me before, but then I've never cared this much either.

"Good!" Adaya steps away from Liv's side then kneels back between her legs. "Push on the next contraction, Liv!"

Liv pushes, and I back my magic off just enough that she can feel the pressure of her baby and the contractions that will help her bring the new life into this world.

"Good, good. You're doing good, momma," Adaya says.

"You've got this, baby," D whispers as he presses a kiss to her hand.

"Another push with the next contraction," Adaya orders.

At her nod, my guys file out. I can only hope that means we've done it. That Liv and the baby are going to be okay.

What feels like hours later, the wailing of a baby fills our ears. Liv relaxes against her pillows, a smile on her face as she stares at the baby Adaya is holding in her arms. D cuts the cord, and Adaya clamps it then comes around and hands Liv her baby.

"A little boy," she says with a smile. "A son."

"A boy?" Liv cries. "We have a son," she tells D, her voice cracking with emotion.

"We do." He stares down at the baby with a mixture of fear and awe. Love and amazement.

"Hi, little one," Liv sniffles. "I'm your momma. My little Reyes," she coos.

"That's a beautiful name," Adaya says softly.

"It means king," she replies. "A royal name for our little prince."

D presses a kiss to the top of her head then leans down and does the same to their sweet boy.

I step away, but Adaya stops me from leaving. She wraps her arms around my shoulders. "You did amazing, Sway. Thank you for coming through."

I glance over at D, who looks up from the baby long enough to shoot me a relieved look. "We're grateful for your help," he says quietly.

"I would do anything for Liv," I tell them even as there's a dark part of me reminding me that this is how it starts.

The power impresses people, and then it gives them grand ideas that lead to power cravings—and being willing to do anything to get more of it. The Ringmaster might not have planned to ask for favors from me before, but what about now that he's seen what I can really do? What if my lions aren't enough to protect me after all?

Sway

The days pass with both blinding speed and torturous slowness. Between shows and practice, Bracken, Duncan, and Killian consume my body and most of my thoughts, but in the small, quiet moments, I think about what I did for Liv.

Her baby boy is healthy and thriving, thanks to my help, but that doesn't overshadow what I've given away about the true scope of my power. I know because, more than once, I've caught D watching me when he doesn't know anyone's looking. The way he studies me makes my fears come alive.

Like a death sentence, the end of my ninety days looms.

In the meantime, Bracken, Killian, and Duncan are attentive, passionate, and completely devoted to my happiness. Bracken woos me with flowers and chocolate regularly. Killian writes me a song that he performs on a guitar I didn't even know he owned. And Duncan whispers promises of violence about the man standing in the way of my freedom.

None of them notices my growing fear about what D will do with me when my contract ends. Maybe because they're all so caught up in catching Robert. Keeping their gaze on the devil that's made himself known rather than the potential one right in front of their faces.

They all want so badly to make me free, but they have no idea it's not just Robert who's caged me. It's this power—and now that I've woken it, the magic doesn't want to go back to sleep.

With two weeks left to go, I know I have to start thinking about what I'll do if D actually gives me the chance to walk out the door. There was a moment before I exposed myself that I might have asked to stay. But now, it's too dangerous. If history has shown me anything, it's that the temptation to use what I have for personal gain is only resistible for so long.

Powerful men remain that way because they constantly seek more power.

Walking away from my lion protectors will break my heart, but I refuse to allow my power to corrupt anyone else. Robert called me a parasite, and while I wouldn't exactly consider myself that—I do believe that even if it's not intentional, my power does corrupt. And the Ringmaster isn't someone who would let power like mine go to waste.

I spend part of my day off with Liv and the baby, careful to time my visit when D isn't around. "He's so adorable," I tell her.

"He is," she replies. "The picture of perfection." She sniffles. I notice the dark circles beneath her eyes but chalk it up to the lack of sleep that comes with the territory.

When the little guy starts to get fussy, I push to my feet and head for the door. Liv's half-hearted, exhausted smile as she looks down at her baby and cradles him for feeding tugs at my heart.

"I'll see you tomorrow, momma," I tell her.

"We'll be here," she calls as I slip out.

In the hall, Bracken strides toward me, his expression lighting up when he sees me.

"There you are. Been looking everywhere for you."

"I just wanted to get my baby fix," I say.

He grins, glancing behind me toward Liv's door. "Can't blame you there. Little monster's a charmer already, isn't he?"

"I didn't peg you as someone who likes kids," I tell him.

"I didn't either," he admits. "But seeing the magic of creation between mates is something special." His gaze holds mine, sparkling with something intimate, and I suddenly wonder if his baby talk is more like baby fever.

The idea is so unexpected and wild that I shake it off.

Bracken cares for me, he's made that much clear, but babies?

Besides, he said creation between mates, and I can't possibly be that for him.

"You okay?" he asks, and I realize I've been silent too long.

"Yeah," I say, forcing a smile.

"Good, because me and the guys have a surprise for you."

"You and your surprises," I say, but I let him sling an arm around my shoulders and lead me down the hall. As we walk, I glance over at his dress slacks and white, button-down shirt. The top two buttons are open, which is the least scandalous thing ever but, for some reason, turns me on harder than it should.

"Does this surprise have something to do with why you're dressed up?" I ask, hoping like hell it also involves undressing.

He gives me a secretive smile. "Can't I just look good for my girl?"

"Of course. But do I need to remind you I don't like surprises?"

"You didn't like them before you met us," he corrects. I shake my head, getting ready to argue as he adds, "Name one surprise we've given you that you haven't liked."

Since there hasn't been one, I don't answer, and he grins, swooping in to plant a kiss on my nose.

"I rest my case. Now, come on. They're waiting for us, and you know how Duncan is about schedules."

Bracken leads me to the stairwell, but instead of taking me back to their apartment—which is pretty much *our* apartment at this point—he leads me to the top floor and through a door marked "Roof Access."

"Let me get that." Bracken holds the door open for me, and I step out into the open air.

I stop as Bracken closes the door behind us and just take in the sight before me. Dressed in slacks and button-down shirts just like Bracken, Duncan and Killian both stand on the far side of the roof with hands folded in front of them.

Between them on the ground is a blanket laid out with platters of food and glasses of wine. At the edge of the spread, cushions are set out in a circle, one for each of us. Beyond that, white candles burn, flickering against the dying daylight. The sunset has already streaked purples and pinks across the sky, and the effect of it combined with the setup they've lain out is breathtaking.

"What is all this?" I ask.

"A celebration," Bracken says, tugging me forward.

"What are we celebrating?" I ask.

Killian reaches for me, pulling me against him. I inhale the scent of his cologne, my mouth watering at the way his shirtsleeves are rolled up to reveal the ink on his arms. "It's our anniversary, baby. Two months."

He bends to kiss me, his tongue sweeping over my lip before he pulls away. Heat builds inside me, but he only steps back to let Duncan take his place. Instead of continuing the fun, he presses a quick kiss to my cheek and holds out a glass of wine.

"Two months," he echoes, "of the happiest days of our lives."

I take the wine glass, and they all reach over and grab one for themselves then hold them up in a group toast.

"To Sway," Bracken says, "the best surprise ever."

"I'll drink to that," Killian says.

"I can't toast to myself," I protest.

"Why not? You're fucking amazing," Killian says. "Okay, fine, we could toast to your pussy if that makes you feel better."

Bracken punches him, nearly spilling the wine he holds.

I hide a smile.

"To us," Duncan says, and when I look up at him, his eyes pierce me until I'm sure he's seeing right into my heart and soul.

This picnic feels much more significant than just a

fun way to celebrate two months of … whatever it is we're doing.

"To us," I repeat. Then I put my wine glass to my lips and tip it back, watching as all three men do the same with theirs. The way they watch me as they drink sends my heart fluttering, but it also makes my pulse thrum in apprehension.

Something else is going on here.

I can feel it.

My power responds by surging to the surface, eager to help me probe for the answer. Uneasy, I shove it back and focus on enjoying the food.

Everything's delicious.

The food, the view as the sun sets and the stars come out, twinkling along with the dancing candlelight. And the company.

Bracken sits on my left, Killian on my right, and Duncan straight ahead. He watches me with added intensity as the others talk and joke throughout the meal.

Killian does, in fact, toast to my pussy at one point. So, I toast to all of their cocks. That makes Killian laugh so hard he falls over.

When I'm stuffed, I sit back and pick up my wine glass—just as Duncan sets his down.

I brace myself, knowing something big is coming. Even without my magic, I can feel a shift has already happened among the three of them. Maybe they're done with me already. And they've come together for a farewell dinner. The thought sobers me instantly.

"Sway," Duncan says quietly, and my heart hammers in my chest.

"Yes?"

"We chose this spot to celebrate tonight because it represents what you want most. Freedom."

My heart plummets. They're setting me free after all. I knew it.

"I see."

"We want you to know that your wants and needs are important to us," he says. "Which is why, for the past few weeks, we've been trying our best to show you we care." His expression darkens.

"We know you only have two weeks left on the contract you made with D," Bracken adds. "And we'd planned to wait until then to have this conversation or at least until we put that fucker Robert down, but we can't wait any longer."

My heart squeezes, and I bite my lip.

"We want you to stay," Killian says, taking my hand in his.

"What?"

It's the opposite of what I'd expected, and my brain can't seem to process it.

"We want to give you everything, love," Killian says. "Not just a rooftop but the whole world. And we don't want to give you up in two weeks. We don't want to give you up ever."

"You want me to stay at the circus," I say carefully. "With you."

"If you'll have us," he says.

"I..."

They all watch me with an intensity that makes it hard to think clearly. The wine buzzes inside me, thrumming through my veins like a livewire.

"I don't know what to say," I tell them. "I was scared you brought me up here to—" I break off, needing a few deep breaths to steady myself.

"You thought we were going to end things." Duncan's words are low and, if I'm not mistaken, angry.

I look over at him. "You told me you like to share women. None of them lasted either, so I assumed..."

Duncan's expression is dark and stormy as he says, "We've never asked someone into our lives, Sway. Only into our beds."

"I see." I frown, still trying to process.

"We share you, Sway, because your happiness means more to us than anything," Duncan adds. "You are our entire world. We believe that, where one of us fails to be what you need, you'll have two others who can step up."

"None of you have failed me," I tell him, my chest squeezing at the complete devotion shining back at me from their intense expressions.

"Then how could you doubt us?" Bracken asks. "After everything."

"I don't doubt you," I tell him. "I doubt myself."

Even as I say the words, my power whispers its way into my head.

"What does your magic say?" Bracken asks.

"Excuse me?"

"Use your magic on us," he says. "Read what's really inside us."

"No," I say quickly. "I can't. That would be—"

Without meaning to, the magic unfurls, and I read their feelings for the first time ever. Immediately, the depth of their devotion and commitment slams into me so hard that I gasp. Duncan's iron determination to protect me, Bracken's yearning to show me I'm loved, and Killian's aching need to prove to me I deserve it all. The magic shows me all of it until I can't deny the depth of their feelings for me is exactly the same as what I feel for them.

Shoving it out again, I struggle to get my bearings.

"Sway?" Killian's hand tightens on mine. He scoots closer.

The other two jump up and crowd around me, all of them wearing expressions of concern.

"What's wrong?" Killian asks.

"It's my magic," I explain. "Ever since that night with Liv and the baby, it's been at the surface, leaking out. It's like I woke it, and it's refusing to be sidelined."

"Is it hurting you?" Duncan demands.

"It scares me," I whisper. "I don't want to slip up. You saw what I'm capable of."

Bracken takes my chin in his hands, drawing my gaze to his. "All we saw was an incredibly caring and kind woman willing to do whatever it took to save her friend. There's nothing to be ashamed of about that."

"And Zaxby? What about him?"

"He was trying to attack you," Duncan snarls. "You saved yourself."

I know what they're trying to do. Why they're attempting to make me feel better. But it's not so damned simple. It's *never* been simple. "You don't know what it's like," I tell him. "What people are willing to do once they find out how you can be of use to them. At least before, I could put it away, lock it inside me. Now... it won't let me do that anymore. It's not safe."

"Magic was meant to be used," Killian says gently. "Think about it, Sway. If we didn't shift into our lions regularly, the beast would eat us alive from the inside out. It would demand to be unleashed. Your magic's the same. It just wants to be a part of you."

"Well, I hate it," I snap, and he frowns. I sigh. "I think being here with you and using it to help Liv is making it stronger somehow." I look up at them, hating that I'm saying it. "As much as I want to say yes, I don't know if staying is the safest option anymore."

Chapter 26

Duncan

I *don't know if staying is the safest option anymore.* Sway's declaration runs through my mind on repeat today, just as it did all fucking night. I stand on the patio overlooking the carnival that has long since shut down. Its bright lights, now switched off again, give way for much more muted illumination, just enough that we can see if anyone is lurking after hours.

Not that I'm paying much attention to that.

Sway is asleep soundly in my bed, along with Killian and Bracken to keep her warm, so I nurse the drink in my hand, wishing like hell I could feel at least a little fucking drunk. Unfortunately, my metabolism burns it off too damned fast for me to get any real relief.

"Can't sleep either, huh?" Killian steps out onto the patio, and Bracken follows soon after.

"No." My tone is clipped, but I know my brothers

well enough to know they won't take offense to it. Fuck, I can sense their moods, too, and they're feeling just as fucking helpless as I am.

"She doesn't trust D."

Bracken's statement is one I've been battling with both as Sway's mate and D's closest confidant. My entire life, since the moment I met the Ringmaster, has been dedicated to his safety and the security of this circus.

He's another brother to me, and this place is home.

To have Sway not trust him feels like a punch to the gut even if I can understand where she's coming from. Robert used her, tainted her powers to match his own twisted agenda, and now she fears anyone she feels possesses any power over her.

"Worse," I say. "She's scared of him."

"What are we going to do about that?" Killian asks.

I down the rest of the bourbon in my glass. "What can we do? We can't force her to have faith in a man she doesn't know. Especially when he only allowed her to remain here on a contract that is set to expire in days."

"D isn't going to use her for her powers, though," Killian insists. "It's not who he is."

"Isn't it?" I ask, turning to face him. "D sees power, and he ties it to himself. He's spent decades essentially enslaving supernaturals he deems important enough to perform here."

"Enslaving?" Bracken growls. "It's not like that."

I sense his willingness to lay down his life for D, and that has pride swelling in my chest. "I know it's not. But Sway doesn't. I only point it out because she will likely never see it that way. Not after what she's been through."

"You're just going to let her go then? Just throw in the towel and wave as she disappears from our lives forever?" Killian crosses his arms and glares at me. "Because I can't do that, Duncan. I can't walk away and pretend this never happened. That *she* never happened."

"I'm not asking you to," I tell him. "But we're going to have a choice to make."

"What choice?" Bracken questions.

I turn back to look out over the land that has become my entire existence. Never, since I set foot in this circus, did I imagine a day when I'd need to leave it behind. But my soul was never lonely before. Now that it's known Sway, there's no going back.

If she were to leave, I would lose myself.

"You're going to go with her," Killian says, shock shooting through our bond. "Leave the circus for good."

"What choice do we have?" I ask him. "Because I'm not willing to pretend that she never happened either, brother."

"What about D?" Bracken questions. "Everything he's done for us. We can't just throw it away."

I swallow hard. That's been my biggest predicament, too. D gave us a second chance. He brought me in then allowed me to rescue Killian and Bracken. Without him, we'd all be dead or rotting away in some hole we'd placed ourselves in.

Without him, we never would have found Sway.

"We make him understand that there's no other option. He's mated to Liv. He'll understand the power of that bond."

"And if he doesn't?"

"We're not contracted," I remind Bracken. "He can't force us to stay. And if I have to choose between him and Sway, she wins. Even if it'll fucking destroy a piece of me to leave."

"Maybe we can convince Sway to stay," Killian offers.

The three of us remain silent, processing what may need to be done in less than two days. Forty-eight hours from now, Sway's contract will be up, and she'll be walking away from us for good. "She's scared. Of D, of the power in her veins, I don't know that convincing her is an option."

"We have to try," Bracken says.

"We've been trying," I remind them. "For three months, we've done nothing but try."

"Maybe, when Robert is gone, she'll be able to see reason. See that this is the safest place for her." Killian sighs. "Why the hell hasn't that asshole made a move yet? We've sent messages through all the channels we know of. He's not taking the bait."

It's true. Using any old contacts we had, we've sent messages that we're willing to negotiate for Sway's release. Making it seem like we're open to selling her back feels cruel as shit, but it's the only thing a monster like him understands.

Still, he hasn't responded to a single offer so far.

It's making me nervous about what he does have planned.

"He's not as stupid as he seems," I tell him. "He's biding his time, waiting for a weakness. But he doesn't know his time is nearly up. Once Sway leaves, it'll be like finding a needle in a field of fucking hay."

"Except we won't be in a position of power if he ever does find us. Not like we are here." Bracken shakes his head.

"Then we hope he shows up tomorrow and we're able to put an end to this entire fucking problem," Killian says.

"She won't be safe until he's dead. So if he doesn't show up tomorrow, I plan to track his ass down myself."

"We need to do it on our turf, though," Killian reminds me. "That was the deal."

"That was the deal," I agree. "But just like we can't use her as bait, I won't risk her safety once she leaves this place either. He comes tomorrow, or we find a way to get to his ass. House protection or not."

My brothers nod in agreement, and we once again fall into companionable silence.

"Do you think she's figured it out yet?" Bracken asks.

I turn toward him then lean back against the porch railing. "No."

"But she will," Killian interjects. "She has to figure out that it's our bond making her stronger."

"I don't know that she even has the knowledge to make that assumption," I say honestly. "I doubt she was raised to know about the mate bond and its effect on power. Otherwise, she would have already figured it out."

"Do we tell her?" Killian questions.

I stare at my brothers, pondering yet another predicament. If we don't tell her but we follow, her power will only continue to grow. If we let her leave, it will likely fade with time. Since we already decided that letting her go isn't an option— "I don't think we have much choice," I tell him.

"When?" Bracken asks.

"Tomorrow night. After her final performance and the party. We tell her what she is to us and what we're willing to do to prove it."

"And if she refuses us once we've told her?" Killian's fear is clear as day.

"Then we find a way to get her to reconsider." I move past them. "Get some sleep." I slip into my room and listen to the sound of Sway's soft breathing.

After her refusal on the rooftop, I'd planned on

leaving her be. On letting her process whatever it is she needed to process, but now—I pull the covers down over her body and slip between her legs. She moans, spreading her legs even further for me as I run my tongue over the sensitive flesh of her inner thigh.

I can smell her arousal already, and it calls to me. Beckoning me forward with powers far stronger than any magic in existence. Such is the strength of the mate bond. I can feel her. See her. Sense her. And I damn sure can't resist her.

Gripping the inside of her thigh, I raise it over my shoulder and slide my tongue over her wet heat. She moans, her fingers threading through my hair as I draw her clit into my mouth. I take my time, making long, languid strokes of my tongue over her pussy.

"Yes," she pleads, her grip tightening on me.

I slip a finger inside of her, fucking her slowly with it as I suck gently on her clit. I want to make her feel. Make her remember what it is we can offer her so she'll be just as attached to us as we are to her.

I increase the tempo, and she begins to rock her hips against my face. It's such a fucking turn-on to know that I drive her so damned wild she can't stay still.

I can feel Bracken and Killian's approval through our bond though neither comes in here. They want her too, but they sense my desperation and let me take what I need.

"Yes. Please don't stop." She rocks against me one

final time then stills, her orgasm on my tongue. It seeps into me, invading every single one of my senses until I'm surrounded by it. By her.

I draw out every moment of pleasure, devouring her the same way she's consumed me. And when she stills, falling silent once more, I climb up her body and pull her against me as I silently hope this whole thing won't blow up in our faces.

Chapter 27

Sway

The roar of the crowd seems extra loud tonight as I finish my performance, which signals the end of the show. My heart thumps like it always does at the wild applause, my lips tipping upward in a triumphant smile at the way they push to their feet, clapping, cheering, and screaming for an encore. Instead of giving it to them, I swing upward into the rafters and disappear from their view, chest heaving with breath after the exertion of soaring one last time beneath the Big Top. My magic, ever-present now, whispers to me about the adoration from the crowd. They're inspired by me, exhilarated by the way I move through the air on nothing but a metal ring and a flimsy stretch of fabric. I ignore the awareness just as I've been ignoring all of the other things my power has inadvertently shown me. I don't need to know any of it.

As of this moment, I'm finished here.

The thought sobers me, stealing my joy and my usual post-performance rush. The weight of leaving this place threatens to crush me, and my knees buckle as a sob rushes up from where I've managed to keep it locked tight all these weeks.

Not now, I tell myself, darting glances at the other performers busy with clean-up. The curtain has fallen below me, but I'm not yet alone. Keeping my head down, I hurry to secure the rigging lines, silks, and lyra in their proper places.

No one bothers me.

I've kept the crew at arm's length for three months, which means no one else either notices or cares that I'm officially done here. It's better that way. Though, realizing it now only makes the lump in my throat bigger.

It's too late to do it differently. Besides, it's better this way. A clean break. It's what I'll have to do anywhere I go next.

As I finish up, I catch sight of Duncan standing guard at one of the exits. He scans the crowd and then glances up at me. My heart pounds, my magic surging, and I look away before his gaze can hold mine.

A clean break, I repeat to myself.

But my heart threatens to cave in at the thought of leaving him and the others tomorrow. Before I know it, hot tears sting the corners of my eyes.

Not so clean after all.

I knew better, and I gave myself to them anyway. Worse, I went and fell in love with them. A mistake that will undoubtedly cost me my heart. Because after knowing those three men? There's no way I could ever feel what I do now for another. Even my power grieves the thought of leaving them. It's attached to them in a way I still can't make sense of. Like it has feelings of its own.

When I'm finished up, I look around and realize the performance tent is already nearly empty. Even Duncan is gone from his post. *Weird.*

I stride toward the exit, fully expecting Killian or Bracken to appear. They've made it almost normal for me to be with one of them every waking moment—and every sleeping moment too, come to think of it. But no one appears, and I make it to the hallway alone.

My skin prickles at that.

It's a bit unsettling to see the tent so empty right after a show.

Just then, Brad pokes his head out of one of the dressing rooms. He grins when he sees me. "Hey, amazing job tonight, babe. That standing ovation was all you."

"Thanks," I say. "Have you seen Duncan?"

"Yeah, he said to tell you to meet him at his place."

"Oh." For some reason, disappointment slams into me as I realize they've decided not to escort me everywhere anymore. "Okay, thanks," I mumble.

"Give me a second, and I'll walk you up," he says.

"No, that's okay."

"It's no trouble. I just need to get these tights off—"

"I'm fine on my own," I assure him.

"Okay." He frowns. "Well, see you."

He disappears back into the dressing room, and I continue down the hall, my mood plummeting. If they've given up their constant protection, it can only mean they're done with me. They know I'm leaving tomorrow—or at least suspect it since I never gave them an answer to their question on the rooftop about staying —and this is their way of letting me go.

Now, the tears don't just threaten; they spill in tracks down my heavily made-up cheeks.

I hurry through the door to the stairwell, but instead of heading to the apartment, I race upward all the way to the top. Bursting out onto the rooftop brings a rush of fresh air against my skin that feels good after the hot tears that blurred my vision all the way here.

I blink them back as I make my way blindly to the spot where we had our picnic. It's the last happy memory I have here. Or the one with the most freedom in it. A moment where all possibilities still existed— even one where I got to have my own happily ever after.

It was a fantasy, sure, but for that moment, it felt real. I'll always have that, I guess.

"Fucking finally."

The snarling voice is so unexpected it takes me a

second too long to register its owner. The moment I do, strong hands wrap around my arms and I'm yanked backward then spun and slammed against the retaining wall.

I let out a yelp as my face hits the concrete with a painful thud. My eyes squeeze shut, and when I open them again, my wrists are being dragged behind my back and secured with a thick cord that digs painfully into my skin.

I don't need to see his face to know who's taken me hostage. But he leans forward anyway, grinning when our eyes meet.

"Robert," I say, trying not to sob. Or panic.

He leans in and plants a wet kiss on my mouth so hard there's no chance of me pulling away. "In the flesh," he says when he pulls back. "Mm. I've missed you, baby."

"How did you get up here?" I demand, my thoughts racing.

Duncan. Bracken. Killian.

They have to know the wards have been breached.

"Don't worry, I didn't hurt your precious fucking lions. Yet. No, they're up next, baby. But I couldn't keep myself from you any longer."

Panic turns to anger then, and when he finishes tying my wrists and spins me around, I use the momentum to slam into his shoulder, driving him backward.

"You won't get away with this," I yell as loudly as I can, hoping that someone—anyone—will hear me.

He stumbles but gets his balance quickly, eyes narrowing. "You think your boyfriends are going to stop me? Too bad they're down in their apartment with every other fucking member of this fucked up circus, oblivious to what's happening up here."

My eyes widen, and his smile turns cruel.

"Oh, you didn't realize they decided to throw a party without you?" he adds. "Guess they're done with you." He leans in and whispers menacingly, "But I'm not."

I yank away from him. "I'm not going anywhere with you."

His eyes gleam with something that sends a true shiver of fear down my spine. "Who said anything about going?"

He shoves me with enough force to send me tumbling to the ground. My wrists are tied too tight to break my fall, and I land on my hip and elbow hard enough to make me whimper.

It's not until I sit up that I realize he's tossed me inside a chalk outline of some sort. Around the edges, a few candles are scattered. He goes to work lighting them, and I look past him to the door, gauging my chances.

Before I can make a move, Robert crouches in front of me. "Don't fucking move, you little bitch. I plan to suck every last drop of juice from your body before I kill you, but if you don't behave, I'll skip to the end and just kill you now and be done with it."

Real fear slams into me then. I can see in his eyes that he means every word he's saying. More than that, I can feel it when I let my power test his mind. He didn't come here to drag me back. He came here to take revenge. Knowing I have nothing left to lose, I unleash my magic, exploring deeper into his mind for some foothold of intention I can use to free myself.

But there's nothing.

Every part of him is dark and full of hatred. There's no way he'll ever let me go.

I manage to choke back a sob that seems to satisfy him.

As if I've somehow agreed to his terms, he goes back to work, setting out tools just inside the chalked circle. One is a long, jagged knife that nearly paralyzes me with terror as his earlier words sink in.

"If you're hoping to buy time until your lions show up?" He throws his head back and laughs. "Then you've clearly forgotten who I am. That bitch witch's wards are fucking nothing compared to my power. And, thanks to whatever magic is shielding you from me tracking you with a spell, we'll be nice and cozy up here for a while before anyone thinks to check."

"What do you plan to do with that?" I ask. "What are you taking from me?"

"The only thing I ever actually needed from you," he says. "Your magic."

"You can't..." I shake my head, trying to think through the panic. But the proof is right there in his mind. It's the strongest desire he holds. "That's not possible."

"It is when you're a warlock who finally uncovered a lost book of dark magic. And it just so happens one of the spells is a perfect fit for what I intend to take from you."

"Why are you doing this?" I ask, my voice wobbling. The pain in my elbow is getting worse, and I'm pretty sure I broke something, but I can't afford to let that distract me right now.

"You're nothing but a fucking headache," he snarls. "I don't need your ungrateful bullshit. Nothing about you makes you worth the time I've spent hunting you down. Or the trouble I went through, planning how to get to you without interruption. This finishes it once and for all. Tonight. And I'll have everything I need to win the favor of my House and take my rightful place of power."

"You'll never get away with this," I whisper, but the longer we sit here without anyone coming to find me, the less I believe it. My magic writhes in pain at the thought. Whatever attachment it felt to them only makes their absence hurt worse.

Maybe the guys really are throwing a party without

me. Serves me right for turning down what they offered me. Not just safety and protection but love. And I was too much of a coward to take it while it lasted.

Now, I'll die alone and forgotten.

I refuse to do it willingly, though.

The next time Robert turns his back on me, I make my move. Jumping up is awkward and painful, but I manage to get to my feet. The moment I do, I race toward the door, hoping I can at least get into the stairwell before he catches me. Maybe at least one of the supernaturals partying on the floor below this one will hear me scream.

Robert catches me before I make it halfway.

Hands grab at my hair then my arms, yanking me painfully to a stop. Pain shoots up my arm, but I ignore it and contort my body around, bringing my knee up into Robert's groin. He groans, his hold on me loosening.

I take off again, but this time, instead of grabbing me, something sharp slices through my hip. I don't stop, but the pain makes me stumble. I go down hard, rolling to lessen the impact. Lying on my back, I look up as Robert stands over me, his eyes blazing with a crazy violence that leaves me no doubt he intends to make me pay for what I just tried.

"You're done, you little bitch," he says, spit flying from his mouth. He reaches down and picks up whatever sliced into me. The knife. Its rough blade gleams in the moonlight, a dark and twisted promise of more pain before he'll make sure I escape it all forever.

"And now you fucking pay," he says, looming over me with the blade clutched in his hand.

I suck in a breath, squeezing my eyes shut.

"I love you, Duncan, Bracken, and Killian," I whisper as I brace for what comes next.

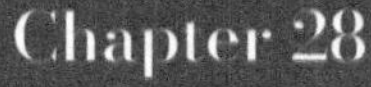

Chapter 28

Killian

Fear hits me like a bullet train, and I stop in my tracks. It churns in my gut, eating away at my nerves, and I scan the room for my brothers, noting that they're also frozen in place. Around us, the surprise party for Sway carries on without her, but deep inside, I'm stone-cold.

Terrified.

Only, it's not coming from me.

And it's not my brothers.

"She should have been here by now," Duncan sends through the bond.

Just then, the door opens, and Brad walks in. Alone.

"The fuck," Duncan growls at him. "You were supposed to bring her up. Where is she?"

"She didn't want to wait for me to change." Brad blinks. "She's not here?"

"What the hell," Bracken growls through the bond. *"Where is she, and why do I feel like I might vomit?"*

And then I know exactly what this feeling inside me is trying to say.

"Sway," I send through our bond as I drop the cake in my hand and sprint for the door. It splatters, but the heavy thud barely registers compared to the heavy thundering of my heart.

Behind me, D steps into Duncan's path, but the distraction is only seconds before Duncan is right on my heels. I reach the stairs first, taking them two at a time as I palm the two blades I always have on me.

Now, the feeling coming through the bond is clear. Sway is in danger. I can feel her pulling me toward her like a beacon. Whoever is hurting her is going to fucking *pay.*

I'm going to rip them to fucking shreds.

Our bond leads me to the roof, and I hit the door with everything I have—but it doesn't budge. I try it again and again, but even though the handle turns, the door remains sealed. Panic ices my veins.

"What the hell is going on?" Bracken demands.

He tries the door, too, as does Duncan.

"Sway!" I bellow as I beat the door with my fist.

"Help!" she screams, a tortured cry that has the predator in me surging to the surface.

"We're coming, love!" I call back as I slam my boot

into the door. Duncan and Bracken do, too, and it begins to buckle right down the middle.

"Come through that door, and I'll cut her fucking heart out!"

The three of us stiffen. And even though we've never heard the fucker speak before, we know without a doubt who has her.

Robert. He found her. He got to her.

"How do we get to her?" Bracken asks through the bond.

"I can scale the wall," I tell them as I back away. *"I'll go up and catch him off guard. Stay here for now, and keep him distracted. As soon as I can unblock the door, you guys get your asses through."*

"Be quick," Duncan replies. *"We'll come after you if it takes too long."*

"Agreed," Bracken adds.

"Understood."

I turn and move quietly back down the stairs, keeping my blades firmly in my hands as I reach the landing. I push onto the empty floor then kick in the door to the nearest apartment. The balcony is wide open, so I waste no more time, rushing outside and scanning for the quickest way up to her.

The quietest way, too.

Because if that fucker hears me coming—

Sway screams, and more pain signals through our bond.

I put one blade back in its sheath then place the second between my teeth before pulling myself up onto the railing. With both hands free, I stretch up and grip the emergency ladder. It moves slightly with my weight, creaking as it does, but at the same time, I hear Robert laugh.

"And you thought they'd come through for you. You always were pathetic, Sway. Weak, idealistic…I should have done this years ago."

She screams again, and in one upward motion, I pull myself onto the edge of the roof, crouching as I take in the scene before me.

I'm surprised to see Robert is alone. I'd half-expected an army of Crimson Hunters to distract us, but there's only one figure standing between me and my woman. Robert's back is to me, so I can make out the ritualistic markings on his naked torso. Warlock then. With a considerable amount of magic etched into his flesh at the moment.

Sway lies bound in the center of an outline drawn in white chalk. Candles surround her, and while I cannot see her face, I can make out the distinct tang of her blood clinging to the air.

A low growl leaves my lips, and Robert whirls on me.

Sway's chest is bare, her blood showing the marks he was carving into her milky flesh.

"I'm here, baby," I tell her as soon as I've removed

the blade from my mouth. I jump down onto the roof and withdraw my other blade.

Nothing is physically blocking the door, but the red rune painted on it alludes to strong magic. Robert straightens fully. He's shorter than me by a few inches. Not overly muscular either, though I take note of the additional ink on his chest and the magic exuding from it. "You don't stand a chance against me, *kitty*."

I grin. A carnal smile that promises a slaughter. "Every single one of you fuckers is exactly the same, you know that? Warlocks are so fucking arrogant that they don't ever know their true place on the food chain."

"I know my place," he retorts as he snaps his fingers. Power flares to life in the palms of his hands. Mild worry streaks through me because, if this fucker was ballsy enough to come alone, it means he's got some actual power up his sleeve. Which is why I desperately need to get that door open so my brothers can join the party.

"It's way the hell above yours," he adds. "After all, I had her first."

"And I'll have her forever," I reply.

"No," Robert says. "You won't." Magic slams into me, knocking me back a few steps. But I don't stay down. I flip up to my feet and sprint toward him, blades out. Shifting will only make me a larger target, and I'm deadly enough without the claws.

He sends more magic flying toward me, but I dodge

it, sliding down to the ground. I send a dagger flying end over end toward the door, burying it directly in the line of his rune.

The magic falters, and the door flies open. Duncan and Bracken shift the moment their feet touch the ground.

They sprint toward him, feet padding, while I rush for Sway. "Hey, baby, sorry I'm late."

I rip the shirt over my head, trying not to focus on the blood covering her body as I cut her wrists free from the cord binding them then slip the fabric over her. She wraps her arms around me, sobbing as tremors shake her body.

"I'm sorry I came up here. I'm sorry."

"It's okay, love, we'll handle him." I carry her to the stairs, ready to get her to safety, when the door slams shut.

I whirl, Sway in my arms. Duncan is on his side, his lion's breathing ragged. Blood soaks his side. Fear churns in my gut even as I can still sense him through our pride bond. Bracken stalks toward the fucker, teeth bared in a low growl, but Robert ignores him and glares at me.

His face is bloody, his chest damn near shredded, but magic swirls around him, snapping like lightning. "Do you really think I am that easy to kill?" he bellows, spit flying out of his mouth. He whirls on Bracken, magic snapping at his fingertips.

Bracken readies to strike.

Sway slumps against me. Shifting her in my arms so I can free my other hand, I send my second blade flying, and it buries into the back of Robert's hand. He yells in pain but uses his other hand to send a web of power surging toward my brother. Bracken dodges—but it catches his shoulder, and he roars in agony.

The pain slams into me then. I set Sway aside and prepare to shift. Robert rips the knife free and sends it flying toward me. I reach out and grab it, my hand closing around the hilt. Then, I rush toward him.

I promised Sway I'd make him pay.

That he'd suffer for what he's put her through.

Sprinting full force, I duck down to avoid another shot of power from Robert's only good hand then throw the blade straight into the fucker's gut. He goes down to his knees and I stalk closer, standing right in front of him.

He seethes through clenched teeth, one hand wrapped around the grip of my dagger, the injured one cradled against his chest. "Pathetic fucking animal," he spits out. Blood drips from his mouth.

"I'd rather be an animal than a fucking monster like you."

He chokes on a chuckle. "I. Am. Power."

"Not looking too powerful now," I spit back.

Bracken stumbles over to me, having shifted back to his human form. "Why is this fucker still breathing?"

His shoulder is slick with blood, but otherwise, he looks fine.

"Because I want him to know that, even as we swore to Sway we'd make him suffer, he's getting off easy." I glare at Robert. "I would rip you limb from limb and enjoy every moment of your suffering. But she deserves the peace of knowing you're no longer breathing."

"She will destroy you all," Robert spits out. "She's a fucking parasite." His gaze shifts over my shoulder to where Sway sits, her eyes glistening with tears.

It infuriates me.

"You're the fucking parasite," Bracken growls. "Taking her power like it belongs to you. She is a gift to be cherished, and you're a fucking bug to be squashed."

Robert snarls, releases the handle, and raises his hand. In a blur of movement, I drag the blade across his throat. Blood spills free, and Bracken slams his foot into Robert's head. He goes down to the ground, choking on what's left of his life.

I don't wait for him to fall silent before I rush back over to Sway. I gather her into my arms and carry her over to where Duncan lies on the ground, his breathing ragged. The moment I set her beside him, he shifts back to his human form, groaning as he does.

"Fuck, dude, I told you we needed to work on your reflexes," I say as I study the chunk of flesh torn from his side, thanks to whatever magic Robert hit him with.

"Fuck. You," he chokes out as he tugs Sway against him. She crawls into his arms and holds on tight.

"Are you okay?" she asks.

"Fine, baby," he replies, closing his eyes and burying his face into her hair. "Just fucking fine."

The door opens again, and D rushes out onto the roof, Adaya and Fiona on either side of him. The water fae surveys the roof then rushes over toward us and kneels beside Duncan.

"He going to live?" I ask as she takes in the damage on both him and Sway.

"He'll be okay," she replies. "But we need to get both of them downstairs so I can get to work. This cut is poisoned with dark magic."

D steps up at my side and reaches down to help Bracken pull Duncan to his feet. Between the two of them, they manage to cart him off the roof and down the stairs.

"Arms around me, love," I tell Sway. She obeys, and I lift her, cradling her slight body against me.

"You left me no fun," Fiona complains as she kicks the headless corpse that was once Sway's fiancé.

There is no humor in my laughter as I stare at his limp body. Honestly, he got off far too fucking easy for my taste. But what's done is done.

And that asshole will *never* hurt Sway again. I lift my gaze to her. "Sorry, berserker, but that one was ours."

S WAY IS PALE AGAINST THE BEDSHEETS. S HE'S TUCKED against Duncan, her head on his shoulder while Bracken sits on her other side. I remain standing, too damned tense to sit as we wait for D to report back after his virtual meeting with Nicki.

The agreement was solid, but if she were to go back on it—I shake my head. She won't. Everything will be fine. And if it's not? Well, then we'll fucking handle it.

"I can feel your irritation from here," Duncan complains.

"Are you okay?" Sway asks.

"Am I okay?" I cross over toward the bed and plop down on the foot of it. Her face is still bruised, her body damaged from what Robert put her through before we got to her. "Don't worry about me, Sway. I'll be just fucking fine. You—I can't even think about what almost happened. Those cuts... What the fuck was that monster trying to do, anyway?"

I share a look with my brothers because we already know the answer from years of experience giving it: torture.

So, Sway's answer surprises me when she says, "He was going to take my magic."

"Take it?" I frown. "How is that even possible?"

"He said he'd found some dark magic spell that would allow him to pull it out of me and take it for himself." Her voice shakes, and she shudders as she adds, "Then he was going to kill me."

"Like fuck he was," Bracken growls.

Sway takes his hand and squeezes it, and I am struck by how, even in the midst of her own fear, she's comforting him. "I'm sorry I went up to the roof," she says for the hundredth time since we rescued her.

"We're sorry we left you," Duncan says as he grabs her other hand and links his fingers through hers. "Brad was supposed to bring you up to the party. We thought you'd be safe enough and we could surprise you."

"He tried," she admits. "I told him no."

"Which is the only reason he's still breathing," Bracken snarls. "That and D's contract preserving his life."

"Don't hurt Brad," Sway says, looking stricken.

"He's just talking shit, love," I tell her. "Blowing off steam."

I don't tell her there's a part of him that actually wants to follow through. And part of me too. We won't. For her, we won't.

"I can't believe it's over." Sway snuggles in closer to Duncan, and he presses a kiss to the top of her head. "That he's really gone."

"He is," I tell her.

"And no one will ever fucking hurt you again."

Bracken's gaze meets mine. *"Do we tell her now?"*

he asks. *"That we're following her to the ends of the earth?"*

"Not yet," Duncan says. *"She's been through enough. Let's let her heal first."*

My phone dings, so I pull it out and stare down at D's message, my nerves melting away as I read the four simple words.

D: We're in the clear.

Chapter 29

Sway

I spend two days in bed to "rest and recover" as they all put it. Adaya comes every day to check on me and Duncan. The dark magic coating Duncan's injury is slow to dissipate, so his recovery is slower than mine. Adaya orders him on bedrest and makes him swear not to exert himself—which he complains about constantly.

I, on the other hand, am at least allowed to walk, eat, and bathe on my own. The cuts Robert made on my chest heal quickly, thanks to Adaya's tea and, within two days, become nothing more than fading scars. My energy returns. And with it, my heaviness at knowing my time here is past done. The magic inside me is stronger than ever, and it takes all my willpower to keep it from exploring the desires and intentions of those around me. The cage I kept it in before is smashed to pieces now, and I have no idea how to trap it inside me any longer.

On the third day, Killian returns from a security meeting to tell me D wants to see me.

"Am I in trouble?" I ask, heart thudding at the mention of the Ringmaster.

"Of course not." Killian chuckles then presses a kiss to my forehead. I'm in Bracken's room today, a change of scenery after being pressed into Duncan's side for the last two days. The four of us have taken to sleeping together in the same bed, but last night, I needed some space. Maybe to prepare myself for what I have to do next.

"Is everything okay? Is Liv--"

"Liv is fine," Killian assures me. "Her first performance back is this weekend as a matter of fact."

"Oh." The news hits me like a punch in the gut.

"Relax, love. Everything's fine."

There's a knock at the apartment door, and the sound of it makes me jolt.

"Be right back." Killian leaves to answer the door.

I have a stark mental image of the Ringmaster coming to the apartment, standing over my bedside, and ordering me to pack my things.

A moment later, I hear Adaya's voice from the living room, and a sigh of relief escapes me. I listen as she goes first to check on Duncan. The murmur of their voices drifts through the wall, but I purposely don't listen to their conversation. Even the sound of Duncan's complaints tugs at my heartstrings.

"Hey," Adaya says, smiling as she comes into Bracken's room a few minutes later.

Killian isn't with her, which surprises me, but I'm glad for the momentary quiet.

"Hey."

She smiles softly and pulls the blankets down to check my injuries. "Your men are worried about you."

My men. I start to respond, but my magic catches a longing within the water fae. A desire to love and be loved in return, though it mixes with something darker. Fear. My heart aches for her, but I rip the power back and shove it deep inside of me. That's one of the worst things about being what I am—the constant feeling that I am invading someone's privacy.

"Are you okay?"

I look up at her. "Fine. Sorry."

She smiles. "You deserve every moment of the peace headed your way now that your asshole ex is in the ground."

A few minutes later, Adaya sits back from where she leans over my abdomen, tending to the healing cuts that make a jagged pattern across my skin.

"Everything seems to be healing nicely," Adaya says.

"It's that disgusting tea," I tell her, earning a laugh.

"I'm glad you're following my orders."

She gathers up the wrappers from the fresh bandages she's just used on me. I sit up, careful not to put too much weight on my hand since my elbow is still sore from my fall. That, along with my hip, is still tender, but thankfully, the fracture in my hip is slight and doesn't require anything beyond taking it easy.

"Thanks, Adaya," I tell her as she packs up and heads for the door. "For everything."

"I'll tell you what I told Duncan," she says, "You all are lucky to have each other. The bond you share saved your life."

"Bond?" I ask, confused. "You mean the one they share with each other?"

Her brows dip. "And the one they share with you."

"I don't understand."

"They felt your distress," she says, angling her head as she studies me. "Do you not realize that you share a mate bond with your men?"

"I..."

I blink, completely caught off guard by her words.

Mate bond?

"That's not..." I shake my head. "We haven't, uh, mated, in that way," I say, stumbling over the words.

Have we?

Wouldn't I know if they were my mates?

Her lips quirk up in amusement as she watches my expression. "That may be, but there's a bond between you nonetheless."

I open my mouth to argue and then decide it's not worth spilling more of my sex life—not when I have a feeling Killian and Duncan can probably hear every word of this conversation anyway.

"Be well, Sway," Adaya says, a gleam in her eye.

"You too," I tell her as she lets herself out.

I brace myself, fully expecting Killian or Duncan to return with some comment or explanation about Adaya's wild claim. But no one comes, and the longer I sit here, the more restless I become.

I didn't agree to a mate bond, nor can I afford it. Not when I have no choice but to leave them all behind.

Finally, I realize sitting here in this room is only prolonging the inevitable. Every day that passes is another debt I owe D for letting me stay past my contract date, and now that he's summoned me, I know I can't put off the inevitable anymore. But I refuse to let this end on his terms.

Tossing back the covers, I make my way to Bracken's closet where all my worldly possessions hang on very few hangers. After pulling on a shirt and pants, I snag a bag from the bottom of the closet that Bracken brought home with us last time we went to the carnival and stuff my remaining clothes inside.

If the Ringmaster intends to kick me out, I'll take my leave standing on my own two feet and my chin held high. I might have come here broken and in a heap of mangled limbs, but I intend to walk out with my pride.

In the living room, Killian looks up from where he's helping Duncan onto the couch. "Moving from a bed to the couch is not the kind of mobility I asked for," Duncan grumbles.

My heart squeezes at the sight of them, but I shove away the emotion that bubbles up at the thought of saying goodbye.

Their gazes both lock onto the bag I carry.

"What's going on?" Killian asks, his voice uncharacteristically cool.

"You said D wanted to see me," I say, my voice wobbling.

Duncan's eyes flash with a heat that prickles my skin, but he doesn't say a word.

"He does," Killian says carefully, still eyeing my bag. "You have plans after?"

I swallow hard, trying to formulate the words, when someone knocks on the door.

Killian scowls but strides over to pull it open.

The Ringmaster stands in the doorway, and I stiffen as he looks right at me and says, "I need a word with you."

"Not sure now's the best time, D," Killian begins.

"Now's fine," I say quickly, stepping forward.

Killian looks ready to argue, so I drop my bag to the floor and say, "I'll be back in a minute."

He doesn't look happy, but he doesn't argue when I

step around him and follow the Ringmaster out into the hall.

The moment the door shuts behind us, I plant my feet and ready myself for battle.

"Come with me," he says, throwing me off by turning and striding down the hall.

I hesitate and then hurry to catch up, my heart thudding as I try to keep control of the conversation. We head into the stairwell where I'm forced to slow my pace, thanks to my injured hip.

"Look," I say as we walk, "I know I've outstayed my welcome these last couple of days. My contract ended, and I'm done here."

"This way," he says, ignoring me and exiting the stairwell. He leads us across the Big Top to his office there.

Realizing he's taking me all the way to his office makes my nerves rattle harder. I have no idea why he'd bother bringing me all the way back here if he wants to throw me out. The exit is behind us.

I try again with a graceful exit speech. "So, yeah, I appreciate the hospitality, and I'm happy to send along any payment you require for it once I find my next position and get settled somewhere--"

"She's inside." He pushes open the door and ushers me through it.

"Who?"

"Liv."

I step inside to see Liv seated in a chair. Déjà vu hits me. It's the same chair she sat in the night I arrived when she pleaded with the Ringmaster to let me stay. She'd smiled at me that night; a genuine, friendly gesture I still hold dear as it was the first one I'd experienced in years.

Now, her smile is forced and tight. There are dark circles underneath her eyes, and there's a tension in the set of her brow I've never seen before.

"Liv? Is everything okay?"

She sighs, and her gaze flicks past me to the Ringmaster. "I'm fine. D insists on making everything a major ordeal."

"You're not fine," he says firmly. And then to me, "Can you help her?"

"I don't understand." I look from him to her. A quick skim of her body reveals no obvious injuries. Besides, even if she was injured somehow, that would be Adaya's area of expertise, not mine. "What's wrong, exactly?"

Liv sighs. "I feel … off. Emotionally. It started after the baby came."

I sit down in the chair across from her, concern distracting me from my earlier anxieties about coming here.

"What started?" I ask.

"Frustration. Disinterest. Exhaustion," she admits. "It's like nothing I've felt before." She stares down at her clasped hands. "I don't even know who I'm mad at. Or why."

"Tell her the rest," the Ringmaster urges.

"I find myself resenting the baby," she says quietly, tears streaming down her face. "Like it's his fault somehow. It's not fair. I wanted to be a mother. From the moment I found out."

She refuses to meet my eyes, and I can tell she feels terrible about what she's saying. That the weight of her words is burying her.

"Liv, it's okay." I take her hand, offering it an encouraging squeeze. "You don't have to feel bad about telling me this. But... I'm not sure how I can help."

"Adaya says it's post-partum depression," the Ringmaster says.

I turn to meet his eyes, refusing to shrink back like part of me wants to do when confronted with such an intense stare.

"That sounds like a condition best left to a healer," I say.

"Adaya's talents lie in physical healing," Liv says.

"But your talents," the Ringmaster says, "might work."

I stare at him, shock then fear rippling through me as I finally understand what he wants from me.

"I don't—"

"I know using your gift makes you uncomfortable," Liv says. "So, please don't feel like we're forcing you.

We just thought... if there's any way to help me get past this, I'd appreciate the help coming from someone I trust. I just want to feel whole again. I need help."

I swallow hard, my heart pounding at what she's asking from me.

She's right. I've already used my magic on her once, and even I can't deny it helped her and the baby through what would have been a very dangerous delivery. But to call it a gift isn't quite accurate.

"Liv," I begin, but the Ringmaster interrupts.

He drops his arms from where he'd crossed them over his chest. With hands hanging limply at his sides, his stoic expression falls away, and his desperation is unmistakable. "Please, Sway," he says quietly. "I can't stand to see her suffering."

"Okay." I hear myself say the word, feel myself nodding even before I realize I've done it.

Fuck.

With a breath that does little to steady me, I turn back to Liv and slowly ease open the door on the cage where I've stuffed my power. It responds instantly, reaching for Liv eagerly. Biting back a cringe, I wait while it explores her desires, reading her most dominant feelings and intentions.

The darkness she described clings to every thought and feeling, but it's clear to me that it's not a natural part of her. Chemical, sure, but not in her nature. My power separates it from the underlying joy and love that I've always so readily felt from Liv. The excitement she felt from the moment she learned she carried D's baby within her womb.

My skin warms with my effort, and I force myself to concentrate as I slowly pull apart the pieces and remove the dark coating from Liv's psyche. A moment later, Liv exhales, her shoulders sagging in outward relief.

A huge smile breaks out on her face, and she grabs both my hands in hers, holding them tight.

"I feel so much better already. More like myself again."

Finished, I pull back my power, grinding my teeth at how badly it wants to remain free, and return it to its cage.

"You okay?" Liv asks, studying me carefully.

"I'm fine," I tell her.

She looks ready to argue, but the Ringmaster interrupts. "Can I speak to Sway alone?"

Liv looks at me, and I nod once. Only then does she rise and go to her mate. He pulls her into his arms and presses a smoldering kiss to her throat, murmuring words only meant for her. She replies quietly, and then she's gone, pulling the door shut behind her.

The Ringmaster comes around to face me, and my nerves return, thanks to the silence that rings out like a drum between us.

"You still resist what you are," he says, startling me with his directness.

I frown. "What I do is dangerous."

"No," he says so firmly I blink. "No power is inherently dangerous on its own. That comes from the way it's wielded."

Guilt weighs my shoulders heavily. "I agree. What I've done--"

"What you were forced to do," he corrects.

I frown. "At the end of the day, what matters is that I used people. Manipulated them."

"Wrong. You did what you had to in order to survive." When I open my mouth to argue, he says, "Do you fault Duncan, Bracken, and Killian for what they did to survive before coming to live here?"

"No," I say, "Of course not."

"And how are your sins of survival any different than theirs?"

I don't answer. Dammit, he has a point.

"What matters is what you will do with your power now that you have a choice," he says. "Just like it mattered for them. They chose not to hurt anyone else who didn't deserve it, and they've lived by that code ever since. What will you choose?"

"I would never use, manipulate, or hurt anyone."

"I would never ask you to."

His words settle inside me, and I realize with a jolt that I believe him. Suddenly, I realize my weeks of worrying that staying here will only tempt him to use my power for his own gain has been completely off base. He would never force me to do the kinds of things Robert did. That's not who he is. And it's certainly not who Duncan, Killian, and Bracken are either.

I'm safe here. Truly.

The Ringmaster studies me as if sensing everything I'm working through in this moment. "What you have is a gift, Sway. But until you can see that, you've only replaced one cage for another."

I sigh. "You're right. I just don't want to put anyone else in danger again."

He cocks his head at me. "You were planning to leave today, weren't you?"

"Yes," I admit. "I thought I'd overstayed my welcome."

"Bullshit. That's twice now you've protected Liv from suffering. You've more than earned your right to be here. You've proven yourself a valuable member of this crew. If you want it, you have a place here permanently. And I'm not one to ask favors, but you should know that, if you refuse me, you'll cost me an entire security team."

"What?"

"Your men aren't as slick as they think they are with their *secret* plans," he says with a snort. "If you leave, they'll go with you. And I can't have that. So, for all our sakes, stay.

I stare at him, shocked. "They plan to come with me if I leave?"

"Yes."

"What if I refuse them?"

"If you refuse, they'll follow at a distance instead of beside you. You can't stop them. Not unless you stay."

My eyes widen, and before I can stop it, my chest expands with sudden hope. "You're offering me another contract?"

"No, Sway. No contract."

"I don't understand."

"You're one of us now. Part of this place. No contract required. Will you take the family I offer you?"

Chapter 30

Sway

amily.

I nearly choke on the word as I make my way back up to the apartment. Truth is I never thought I'd have it again after my parents were killed. Robert was my attempt at creating my own, and, well, that turned out fucking terrible.

I wasn't looking for connections when I ran here.

Protection.

Salvation even.

But family? It was an impossibility.

I pause outside my door for a moment before pushing it open and stepping inside. All three men look up at me. Duncan still sits on the couch, but Bracken and Killian stop pacing to stare at me.

The bag I dropped near the door is nowhere to be found.

"If you refuse me, you'll cost me an entire security team."

"Were you planning to follow me if I left?" I blurt, my gaze raking over all three of the men. Each of them wears his own expression that betrays the truth. "You were, weren't you?"

"We won't lose you," Bracken tells me.

"But this is your home."

Killian crosses over and brushes his finger over my cheek. *"You* are our home, Sway."

I start to ask them how they'd even know where to find me, but then my power stirs, and I realize with a jolt that the answer has been sitting inside me all along. The awareness, the attachment I've felt to these men wasn't the magic inside me gaining control. It's been a mate bond all along. A tether tying me to the three lion shifters I know now I can never walk away from again.

"Do you... Am I..." I shake my head at how scary it feels to say the word out loud, but I have to know. "Am I your mate?"

Killian's expression softens. "Yes, love."

"You didn't say anything," I whisper.

"We didn't want to scare you off."

Tears spring to my eyes as I look past him to the others. "When did you know?"

"We've always known," Bracken says.

Killian nods, and Duncan pins me with a look that sends a shiver through me. Always. I don't know what to say to that. "I feel it," I whisper. "The bond. The connection. It wasn't my magic. It was this."

All three of them nod, grinning.

"Finally," Killian mutters, but I can only laugh, happiness bubbling up to replace all my fears.

"D—"

"What did he want from you?" Duncan questions.

"To show me that my power is not the weight I've considered it to be all these years."

"And do you believe it?"

"I don't know what to believe." I close my eyes briefly and take a deep breath before opening them again. "I know that Robert used me. That I believed for so long it was my fault he turned out the way he was, and now I'm not sure what to think."

"That bastard was evil long before he met you," Bracken growls.

I don't argue with him because some small part of me knows he's right. Still... "My power has been used to manipulate."

"It can also be used to heal," Killian reminds me. "You helped Liv with the birth." I recall the relief she'd felt when I unlocked the darkness from her mind. The part of her that whispered horrible things about what a terrible mother she'd be. I helped her move past those doubts and right into the love and affection she carried beneath it all.

"The power isn't good or bad," Duncan says quietly. "We get to choose how we use what we're given."

Something inside me lifts at his words. I think he's right. I want him to be right. "But at the carnival," I say, still hesitating as I look back at Bracken. "I cheated. I... couldn't help my power surging. Couldn't control it."

"That's because you'd locked it away," Bracken says. "You stopped letting it be a part of you. Stop fighting it, and take back your control over it."

"I don't know how," I whisper.

"We'll be here to show you." The hope that shines in Bracken's eyes as he says the words is like a beacon drawing me in.

"He offered me a place here."

"A contract?" Duncan questions.

I shake my head. "A family." My throat constricts, emotion burning me from the inside out.

Killian smiles so brilliantly it nearly blinds me with love. "And you said yes."

"He didn't give me much of a choice," I say with a chuckle. "Since you all were planning to abandon him."

"I assumed he knew." Duncan shakes his head.

"Not much gets past D," Bracken agrees. "Will you stay with us, then?" he asks as he ushers me toward the couch and pushes me down near Duncan. I sit beside him as he wraps an arm around my shoulders.

The idea of staying here with them—of being loved

by them for the rest of my life—brings me more joy than I ever thought possible. "If you'll have me."

"Fuck yes we will." Killian drops to a knee and Bracken kneels beside him. "Ignore Duncan, he's too broken to join us."

Duncan glares at him, but Killian merely grins. Then Duncan moves enough to reach into his pocket, withdrawing a small ring with a citrine stone settled in the center of a trio of diamonds. "Will you marry us, Sway? Be our mate? Our family?"

Tears stream down my cheeks as I stare at the piece of jewelry. Not too long ago, I wore a ring on the same finger they are asking me to slide that one on.

The difference, though? This isn't a shackle given with strings attached. It's a promise offered to me freely.

Freedom.

Hope.

Love.

That's what Bracken, Killian, and Duncan are offering me.

"Yes. I will absolutely marry you guys."

Duncan beams and slips the ring onto my finger. I stare down at it as Bracken moves to the couch on my other side, and Killian settles between my legs, the three men closing me in just as the citrine is shielded by the diamonds.

Four pieces that make up a whole future of possibilities. All of them shining brightly with joy I never thought I'd experience.

WANT MORE OF THIS WORLD? GET YOUR COPY OF Hunt Me!

To get more of these characters, check out SLAY ME BY JESSICA WAYNE! See where Dante and Liv started and get your copy today.

For more why choose from Heather, download Goddess Ascending!

About Heather Hildenbrand

Heather Hildenbrand lives in coastal Virginia where she writes paranormal and urban fantasy romance with lots of kissing & killing. Her most frequent hobbies are truck camping with her goldendoodle, talking to her plants, and avoiding killer slugs.

You can find out more about Heather and her books at www.heatherhildenbrand.com.

Or find her here:
TikTok
Patreon
Facebook group
Instagram

Also by Heather Hildenbrand

One Dark Spark

Two Blazing Hearts

Three Scorched Kingdoms

Dark Wolf Soul

Deadly Wolf Bite

Broken Wolf Heart

Protect Me (Immortal Vices & Virtues)

Hunt Me (Immortal Vices & Virtues)

To Hunt A Wolf

To Kiss A Wolf

To Keep A Wolf

Midnight Cursed

Midnight Hunted

Midnight Bound

Wolf Cursed

Wolf Captive

Wolf Chosen

Wolf Revealed

A Witch's Call

A Witch's Destiny

A Witch's Fate

A Witch's Soul

A Witch's Prophecy

A Witch's Hope

Twisted Tides

The Girl Who Cried Werewolf

The Girl Who Cried Captive

The Girl Who Cried War

The Girl Who Never Cried

The Winter Witch

The Spring Witch

A Witch's Heart

Midnight Mate

Goddess Ascending

Goddess Claiming

Goddess Forging

Kiss of Death

Knock Em Dead

Death's Door

Dead to Rights

Dead End

The Girl Who Called The Stars

The Girl Who Ruled The Stars

Alpha Games

Alpha Trials

Alpha Chosen

Dirty Blood

Cold Blood

Blood Bond

Blood Rule

Broken Blood

One Hour: bonus novella

Imitation

Deviation

Generation

Guarded by the Alpha

Alpha Undercover

Mated to the Wilde Bear

The Bear's Fated Mate

Protected By the Bear

The Badge and the Bear

Tragic Ink: A Havenwood Falls story

Small Town Contemporary Romance (Heather Hildenbrand writing as Violet Stafford)

Stay for Summer

The Breakup Bet

Contemporary RomCom (writing as Moxie Rose)

Quarantine Crush

Corporate Crush